This book should be returned to any branch of the
Lancashire County Library on or before the date shown

2 1 APR 2018

1 0 JUL 2021

SARAH MARIA GRIFFIN

TITAN BOOKS

Spare and Found Parts
Print edition ISBN: 9781785657054
E-book edition ISBN: 9781785657061

Published by Titan Books
A division of Titan Publishing Group Ltd
144 Southwark Street, London SE1 0UP

First Titan edition: February 2018
10 9 8 7 6 5 4 3 2 1

This book is a work of fiction. Any references to historical events, real people, or real places are used fictitiously. Other names, characters, places, and events are products of the author's imagination, and any resemblance to actual events or places or persons, living or dead, is entirely coincidental.

Permission to reprint excerpt from "Sharp Things"
granted by the author.

A CIP catalogue record for this title is available from the British Library.

Printed and bound by CPI Group (UK) Ltd, Croydon, CR0 4YY

TO KATIE

I recognize, I must tell you, the ways
I have taken after my mother,
the ways I know I have become her,
my head tilted towards the clouds,
hips raw like the aftermath of falling into a rose bush.
FROM "SHARP THINGS," BY NIC ALEA

PROLOGUE

When you grow up, you'll never be sure if this happened or not. Never sure if it was just something your grief stitched together from the parts of her you remember and the questions still in your throat. Your doubt comes up against the image of her, flickering behind your eyelids.

This is the last time you see her.

You've managed to steal up into her room, though you know it's bold to go up there, though you know she needs to be resting. You haven't been near her in so long. You'll rest with her, you think, climbing up into her bed and across soft cotton plains. She laughs, deep, when she sees you, leans over. "Come here to me, come here to me!"

She is beautiful.

She holds her hand up in front of your face, inches from your nose. At her fingertips, there are *lights*.

Blinking green sparks, pinprick. She brings her touch to your face, cradles your cheek and your jaw. You feel small, hard lumps beneath the surface of her touch. Her skin, once warm, is now ash. There is green at the edge of your vision. Green like a frog. Green like leaves. Green like nature but unnatural, artificial instead. You have never seen these before.

There are gaps where the teeth at the edges of her smile should be. Her eyes are still soft, if far away. A green pinprick flickers above the arch of her left eyebrow. Her hair is wrapped in a scarf, escaped black tendrils here and there.

Her lips are chapped. Your cheeks are wet with tears; she thumbs them away. "Don't cry for me, Penelope," she sings, rhythmic, lullaby. "Don't cry for me."

A strange light sits in the center of her chest: a bigger one, round as a penny. It sits like a jewel amid chalky scar tissue. It doesn't flicker, but rather flashes, framed by the softness of her nightshirt. Her veins are risen and pattern her skin, tiny black rivers.

"There's nothing to be sad about. I am *so* happy." She's whispering, she's laughing. "I wish you could hear the things I hear. I have spoken to electric gods. You will, too; I know it." Her finger is hard on your jaw now; it starts to hurt. "You'll find a way. You're cut of my cloth, girl."

Her voice is thick. You climb over the duvet landscape

to her lap, and she cradles you. You put your ear to her chest, looking for warmth, listening for a heartbeat. There is none. A hiss comes from under her skin, a static thrum. She smells like burning, like copper.

"Can you hear the machines, Nell?" she whispers to you. "Can you hear what I hear? They tell me you'll do great things. They tell me that I am dying but that my questions live on in you."

"Who are they?" you ask.

"They have voices like falling stars," she says, her hand on her chest.

"Who are they?" you ask again.

Your mother holds her hand above your face, sparks in her fingerprints, filaments alive. "The questions. You've started already."

A door swings open. You are lifted away.

They argue, your da and your ma.

"Don't be talking to her when you're like this; you'll poison her worse than she already is," he says, and she swears at him.

"She's more like me than you; she has my eyes."

And you're out into the hallway, down the stairs in his arms, floods of tears, green still at the corner of your vision. Green like the parklands, green like poison. Like electricity.

Green like Go.

There are three rules:

1. The sick in the Pale, the healed in the Pasture.

2. Contribute, at all cost.

3. All code is blasphemy.

ASSEMBLY

Just under the surface of the waves where the ocean met the land, a hand without a body reached out for someone to grab it. The hand was wrapped in plastic, so time and water hadn't eaten it, and its fingers, unmoving, were poised and ready to be held. Nell Crane picked it up out of the foam. She placed it quietly into her satchel.

Right where the black river split into the big wild blue, Nell and Ruby Underwood were collecting bits of treasure from the foam. They were farther out than they were supposed to be, out on the city's jagged edge, the pair of them charged with rebellion. Besides, this was where all the best stuff washed up. Right before the hungry sea gobbled the old pieces of the city into oblivion, the estuary caught them and spread them all out on the beach. Treasure among the pebbles.

Nell wouldn't take her boots off and stood at the kissing lip of the water, keenly eyeing the drift. A lightbulb, a coil of wire: she snatched them and tucked them away. Only useful things. Maybe they'd be the very things that would spark off a great idea— she needed one, and fast. Summer would be over soon. Days like today were a distraction from the forms Nell had not yet filled out, the letters she hadn't answered, the end of apprenticeship project she had not yet begun. Here by the waterside she could forget, at least for a little while.

Her small pet stoat, Kodak, was far more courageous, leaping about in the foam. Ruby, however, bravest of them all, was in up to her knees, a net in her left hand, a long stick with a pincer at the end in her right, and a basket thrown over her shoulder. She was a round, bright pinwheel in the water, and Nell was drawn out like her long shadow on the land.

The shoreline was pocked with dilapidated signage roaring impotent scarlet warnings like TURN BACK NOW or NO ENTRY. The girls ignored them. Quarantine was over; there hadn't been an aftershock in years. The two of them had been touched by the epidemic in different ways, both their families scarred by the toxic electromagnetic pulses of the Turn, but these times were for healing. This water was theirs.

The fat old sun wouldn't lower into the horizon for another hour or so, and the heat of the day was beginning to weigh heavy. The salty air helped, alluded to a breeze, but it was still so hot. The sky had been a too blue blankness for months now, so quiet that it had long since become suspicious. Sweat beaded down Nell's forehead and nose, gathering at the tip of her chin, where a chalky ashen scar began.

Despite the heat, she was covered almost head to toe in linen and cotton. Her hair was a black crow's nest, impossibly thick and just about persuaded into a bundle, speared with a thick graphite pencil. She'd deal with the sweat; it was the price she paid for invisibility. She'd never shown anyone the whole scar, the path of it down the center of her body. Her chest cavity at least ticked only faintly this afternoon, a soft metronome against the laughter of the waves. She would have traded the scar and the ticking for a mechanical arm, or leg, in a heartbeat—or whatever the machine did, close enough to a heartbeat that her body believed it was real.

It was commonplace to sport an arm, a leg, a set of ears, two fingers, or even the bottom half of a jaw crafted from exquisite, intuitive prosthetic. Absent limbs were part of the price the people of Black Water City paid for surviving the cruel touch of the epidemic.

Nell, however, was the only person with all her metal inside. She was the only person who ticked.

Ruby surveyed the murky water. She dug up hunks of sea glass and other shining scraps, sometimes whole objects that had been fed to the Livia River by accident, or perhaps sacrifice, during the Turn. With salty fingers, she adjusted the patch that sat comfortably over her right eye socket. Ruby staunchly refused prosthetic or augmentation, wasn't keen on the machines; she always said, "What's good for the rest of you is good for the rest of you." Thick eyelashes framed her left eye, so dark brown that it was almost black. Today she had painted all around it in gold and jade powders a proclamation: "You'd better look right at me. I survived!"

Ruby looked up. Kodak had gone and got himself into a spot of bother. The stoat floundered barely a foot offshore; something had caught his tiny leg. He barked softly, fighting it but losing. She stomped toward him and pried his leg free as he squirmed.

"Ah, would you look!" she exclaimed, tossing the offending object to Nell. "That's for you!"

The tall girl shrieked and clumsily batted away the slimy, cold web of seaweed. Ruby cackled, and Nell thought for a moment about rushing in and splashing her as watery revenge but looked down at her boots: not going in there proper, not today. The beach was good for combing, but farther in, you never knew what you could find or what could find you.

Not that they'd ever come across anything made of flesh and bone, but the abandoned pieces of people's lives were sad and terrible enough: drowned blank books, washed of ink, useless pieces of unconscious technology, scraps of the old world swallowed up while the town was burning.

Behind the girls and the beach and the dunes lay ghostly industrial estates, tall and gray, with scorched black windows like rows of blank eyes. Beyond and to the west, past the factories, stood a stone monument—a woman, towering more than a mile high over the rest of Black Water City. Beyond the devastated capital, western still, sat the Phoenix Parklands, where Nell's and Ruby's homes lay. It was a long ride back, and the girls' bikes waited for them in the pebbles, like spindly steel horses.

"All right! I'm done!" announced Ruby, storming back to shore. "I won't be able to carry all this if I keep at it!" She staggered a little under the weight of her basket as she strode from the water. "Ugh." The seaweed was oily on the soles of her bare feet.

Nell was glad she'd kept her boots on. As they walked up the stony shore, Ruby said, "Well, give us a look at what you found."

"Just scraps. And this." Nell took the hand she'd picked from the drift. Kodak flounced out of the water and ran in circles on the beach, shaking himself off with the disgruntled gait of a wet cat and the enthusiasm of a puppy. They planted themselves on the stones by the bikes for a moment. Ruby was panting a little, and her basket landed on the beach with a thud. It was almost completely full of smooth glass shards but for the occasional iceberg of bright plastic breaking the little sea of green.

Nell peeled the briny plastic wrap from the hand, cellophane strips placed there in some attempt at preserving it. The plastic was old but held strong. She unwound it like bandages and revealed the too pink painted skin. The hand was posed as though it were holding something invisible, painted crudely but with the intent of looking marginally lifelike—pinker nails, clumsily engraved knuckles. It stopped just below the wrist, with a screw protruding from a flat base. It was weirdly big, an ungraceful thing. Nell turned it over and over in her own hands, fascinated.

"What do you think, Ruby?" asked Nell, locking her fingers with it, her own hand small against it.

"Well, it's useless to me," answered her friend, absentmindedly combing through her basket of treasure. "If it were a bit more elegant, I'd use it for displaying rings, but it's too masculine for what I'm working on right now."

Nell hadn't thought about giving it boyness or girlness, but now it certainly seemed boy*ish*. A boy's hand.

"Huh, I suppose so," she mumbled.

"Look, you can keep him. Show him off down the Bayou; take him home to meet your father. Then all your problems will be over!" jibed Ruby, planting an elbow into Nell's ribs.

"Piss off." Nell elbowed her right back.

"Get him involved in the family business. Break Oliver Kelly's heart once and for all."

Oliver Kelly. Trust Ruby to conjure him to their quiet afternoon—in revenge, she placed the long, strange fingers of the hand on Ruby's face. She shrieked, and Nell cackled. Ruby had meant it, though, had thrown Oliver Kelly's name like the seaweed, slimy and cold, unpleasant.

"Can we go home?" asked Nell, retreating and discreetly placing the hand back into her satchel. She eyed the tide, a little greedier now, eating further into the land.

Ruby rolled her eyes. "So early."

"I know, I just . . . Da worries."

"It's what, five o'clock? It won't get proper dark until

ten. Your da needs to calm down."

"I know," Nell repeated, her voice sinking quietly in her throat. Her ticking escalated ever so slightly; she could just about hear it.

Ruby groaned and stood. "Fine, fine. Let's go."

They affixed their belongings to their bikes and took off in silent flight down the beach and out onto the deserted roads. They didn't say much as they shot along, their empty shadowbox city offering a meager welcome.

The population sign at the leaning harp of Godot Bridge boomed: Welcome to Black Water City, We're Well Again! Population 10,07**6**. It had been 74 that morning, and the paint was still wet. The number hadn't taken a significant dive downward in quite some time. It flickered week to week—three up here, three down there—marking the revolving door on the city. Nell took small reassurance from it; chances were that the babies had arrived safely, maybe had even been born without missing any parts. Or maybe it would be just a missing finger or toe or a cavity somewhere innocuous—lower back was common and easily repaired. They'd be due a good life in the Pasture; a whole body could be a ticket out of the Pale. The number would waver but would never plunge deep again.

Every time the number on the sign rose, though, their city gained strength. Glasses would be raised in the three taverns; the bands would play later. For all the gray and gloom, the people who remained in the city were happy and eager and strong. Their world was small, but they were content to try to make it bigger, one brick at a time.

By the looks of it, the construction workers were being let out an hour early, too. The girls found themselves cycling amid the daily exodus from the site of the giant woman.

Strong, stony-eyed folk, decked out in flannel and denim, hard hats under their arms, marked out with neon vests and heavy boots, strode toward the city in clusters. The women wore their hair in efficient braids; the men were largely bearded. They'd a style of their own, a culture developing all along the skirts and curves of the monument. Their kinetic limbs were bigger and gaudier than the rest of the civilians— part statement, part function. Their smart biorobotic arms and legs needed to support more movement, lift heavier things.

Altogether around a thousand people worked on the statue and would work on the next when this one was finally done. Some were older than Ruby's and Nell's fathers, some were just about their age, a couple here and there were younger. They were a vast collective, a village almost, working together to erect the closest thing their island had to a beacon. These folks had hope. Some sang their way home, others chatted. The news of the two births had spread.

The giant woman was Nell's titanic sister; her plans had been Nell's mother's contribution to Black Water City. Like any sister, Nell wasn't sure if she loved her or hated her and was almost certain she'd never live up to her. Best to admire her from a safe distance. The scale of her importance was staggering when she got too close. Nell's achievements—or striking lack thereof—were shameful in the shadow of what her parents had made.

Each lamppost they passed had the same stack of flyers hung on a shiny nail, declaring, "Dr. Julian Crane's Marvelous Augmentations—Present This Flyer and Construction Collective Membership Card for a Free Strength Upgrade!" Nell's father's sharp cheekbones and glinting eyes and round spectacles peered out from the ink. A genius, folks would say, but *so* reclusive. Such a shame what happened to Cora Starling-Crane! He must *still* be heartbroken. She was so young, they'd say. It was her death that drove him to be so passionate about his work; it was he, you know, who brought the first prosthetic to life! The augmentation! A miracle! And he was only *twenty-one* when he came up with it! Unheard of, that level of prodigy. And his tiny daughter! Well—

Somebody called out, "Look, it's Nell Crane! Heard you'll be joining us soon!" A ricochet reply: "Nah, she's going out to live with the preachers in the fields, aren't you, Nellie?" Other workers hooted and cheered, but Nell kept her head down, her skin crawling. Under no circumstances would she be joining them *or* going out to live in the Pasture. Ruby didn't say anything.

The pair coasted up the boardwalk alongside the Livia River, past the hodgepodge markets of downtown. The city was a labyrinth of burned-out houses littered with small pockets of community. It had taken almost a hundred years for this quiet to fall, for the fires to stop. It had once been so vibrant, so full of technology and ideas. Too much technology, some thought. Too many ideas.

That bright city was a thing of the past. Strictly rationed electricity dimmed the glow of the place to embers. They'd scorched it out, renamed it, started from nothing. But it was a peaceful ash heap at least. The blue turning violet of the sky was scored with black wires that had once carried power and information; now they simply hung there, making the sky a harsh dead grid above them, thin square shadows on the paths.

Nell and Ruby raced up the quays of the murky river

and swung north for the Phoenix Parklands, where their fathers' houses were. The hungry, pulsing trees and tall ferns filled the air with their dense aroma as the girls passed through the ancient iron gates and made their way up the winding road home. The parklands was almost a village scattered throughout a huge forest, pocked with old family houses, just outside the city. It had made a good retreat when the Turn had become violent: a dense, leafy stronghold, bubbling with swamps.

The Cranes and Underwoods were the only families in this neck of the woods. The farther Ruby and Nell rode, the more the greenery gnawed at the path until they turned sharply into the glades cradling their homes. When they pulled up at the messy garden that marked the Crane house, they stopped together.

"Still coming to the Bayou tomorrow, aren't you?" Ruby asked, challenging Nell to say no.

"Yes, I suppose."

Ruby made a theatrical, exaggerated noise. "Suppose! Try and muster up a little excitement for once, would you?"

Nell forced a smile that was all gritted teeth. "Yes. Yes, I'm coming."

"The party's going to be wonderful. Wear something nice like; don't make a show of me all decked out for a funeral. I'll come for you at half six." Ruby clumsily shifted her bicycle back toward the path. "Stick that awful hand in a pot of boiling water before putting it on any of your shelves, too. Never know, it might start creeping around when you're not looking."

Ruby stuck out her tongue and cycled away toward her house, just on the other side of a fat, twisted thicket of briars. Nell watched Ruby disappear, then led her bike to the house.

The Crane house stood with a shabby kind of magnificence on four thick pillars, twenty-odd feet from the ground. The wooden paneling on the walls was stained and dark; the windows were long and covered by blinds. If a wrong kind of magic touched it, it could walk away on its own, a clumsy creature of a house. It loomed. It was home.

It had started life as an elegant holiday home for the Starling family, visited rarely, planted deliberately in the last green lands of Black Water City. When Nell's willful mother decided she wanted to get out of the Pasture and live in the Pale, her parents reluctantly gave her the keys. As time peeled away that history, the house had taken Nell's father's name instead.

Nell checked the postbox. There a crisp, slim letter and a carefully wrapped brown package sat neatly together, addressed to Miss Penelope Starling-Crane. She sighed. Definitely from Nan.

She kicked out the stand and left her bike in its place under the stairway to the porch. Kodak scampered up her arm and onto her shoulder as she took her satchel and trudged up the stairs, her head a thousand miles away.

Through the front door, down the hall, and up another rickety stairway she went, creaking a symphony, up to the crooked landing, to her bedroom.

Nell's room was uncommonly large, with high ceilings and a bay window looking out over the tangled mess that their back garden had become. Just beyond a ridge of full, low-dipping willows, lay a small lake. In the dark, it reflected the night sky so clearly that sometimes it looked as if the whole world ended at the bottom of the garden. The Pasture could begin here really—Nell was sure of it—but healed folk had marked a twenty-mile stretch of land outside the city as sick, too. That whole barren territory was marked as the Pale. The Pasture spanned the rest of the island, ruined and quiet but for the port town to the west. During the island's quarantine a partition that stood to this day had been built around it. Nell hadn't any desire to leave but knew that out there in the western reaches of the Pasture was the Library Complex, towers full of paper from before the Turn, the printed

Internet, being alphabetized, sorted, stored—away from civilian eyes.

Nell had asked Nan in her childhood if she could go to visit the Library buildings, but Nan had just laughed. "You've enough paper here to be contending with, girl, rather than need to see what's out there."

Nell *did* occupy herself with an awful lot of paper. The walls of her sanctuary were covered in drawings and diagrams, proof of Nell's studies; detailed pencil-drawn charts of leaves, a dead mouse, how the kettle boils. Her father had been a distant mentor through her apprenticeship, but she worked hard, if alone.

She drew reams and reams and reams of things on long sheets of butcher paper: thin detailed lines, light gray shading, to scale and then bigger and bigger. Massive spiders stood watch with unmoving eyes from their homes on her papers. A single great rose almost burst into a flood of gray petals above her bed. By her wardrobe were a cluster of self-portraits and a constellation of drawings of her mother, facial comparison studies. They had the same full mouth, the same brown skin, the same nest of thick, untamable hair.

Nell dropped her satchel and sat down by the window at her drawing table to read the letter. It was heavy in her hands. She'd been expecting it. She hadn't replied to the last one or the one before. This table was the quietest space in the whole room: a barren expanse but for a fat stack of similar envelopes in the corner, weighted down by a spare wrench. It was a stark plain in contrast with the mad cavern of her work desk, a quiet place to think. Nell ran her finger along the gum of the envelope and tore it open.

Penelope, dear.

Where has the time gone? Summer again already—the days are so long, a grand stretch in the evening. I'm sure you're as surprised as I am that contribution season is almost upon us. For so many families in the city this must be such an exciting time, the next generation of apprentices ready to contribute to the healing. Out here in the Pasture everyone is positively humming with curiosity about what the contributions will be. There is stone fruit on every altar, and my rituals have mostly taken place outdoors.

I would love to be as excited as my neighbors, but sadly I have a great deal of trepidation about your seeming unwillingness—or inability—to provide any progress reports on your project to either the Youth Council or to me.

This is not easy, but I must be stern in the face

of your recent silence. I'm unsure what kind of point you're trying to make. Is this a silent rebellion, or pure laziness, or a cry for help? I certainly hope it's not a deliberate attempt to cause Julian Crane—or me—any anxiety. If you believe there to be some charm or honor in working the stone woman site, then you are sorely mistaken.

You are from the line that drew the stone woman. Our Cora was a pioneer. She found a way to employ hundreds of people, to give them hope. You'll bring nothing but shame on us. My own mother and father didn't strive as hard as they did to remain whole and healthy just so the last in the Starling line could throw it all in. Cora had a rebellious streak, but she worked hard. You are simply not doing enough, Penelope.

I've outlined below the only options I see fit for you from here on in.

1. Produce a contribution of excellent standard by the Youth Council's appointed date.

2. Quickly, and without notable fuss, begin a courtship with an appropriate partner whose contribution aligns with your skillset. If you do pursue this avenue, alert me immediately so I can schedule a visit at the soonest possible juncture in

order to approve your selection.

3. Pack up your belongings and relocate to my estate on the Pasture. I can formally employ you as my personal assistant, and you will remain preserved from stonework.

4. Continue to squander your time. In this case, I am unsure if Julian will permit your residence at the parkland house, and I will be ceasing any contact and withdrawing my support. You will not work on the stone site with my blessing.

I will write each choice on a nectarine and place them on the windowsill until the season changes. I hope the fourth rots last, child. This letter has taken me all day to write. I have been reading it aloud to myself over and over. These things need to be said before it is too late. I hope you will make the right decision. Cora would have wanted more for you than the scaffolding and the stoneyard. You could have a very good life out here in the Pasture if you wanted.

Write me soon. My love and blessings are with you.

Nan

CHAPTER 2

The first thing is you are ten years old.

Your last summer in the Pasture is rose and tender until it is sour and wrong.

Your grandmother isn't much taller than you, all long linen jackets in coral and powder blue, all floral skirts. She smells like dry lavender, like aloe vera and safety. She wears rough crystals on her neck, on her fingers. She asks you questions and hangs your drawings around the mirror in her dressing chamber. You love her, and you love the halls of her country home, the high ceilings and the tall, airy corridors, the shiny marble floors, the lush carpets. There's nowhere in Black Water City like the Starling manor. Starling, like the iridescent black birds with bright white tips on the feathers on their breasts, like comets falling on an oily night sky. Starling like your mother.

You wish your chest would sound like a falling star. Instead, *tick, tick, tick,* all along the hallways. It bounces back at you from the shining surfaces. It echoes as if there were more of you. But there aren't more of you. Just one. Nan doesn't care.

You sit on the floor at her feet in the conservatory. All the world is green just past the glass walls, and the sky is spotless blue. Nothing is gray. This is the uncity. Nan is in the grand wicker chair, Kodak resting on the arm beside her. She braids your hair, the masses of it, with dexterity. Your ticking reverberates louder against the glass, and you are trying to ignore it, trying not to let it change the fabric of this quiet afternoon world. Nan doesn't mention it (Nan never mentions it), and you are thankful to her for this. You are thankful for her pearly painted nails on your scalp, knowing and gentle. She hums a sweetness, and it gets behind your eyes and you feel better. You can barely hear yourself when you focus on her voice.

You aren't sure if you believe in magic, but you understand why people say she is an oracle. You understand why they gather in the garden after dark and listen to her prayers. You understand why people come to her with lost objects, broken hearts. Her hands are in your hair, and you are not a clockwork girl; you're her grandchild, protected. The Pasture is endless, and the city is nowhere in sight. You are warm in this prism. You could stay. You think about asking her if she'd let you. She might.

You are without lessons for the season, without Oliver Kelly on weekends and your father's watchful eye, his rules. You are without constant instruction or the fumes from the laboratory, the relentless stench of scorched metal. These things all fade into the concrete city beyond the horizon line of the Pasture.

You wish you could show Ruby these rolling fields, this clear sky. Even still, you are happy. A quiet, ordinary feeling. Nan doesn't say anything, you don't say anything, and the pair of you are linked in the afternoon hush.

Two of her maids bustle in just then, wheeling a gilded tea service. Healed, the pair of them, or just about; you can't spot any augmentations. The elder of the pair, Lynn, who's worked in the Starling house as long as you remember, begins to unload dainty porcelain towers of iced cakes, pink and white and mint. She transfers them to a glass table, low enough that neither you nor Nan has to bend out of your way to eat.

The other girl you've never seen before. She's a teenager, hair cropped close to a pixie face. You don't get too much of a look at her before she exclaims,

"Oh!" and drops a teacup. It smashes empty on the tiles. Her eyes are ice blue; you notice then—only because they're all over you. *Tick, tick, tick.* They're up and down the length of your scar, her pupils pinpoint, her mouth sour, open.

She pales a little, bubbles, "Sorry, sorry, sorry," blushing and stammering. She's still staring, your neck, your chest, a moment, two, then blusters away, leaving the air thick and awful. It is too bright in here. Your skin is too tight. Lynn quickly picks up the pieces of the cup and, producing another, seamlessly pours tea and places two cups at the bottom of the cake tree. But all you can see is the new girl's horror, her shaking hands.

"I am so, so sorry about this, Mrs. Starling," Lynn trills. "I warned Annie about Miss Nell, but she just wasn't prepared. I'll ensure it doesn't happen again."

Nan does not say a word, but her hands are motionless on your head. Lynn leaves the cornucopia of tiny cakes and proud-bellied teapot on the table, curtsies, and wheels the service away.

Tickticktick.

You are old enough now that when adults talk as though you were not there, you are not oblivious. Instead, you are furious, and the sound your body makes is the music of that fury. Nan's hands take up braiding again, and steam rises from the teacups. Perhaps you would like, after all, to go back to the city. You are not like the people in the city, but you are more like them than like the folk here. City people never look scared of you.

"Not to worry. We'll get you some nice, colorful scarves," coos Nan, and you say, "Thank you," but you mean, "Why didn't you say anything?" and you mean, "Are you scared of me, too?"

You don't see the younger maid again, but her eyes are on you always. Her mouth, disgusted. You don't go to the Pasture the following summer. You miss it, the green world, until you don't. Until the gray world is a comfort.

You don't stop missing Nan, though. She sends scarves in brown paper packages, and you wear them around your throat, disguise your scar with softness, with cotton. They come every week. She stops asking you to visit. Eventually she starts telling you what to do.

CHAPTER 3

Far outside the boundaries of Black Water City, a silent, guarded line lay between the Pale and the Pasture. The world changed there. The sick were raised and grew and contributed in the Pale; the healed lived and farmed and prayed in the tall grasslands of the Pasture. Nell cast a look over her shoulder at her tousled bed and thought for a moment about the fresh, expensive white sheets she'd sleep in at Nan's, about the quality of the light out there.

Until now Nan's weekly letters had been concerned, full of questions, but never formal. Never angry. Or cold. Nell traced her fingers over Nan's writing, something worse than guilt catching in her throat. She folded the paper over and placed it back into its envelope, then shuffled it anonymously into the bundle of correspondence. Her wrench, a sometime paperweight, sat in its place.

The package the letter had arrived with was wrapped with such precision that Nell took it apart with reverence, so as not to spoil the embossed paper patterned with tiny birds in flight. It contained a scarf, a wisteria print flecked with tiny sequins, newly woven, not salvaged. A scarf for going out. A fancy scarf, one for the mood lighting at the Bayou. A pretty disguise. Nell pulled it out to wrap around her shoulders, and something fell out of its shimmering folds: four batteries, shrink wrapped. A small square of paper flittered to the ground. Nell scooped it up. Nan again: "Make good use of these."

A smile woke up in Nell. All right, Nan, she thought. I will.

She unpeeled the film and examined the batteries: wouldn't be much use for a big project, but for a small exercise, perfect.

Nell's work desk, oak and sturdy and far older than she was, was nestled in an alcove in the corner of her room, just a little away from her drawing table. It was part immaculate order and part utter chaos and looked as if it had bloomed out of the wall: a natural junkyard, just her size. There were jars full of tiny gears, clusters of springs, careful assortments of screws, collections of tape, coils of wires organized by size on the pegboard on the wall, their metal glinting in the lamplight. There was just enough room for Nell to spread her elbows, a whole inventory of pieces and parts barely even an arm's length away. She knew the geography of this clockwork cove better than any place.

A tiny blowtorch was coupled neatly with an alarmingly toothy set of pliers, overseen by a grand family of hammers displayed on the headboard, all the way from the daintiest of cross-peen pins to a grand, fat joiner's mallet. Nell had never actually used that one; she didn't really deal in large constructions, but it was handy to have it there nonetheless. Hinges of gold and silver and stainless steel and some polluted with rust lay about the place like loose butterflies in a lush metal garden. This was Nell's playground, and her Nan, her furious Nan, had gifted her some new batteries to toy with.

Two sets of goggles hung like neighbors: one for general protection (Nell had torched her eyebrows off on more than one occasion) and the other equipped with adjustable lenses, allowing her to look more closely at smaller parts and mechanisms without having to use one hand for a magnifying glass. Though lupes and spyglasses were helpful, too; a bouquet of varying lenses stood in a vase in the corner.

Nell's gloves (latex, cotton, leather, steel tipped at the fingers) and welding masks all were hung in clusters, where she could change them in a moment as her projects dictated. Her lamp dangled from a thick red cord from the ceiling, a pool of yellow enveloping her workshop.

Two pins, two wee ball bearings. Nell used tweezers to make sure they didn't up and roll away into the crevice between the desk and the wall (it ate more good parts than she could spare). One fresh battery. Some springs, a couple of cogs, three inches of wire. Two buttons painted to look like eyes. Twenty-five minutes of Nell's fingers pulling sense from the scrap, her whole mind empty but for the rising satisfaction of a tiny creature coming together at her hands. It was only a creature because of the eyes. Otherwise it was just a practical exercise in assembly and kinetic movement. She was running scales on the piano here, conjugating satisfying reams of verbs.

The eyes were a tiny flourish, a vibrato on the high note. They were a perfectly rolled *r*. They made the tiny machine more than the sum of its parts. They made it look alive as she connected the copper to the battery, as the tiny pin legs moved one after the other. Alive, rather than simply logic. Just cause and effect. Nell looked down at the bobbly little battery with legs, a mess with no casing or style. She could see how every part of him worked—how every part of *it* worked. It.

There was no magic here. Eyes didn't make it any

more than coils and wire and hinge and metal. Scrap. Practice. The exercise of the steel sprite wasn't enough for Nell anymore. She wanted more than button eyes. She knew that before the Turn machines could think. *That.* That was what she wanted.

The sprite skittered clumsily across her desk. A whispered word for a thinking machine was *computer.* The word sent thrills down Nell's spine. Forbidden, clever metal things.

Computers had brought about the end of the world. Black Water City was so grateful to have survived— even if it was still sick and wheezing—that the very mention of computers was blasphemy. They were brought to life by reams of numbers that conjured thought, and impulse, and memory out of nothing. Whole tomes of language in numbers and oblique symbols that, when lined up just right, could bring consciousness to steel. She longed for access to it, for how huge it could be.

Nell didn't think there was any reason to be afraid of numbers and letters. She'd been raised with a wrench in her hand; there wasn't a thing made of steel that could spook her. She spent her every waking hour listening to the ticking of a machine that kept her alive. She was sure that the rest of the folk in Black Water City were afraid only because they didn't ask questions, because they believed what they were told. If all you'd ever heard about the history of your world was horror stories about gleaming boxes full of bad knowledge, of course you'd be afraid.

Nell knew better than this. Her father had told her that the metal boxes full of magic had been fine. It was people, frightened, angry people, that had brought the world down. Was it just the boxes, she often wondered, that they were so afraid of? How easy it is to stuff myth and horror into a box. Haunted slices of clever steel, something with hard lines, something cold.

Surely, if there was a way to make a computer look like something people trusted, there'd be a chance for a world full of clever machines again. Friendly-looking computers, full of knowledge, full of answers. Nell sighed. "Think of all we could know."

Her wish fell dead in the air, onto the desk. She watched her tiny motion machine dance across the surface and tapped her fingernails against the wood, matching the rhythm it walked in. It was almost endearing, its little eyes blankly staring out. She turned it around, and it walked back toward her, a kind of sweetness to its almost dance.

She imagined it blinking up at her, moving of free will rather than rote.

"Hello," she whispered. It tippled along, silent. Nell

wanted so much more, but all she had was this desk, these batteries. The analogue. The *not enough*.

She sighed, caught the sprite as it attempted to potter away toward a nest of springs. She disengaged the battery, and all movement dropped out of the little creature. A quiet, tiny friend, but not enough.

Kodak nipped at her ankles, not willing to be ignored much longer, then hopped into her lap. This was the specific kind of needy he always became at this time of night. The hunt, then dinner.

"A'right, a'right," Nell conceded, placing the tiny exercise on a shelf above her tools where a space was open, ready, among a menagerie of twenty, thirty steel sprites just like him. None worthy of presentation, none a big deal. Essentially the shelf was full of toys. Nell sighed, looking up at them, knowing they were a waste of battery energy, knowing that her new little pal wasn't what Nan had intended Nell to use her gift for. She tucked Kodak under her arm, grabbed her satchel, and walked across her room, away from her cove, to the great bay window. The sprites were trinkets, just enough to satisfy the parts of her that wanted to bring things to life; what Nell needed was something much bigger. Black Water City needed something much bigger, too.

She swung the window wide and stepped out into the fresh night.

CHAPTER 4

Nell sat on the hot red tiles of the roof, looking out over the parklands and the city. Kodak was curled up at her feet. Out beyond the glistening green of the forest the city cracked open with light against the darkened sky, a pomegranate with a split gut, all jewels. When the city had been rebuilt, dedicating electricity rations to illuminating the streets had been the local council's absolute imperative. Memories of the atrocities had hung around dark corners, and the light kept the deep swaths of national depression at bay. On the roof, Nell kept a little oil lamp by her side (no sense in wasting a battery) so she wouldn't lose footing, and the glow was a cradle against the blackness of the forest at night.

In the distance stood the tall white monument, Kathleen ni Houlihan. Or Kath, Kate, Katie. Stone and majesty, six hundred and some feet tall. Nell's mother,

Cora, had designed her body on paper at the very same desk Nell drew at. Cora had pulled her construction out of her imagination. For her whole life, Nell had been watching her mother's contribution rise over the cityscape from this quiet spot on her roof. Day after day Kate grew, and now all that was missing was the right side of her face, a forearm and hand. She was posed gracefully, reaching one hand back out to the ocean and one arm toward the center of the city, stopping, incomplete, at the elbow. Nell usually came out to say good-night to her. They'd been made by the same woman after all.

Nell's stomach tightened at the sight of her mother's contribution. There really was only a few months left for her own. Her grandmother's list scrolled behind her eyes. Make something. Marry someone. Leave. Shame them all by going to the stoneyard. Of the four, only one was something she wanted to reach out and touch, and that was the making. But *what?* Something worthy and important and powerful. Something that mattered to her as well as to the city.

Nell was a good mimic, had a good eye for structure. She drew excellent plans for all sorts of little civilian machines: cameras, typewriters, useful recreational objects that unfortunately existed already and were in no need of augmentation. Why build something new if one from before the Turn could be salvaged?

"We're trying to *move forward*," her father would insist. "Keep that in mind. You should be contributing something that brings us forward."

Nell wasn't sure it was possible to go forward if they didn't look back to before the Turn. Their island was still disconnected from the rest of the world.

The people of the city lived in a strange, dusty cornucopia. There were so few of them left in a place built for millions that they all had more or less what they needed. Except Nell. She couldn't fish a worthy idea out of the water at the end of the Livia.

Every time Nell mentioned this looming problem to her father, he told her she was "frustrating but capable," that he was *sure* she would think of something and then occupied himself elsewhere.

It was as if the topic of her future were a mild potential inconvenience, preferably one to be avoided, as opposed to a massive shift in Nell's entire life trajectory.

If she chose the monument, Nell would be gone on early or late shift work, laying stones from one end of the day to another. Her only friend would probably be too embarrassed by her to keep her company, and even if she weren't, their lives would look so different. Their worlds, unmoored, would drift. Ruby was already untethering herself anyway, shamelessly unpicking the knots of their friendship to loose herself upon the world, and there was absolutely nothing Nell could do about it. Nobody ever made Ruby do anything she didn't want to.

Ruby would become a tailor or a weaver or whatever she wanted. She could start her own business or marry into a partnership or take ability tests to start life in the Pasture if she wanted; she was whole but for her eye. Ruby stood in a bright atrium with open doors on all sides. Ruby was going to be just fine.

If Nell walked through the door that led to the monument, maybe she would find new friends— once she got over the massive, excruciating shame of falling so far short of the Crane family brilliance. Maybe she could just curl up and disappear. That sounded appealing.

If Nell moved to the Pasture, maybe she could convince the people there that she was an oracle, just like Nan. Give prayer sermons and blessings. Put bird bones and sage in little jars, and call them spells. Be the only augmented living thing for three hundred miles. Get stared at by the healed; get treated like a piece of machinery. Crack up completely. Delightful.

Option three: Oliver Kelly.

Nope.

Nell sighed deeply, opened her satchel, and began

to unpack her spoils from the shore. She laid them out in the lamplight. The thick spool of stiff copper wire. Two large, unbroken lightbulbs. Nell considered taking them apart. Their filaments could be salvaged; she could perhaps cut them open very gently, maybe turn them into terrariums for the kitchen. A handful of sea glass that Ruby didn't want. The headset of an analogue telephone, easily from well before the Turn. It would have been the best find of the day if it hadn't been for the hand.

Nell examined it carefully, curious. It was nothing more than a stray piece of a mannequin. But she admired it. Such a strange piece of the old world. A boy's hand.

Any time Nell thought about boys, or girls for that matter, she immediately sabotaged her fantasy self out of any romance. No beautiful strangers waited in the lamplight to whisk her away from her life, and if there were, Nell was certain that she'd viciously alienate them in less than five minutes flat. If it wasn't her dour expression or the scar that ran from her chin to her gut, then the ticking would send them running. There's not much thrill in kissing a grandfather clock in a girl's dress. Nobody wants to dance with a time bomb.

It all came so naturally to Ruby. Ruby was funny and pretty and didn't tick. She always had a boyfriend—she ate up the thirsty-eyed boys and spit them out, bored as soon as they had made themselves comfortable. She picked her teeth with their bones and cackled scandal to Nell, who usually loved the thrill of Ruby's tales. Or she had when she believed that she'd grow into something like Ruby's charm or come across someone who could see past the height of her family's name, her ticking. Now Nell's hope was dimming, and Ruby's ease seemed so unfair. Plus Ruby had ideas. She was always creating beautiful things.

Nell turned the hand over again and again.

What use was a hand with no boy to go with it? Nell could have launched it off the roof that very moment, sent it plummeting down into the garden to smash or rot or otherwise disappear. She looked to stone Kate on the horizon, mocked throwing it right at her head.

"You can have it," she said to the one-handed stone woman on the skyline, her voice catching with the bitterness. "You need it more than I do."

In the distance, the torchlights of the night watch folk danced around the woman's skirts, her waist, her neck. They were fireflies, phosphorescent and magic instead of labored and repetitive. It looked so much better from far away, Nell thought. She might be a firefly someday soon, a glowing speck waltzing around the still, hard body of the closest thing Black

Water City had to a god. The god people like her grandmother prayed to in the Pasture was too busy with green fields to throw its eyes on the metal and concrete of the Pale. Kate would do. Nell held the hand up to the statue's unfinished arm, the perspective difference between her and the great statue making it almost match. Almost.

"You're not finished yet, are you?" Nell whispered. "It's okay. Neither am I."

Someday soon it would take twenty or thirty people and miles of thick cable rope and sweat and aching muscles to bring the forearm up from the city floor to its position at the end of Kate's elbow. Every day sculptors sat around an enormous hand, chipping away at the stone, detailing her fingers, her palm. Do women of stone get life lines? Love lines? Do their knuckles have marks? Do their fingernails have cuticles? Calluses? Did the sculptors just slapdash the work to make the hand look moderately human, or did they write her life there?

As she mulled over her future with a pick and hammer, with rope-burned hands and shadows under her eyes from the night watch, she began to unspool the wire she'd salvaged. It was sharp, and if she wasn't careful, she would tear her fingertips; but Nell knew how to deal with metal. She loved the smell of it, how it changed against heat. She coiled the wire around the wrist of the useless hand a few times and then extended the spiral slowly around the air, a scaffolding for an invisible arm, a hard copper spiderweb. She reached where the elbow would have been and stopped. She pulled her pliers out of the front pouch of her satchel (with her big magnifying glass and spare leather gloves and knife and the panic whistle Ruby made her keep on her at all times) and nipped the wire free from the rest of the spool. What remained was a wire frame gauntlet, an empty arm for the mannequin hand.

"This will have to do for now," she whispered, holding it up. Kate's face was still missing, but her body was now more or less complete in Nell's gaze. Awkward, partially metal, but complete.

Motes of dust were illuminated by Nell's lantern, and against the dark they seemed like tiny live sprites swirling around the inventor's daughter. She held the copper skeleton arm alongside her own and locked her fingers with the hard, unmoving mannequin hand. She had never held a boy's hand before.

In the dim light his body, from elbow to shoulder to other shoulder, bloomed before her. His throat, his chest, his stomach and hips and legs. His skin, the rise and fall of breath.

Her mother gave this city a six-hundred-foot woman

of stone. Her mother drew the inside and outside of her onto paper and stood in front of the council and told them that building a stone body would remind them of their humanity, after everything.

What could be more human than building something new, more human than making life? An idea lit Nell up then, sparkling like the torches along Kate's stony skirts.

If it was possible to build parts of a person, it was possible to build a whole one. Of course it was. If people were afraid of coded magic in steel boxes, she'd take the magic out of the steel boxes and put it in a brand-new body. Not a stone giant. One just her size. A whole person. Hang limbs on a spine and find a way to give him a brain, a heart—a soul. Could you make a soul out of spare and found parts? Why not?

"Sorry, Kate," Nell whispered, gripping the hand. "I think I'll be needing this after all."

CHAPTER 5

It always happens like this.

You are seven years old. You have a pain in your chest. Or something like it. At least, a murmur of pain, a suggestion. You are coming to, just waking up. You are lying down and looking up, and there is light blinding you; there is something over your mouth. You are having difficulty breathing.

A gray mechanical hand descends on you, and you begin to panic; but it releases you from the mask, and you can breathe easier. You are sure for a moment that your father is standing above you: his blurry silhouette, his tall presence. He casts a warm shadow. There is a noise you can't quite make out, but it is new and constant. Then he is gone.

You try to lean forward, to sit up and reach for him, but you are so heavy. You say something that should be his name, but your tongue is deadened and useless. You pull your new, shocking weight against gravity, and after an eternity, you sit up, and the new sound suddenly makes sense: a clock. A tense, even punctuation. The volume of it ascends like a sick panic, like something terrible.

"Da?" You try to say it again; but nothing comes, and you climb down off the bed—no, the bench— the operating table. Wires lead from your wrists like the strings on a marionette, but you cannot see where the wires go; you are connected to something you cannot see.

You stumble to your feet. You want to walk, you want to run; but fat wires are holding you, and the ticking is deafening. A roulette wheel, a machine gun.

Your bottom lip becomes heavy; your mouth weighs a ton. It splits open, your chin and throat part, your sternum and chest, your gut, and there are birds coming from you, small steel birds flying from the cavity of you. Their song is a ticking and mechanical symphony, ugly and loud. The birds are the last thing; they are always the last thing, gray and red and everywhere, singing a terrible countdown. *Tick, tick, tick.*

When you wake in the sharp of morning, whole and grown, the wires are gone. The dark is gone, your room is quiet and safe,; but the ticking is still there. It is always there. The ticking is always there.

CHAPTER 6

Nell brushed her teeth at the small sink in the poky water closet off her bedroom. When the dream came and the ticking in her chest got so loud it woke her and left her shaking, she knew how to handle it. She couldn't just lie among her blankets and pillows and dwell on it; she had to get up and be a live, mobile person. Her father was rattling around the house somewhere. Kodak must have been down there with him because he was nowhere in sight. She rinsed her mouth and washed her face and pinned away her mad spirals of curls.

She dressed herself from the tall wardrobe in the corner, in front of a gilded mirror. It had been her mother's; aside from underthings and shoes, everything Nell wore had once belonged to her mother. Cora Crane had always dressed remarkably well, even in her daughter's hazy memories of her. It was one of the few trappings of her Pastoral upbringing that she held about her in her city life: good fabric, everything made just her size.

Nell wanted to carry that same grace, the same silhouette. She was tall and spindly where Cora had been short and soft, but things somehow still managed to fit, just about.

Loose culottes, small boots. A blouse with short sleeves and a high collar. A long scarf wound around her neck. Another wound around her hair, to keep it out of her face. Earth tones, all, today. Deep blues and greens and browns and burgundies. If Nell stood out in the thicket at the right time of evening, she'd be invisible. She leaned in close to the mirror and dabbed tincture on her lips, and they bloomed red. The ticking slowly hushed to its usual thrum as she completed her morning routine, her self-assembly, with focused deliberation. It was barely audible by the time she was ready to leave her room and go downstairs.

The hand sat, untouched, on the pillow where she had left it. She stared at it for a moment, considering whether or not she should bring it down for breakfast, rest it next to her mug full of tea and saucer heaped with toast, but decided against it. If her father saw it, she'd have to tell him where it came from, and he wouldn't be impressed. She'd keep it to herself, the warm egg of something terrific. No use in his tapping on it until it cracked. It would hatch when it was ready.

She pottered out of her room and down the steep wooden stairs. The Cranes didn't have a lounge or living room downstairs: just Julian's laboratory and the cavernous kitchen. The house was more or less a two-up two-down, but bigger, and it had become crooked with expansion. The laboratory's door was permanently closed. The kitchen, however, was the most welcoming room Nell had ever known.

It was a hearth and a belly and a hub, a powerful room, all terra-cotta flooring and strong, exposed beams. Drifting spider plants hung in old glass jars from the rafters. Lanky shelves, most neatly packed with books upon books, stood around the walls, but occasional cubbies would be precariously stacked with crockery and pans. The kitchen could have just as easily served as a library in its own right. It basically served as everything else: from principal location of many a town meeting to Nell's childhood playroom, her classroom.

The kitchen table was a huge, stately-looking slab. It had borne witness to so much change. The elbows of giants had rested on it, world-changing plans had bounced back and forth over it, and it had seen more than its fair share of spilled food, water, and wine. The cooker was a gnarled wrought-iron thing, black and imposing. It was scarred from half a century of heavy use. A kettle, bronzed and ornate, stood on a scorching red hob and sang the beginning of a boiling song. Julian stood with his back to his daughter, plucking a pair of mugs out of the cupboard, one in his human arm, one in his augmented arm. He looked tired but not irritated. Nell took this as a blessing.

"Tea?" he asked brightly.

"Yes!" Nell replied. "Have you eaten?"

"No, but there's just enough of that loaf left to sort us both out for the morning. And there's fresh jam. The eggs went off overnight."

Quietly they prepared breakfast, sweet and simple, the same thing they ate almost every morning, depending what had been gifted to them that week. So many of the great tradesmen of the city were indebted to Julian for the limbs he had built them that they were kept in fresh bread, sweet jams, cured meat. Nell's days were regularly punctuated by taking calls from the townsfolk bearing tokens. Part of her apprenticeship seemingly was to act as receptionist to the Marvelous Dr. Crane. It was exhausting: all that smiling and thanking people and taking note of who dropped off what and who paid their debts in tokens and who paid theirs in produce.

Julian was often too wrapped up to take them himself. Or at least he said he was busy. "Ordinary" craftsfolk profoundly annoyed him, and the misanthropic apple didn't really fall far from the antisocial tree; Nell wasn't in the least bit keen on the hostessing bit either. The townspeople often looked her over and asked prying questions about her forthcoming contribution. She played secretive to them usually, as though her great idea wasn't ready to be spoken aloud yet. Her ticking would rise, but she'd grit her teeth, gracious through the panic. Who knew if they ever believed her, but she did what she could, smiling and thanking them for coming all the way out to the parklands, for considering her family in their weekly dues. She'd shut the door softly after visitors, then lean against it, eyes closed, inhaling and exhaling her ticking back to normal.

The Cranes sat at the table with steaming mugs of tea, small bags of dried dark leaves at the bottom, bitter hot cups, and thick slabs of soda bread toast slathered in sweet, fresh nectarine jam. They ate quietly and thoughtfully in the morning warmth.

Their family resemblance rang true, except that Julian was pale and Nell was not. They had the same bags under their eyes, the same heavy lids. He was tall and thin and had a long, sad face, which in public was usually animated with an earnest charm that passed for authentic, that kept people rapt. This was why he could only ever be social in small doses. It exhausted him to be well liked. Nell saw it, and heard the flatness behind his jovial tone.

"Your hair needs a cut, Da."

"Do you think Ruby'd give it a go over for me this afternoon? Tomorrow?" Julian ruffled it with his hand, and it stuck out at all angles.

Nell nodded. "I'll ask her. You look ridiculous."

Julian feigned a grateful bow over his tea, with a flourish of his augmented hand.

Aside from the hair situation, he looked very formal today. He wore a neatly fitting linen shirt, a highly respectable tie, and black suit pants with shiny black shoes. He wasn't working in the lab; he was heading out to the city to fit people with new limbs. He made every single one from scratch, then brought them down to the city twice a week to affix them to new owners at the Medical Center.

His arm was the miracle about him. It was the first of its kind, a fully responsive and intuitive biorobotic limb. It was a tasteful matte gray steel, not painted to match his skin or a gaudy plastic, as many of the more popular models were. It was modest and silent. The formula for his structures was impervious to epidemic traces or aftershocks: it was safe, healing technology.

Nell was never sure whether or not she hated it. When she looked too closely at it, it shone with everything she hadn't been able to achieve. The best contribution their infant city had ever seen. The healer of the nation.

Julian had been looked upon as a boy genius, a maverick: solely responsible for revolutionizing how the survivors of the epidemic lived. He'd been born without his left arm. The legend went that he built model after model until he eventually developed the design that behaved perfectly naturally. He'd started with wood, then advanced to steel, then broken the steel down, and made it cleverer, completely kinetic. Somewhere between wire and steel and organic materials, some perfect formula. His wife's family, the Starlings, hovered above, possibly pulling delicate strings in his favor; what he presented was dangerously close to pre-Turn technology, the kind that their land was still paying for. But it was deemed necessary, and he received an exception from the council. Kinetic augmented limbs were declared nondisruptive.

Nell had just been born when he presented the first model, and Cora still alive. They were young, bright parents on the cusp of a healing world.

Now it was just Julian and Nell. He was still a

hero of the city, and she—well, they all were waiting for her. She couldn't drop by the beauty shop for a replacement kohl pencil without Delia and Janey, the highly painted ladies with soft voices and impossibly colored hair, cooing, "Girl, you got anything exciting in the works?"

Ruby was usually Nell's shield in these circumstances. She'd laugh it off and say something like "Ladies! Would you put a cake on the table before it was iced?" or "There's no point in asking her. Every time she tries to explain it to me, I've not a clue what she's talking about!" But lately even Ruby had stopped trying.

"Having dinner with Daniel and the mayor tonight," Julian said, holding a slice of bread near his mouth. "You going to the Bayou?"

Of course he knew about the party tonight. Nobody Julian's age would be caught dead at the Bayou, but tonight's party was out of the ordinary; murmurings must have eked out to the circles of tradesmen and masters alike.

"Yes. Ruby says it's important."

"Daniel was telling me. She's not wrong. You can't be going and hanging around there twice every week without showing up and raising a glass to the twins. They pulled that place out of nowhere, you know. It was an incredible contribution to the city, given their start in the world."

Nell raised the deep mug to her mouth and closed her eyes. Contribution. The Fox twins *did* deserve a celebration, and yes, the Bayou was important to a lot of people; but she hated it. Noise and clutter, all the bodies and smoke. Ruby always spent the first fifteen minutes with her, a pained look on her face, then excused herself to dance with somebody and was gone. Nell would spend the rest of the night perched at the bar, people-watching, warding off nosy acquaintances. Twice a week, every week. She'd stay until Ruby forgot she was there, and then she'd ghost out without any good-byes. Lately she'd had to stay for less and less time; last week it had only been an hour.

"You should try to enjoy yourself, occasionally, Nell. It's starting to show in your face. You'll never get anything done if you worry all the time; you'll run down your engine from the stress. Wouldn't want that, would you? Besides, how do you expect to create anything if you can't enjoy anything? You're no use to anyone if you're cracking yourself up." Julian finished his tea and the last chunk of sweet, crumbly bread, then wiped his hands, the flesh of the left and augmented steel of the right passing each other without a second of delay or interference, without a telltale creak or hum. It used to hum loudly; this silence was fresh.

Why couldn't he have made the machine in her chest quiet, instead of so imposing and loud. He probably could now, Nell supposed, with the advances he'd made in his designs, but the idea of ever going under a knife again made her sick to her stomach. She put down her tea. Even the quiet wouldn't be worth it.

"I'll swing home in the afternoon to see if you and Ruby are about to sort out this mop"—he ran a hand through his hair again—"and tonight I'm hoping to be back in the house early. I've some new work to go over with Daniel, so don't be surprised if the house is quiet when you get in; we'll be in the lab. Ruby can stay over if she doesn't want to sleep in the cottage on her own."

Her father gathered himself, collecting his dark leather doctor's bag and his bicycle helmet from the rack on the wall by the door to the back garden. He left his plate and mug on the table.

"You look like someone died, Nell." Julian ruffled her hair a little too hard, dislodging her headscarf. "Oh, and this is for you. See if you can get it to light up, will you? I haven't had a minute to look at it, and I thought it'd make an interesting project. Might spark something, you know? You're running out of time."

He opened his bag and pulled out an almost flat silver box, around the size of his palm. Nell took it from him. One side of it was black glass; the other, silver. On one of the thin edges there were two small holes. Nell hadn't a clue what it was.

"Somebody gave it to me on the quiet down at the clinic, thought I'd be interested in it. From the look of it, it's a music box. Digital. Absolutely pre-epidemic, pre-Turn. Contraband of the highest order. Run a few volts through it real gently. See what happens."

"But—" Nell began, wanting to know exactly *how* she would just "run a few volts" through this tiny box without setting it on fire, but he was out of the kitchen and down the hall. The front door opened and closed with a click. She sighed deeply and placed the little box on the table next to her unfinished breakfast.

She plucked the teabag out of Julian's abandoned mug and placed it in her own, the water still hot, pulling more deep, bitter flavor from the damp leaves in the used paper pouch. She sat there awhile, still and quiet. Kodak crept into the kitchen and hopped up into her lap. Nell fed him morsels of the soda bread until it was all gone, then rinsed the mugs and saucers.

She left them to dry and wandered back upstairs to her bedroom, almost forgetting to take the silver "music box" or whatever it was that Julian had left her. She'd pull it apart all right, but she was doubtful that anything on her work desk would be compatible with technology as sophisticated as this. She could stick some eye buttons onto it maybe. Maybe a battery pack and tiny motorized legs. With three batteries she could build a propeller and make it fly, but Nell doubted that she could make it sing.

She wasn't even sure that she liked music that much. The loud clutter of noise and old torch songs the band at the Bayou played made her whole face hurt. Why would she want to take it all back home with her? Why would she want to listen to music from a different time? Surely it was all going to be a mess that she didn't understand.

Nell tossed the box onto her bed and grabbed the hand from her pillow. She sat at her desk and set the hand in front of her. Kodak nestled around her ankles.

She looked at the hand and lifted her pencil to the enormous thin sheet of paper spread out on her workspace and began very slowly to draw. When she was done outlining the angle of each finger, the silent intonation of its gesture, she moved up to a wrist, a forearm, an elbow; before she fully realized it, she had almost turned it into a whole person.

A kind person. A person who spoke softly and made her laugh and liked her just the way she was, who didn't ask her questions she couldn't answer.

Hours melted away as she drew, and the cogs in her head turned and the cogs in her heart turned. This person on the butcher paper developed into a boy with a soft face, and he sprawled out, limb to limb. He took up nearly all of her desk. The ticking in her chest was almost inaudible, a soft, steady peace.

She glanced up at the clock on her wall, and the clock in her chest shot straight up in volume. It was almost four. She'd spent the whole day drawing. She'd done *nothing,* and Ruby would be there soon. If only the peace that came from putting pencil to paper were enough for the rest of the world. For Nan.

Nell begrudgingly stood up to get changed. She looked down at her desk, the new landscape of an imaginary boy with a tender face and no spare parts. As a last detail she drew the line, the line that separated the hand from the body. There. Perfect.

CHAPTER 7

"It'll bring out the flecks of gold in your iris," Ruby said to Nell.

She held Nell's face with one hand and, with the other, very carefully painted a slick of toxic bright purple eyeliner onto the lid of her left eye, biting her tongue in concentration. The two girls sat cross-legged on the kitchen table, facing each other. A small mountain of black hair sat at the base of a tall broom in the corner. Ruby had given Julian a quick once-over with her miracle scissors and had transformed him from Mad Scientist back into a clean-cut Marvelous Doctor. The speed and understanding she had for shape and something more elusive than that—style— were utterly beyond Nell. Julian had remarked that Ruby's taste should be her contribution, and Ruby wholeheartedly agreed.

"I'd paint this town all over, Dr. Crane," she'd said, perfecting the hairline at the back of his neck, blade dangerously close to skin. "You just give me time."

Nell was always a great appreciator of Ruby's gift, but at present, with a long, thin brush flying this way and that around her eye sockets, she wished she could appreciate it with a little more distance.

Ruby added a flourish here and there, then paused to admire her work. "There. Perfect."

"Mhm," managed Nell, in something resembling agreement. Her eyes were brown; she was fairly sure there wasn't any gold in there, but she wasn't going to argue with a girl holding a paintbrush at extremely close proximity to her eyeball. Ruby's forehead was wrinkled in concentration. She'd been twenty minutes doing Nell's makeup because "You can't go out with those big messy black eyes on you; you look like you haven't slept in ten years. Just for once step into the night; don't be hiding."

Ruby smelled like oranges. Her face was flawless; her eyepatch for tonight, a muted black velvet. Her other eye was surrounded by a cloud of gold powder, and her lashes extended long and doll-like. She'd painted up her clusters of freckles to accent them: they popped. Her mouth pouted in focus, a pink that was gold when the light caught it.

Ruby perceived beauty in almost everything and with a few subtle but confident touches could turn anything around. Even Nell. Ruby painted Nell's face regularly; neither could irritate the other when they were quiet like this. Nell tried to enjoy this closeness, to push down the dread of spending the evening in the Bayou.

When Ruby was done, she beamed with pride and said, "There we go. Human after all," and Nell stuck out her tongue. Ruby flashed her a mirror. Nell's reflection looked, unsurprisingly, just like Nell, only Nell with big violet halos around her eyes and some dotted freckles to match Ruby's. The dark moons usually under her eyes were invisible. Her mouth was glossed subtly. Fine, Nell thought. That's fine.

"It's wonderful," she said, mustering enough enthusiasm so Ruby believed her.

As the girls gathered their things to leave, Ruby bopped about in excitement. Nell should have found it contagious, but she couldn't feel a thing other than the heavy sludge of dread. She scooped Kodak up in her arms as they walked out the front door and down the porch steps to their bikes. Ruby gave her a disapproving look, an I-cannot-believe-you're-bringing-an-animal-to-the-bar look but managed to not chide her. Not this early in the night.

Past Ruby's home, a cozy bungalow with a thatched

roof, the district was barren of buildings or life. That was why the twins had chosen the guts of the parkland for their speakeasy, though most young patrons' routes barely touched the long and winding journey Ruby and Nell cycled to get there.

The Phoenix Parklands held acres and acres of wet, overgrown greenery. These swamps had thickened and the ferns grown tall when the temperatures rose during the Turn. Once Black Water City and the country surrounding it had been cold and rainy, but now it was a hot, dense place. It was said that the same sickness that had poisoned the inhabitants had bled out into the atmosphere. This year the hot season had lasted too long; the air around them needed to break. It ached with humidity. The time was coming. The girls' ride through the parklands was tense in the hot, new dark of evening.

Before the Turn there had been a zoo in the parklands. There had been other buildings, too, but concrete falls and wood rots. The animals, however, remained. Even though Nell and Ruby had never seen much more than a tall stray stag or heard more than some rustling or growling from the thickets, they knew there were bigger things lurking. Animals they weren't sure they had the right names for. Animals they had half-whispered histories for. The girls were quiet and respectful when they passed through these less charted lands. They made this journey twice a week in the dark. Nell lately had been making it alone after she could slip out of the Bayou unnoticed. The dark wilderness of the park held a strange comfort for her.

The light from the Bayou appeared in the distance like a flicker at first, but it rose into a bright candle of gaiety the nearer and nearer they pulled. It was a low, old building that had been dressed up in finery and brazen electric lights like a delighted great-aunt at a wedding party. The building had a whole generator of its very own, hard won and, through favors owed and favors done, carefully hidden. The Fox twins, Antoinette and Tomas, had been orphaned by the epidemic. They'd spent their childhood in the city orphanage and apprenticed in the production line at the Tea Factory, but as soon as they were old enough, they had set off into the world.

And eventually, in the dank tangle of the parklands, they'd opened the Bayou. A shred of real happiness in the city again. It changed everything for the young survivors of the epidemic, gave them something to look forward to. The parents and elders in the community steered clear, far too jaded to dance and sing. Two other watering holes opened up in its wake: quieter, more austere venues. This place, however, gave the young a chance to feel young.

The doors had first swung open on the party five years ago, to the night.

The Fox twins, green eyed and blond, had truly contributed something.

Nell hated them. Or something like hated them, something she was too ashamed to call jealousy.

As the girls approached the building, Nell's stomach dropped with dread, heavier than usual. She didn't want to go in. She wanted to go home and draw the hand and its person some more. The ticking in her chest had escalated without her noticing, but now it was all she could hear against the night air, over the hot breeze as she cycled.

Here was the thing about bad feelings: they arrived for a reason, and some people felt them more intensely than others. Some people trusted them; others didn't. Nell, unfortunately, was acutely aware of the things her body did and what they meant, and she knew the tightness in her abdomen only meant trouble. Rising panic. It meant, "Go home now, Nell."

They passed the lanky iron gate that would have been imposing if not for the strings of tiny white electric lights. They locked up their bikes along with all the others on the rails set up specially for that purpose. The garden was chaotic and colorful, full of flowers and plants in big terra-cotta pots. The Bayou itself lay before them, thrumming with life, stretching so far back into the knotted throngs of trees that it was impossible to see how big it really was in the dark of the fresh night.

Nell scooped Kodak, docile and wide eyed, out of her basket and placed him on her shoulders. He made a rumbling sound that wasn't quite a purr, and she was comforted, if only a little. He was well used to this.

"You're ticking fierce loud, Nell. Can you"—Ruby hesitated—"can you get it to shush? A little bit?" Everything in her face was: "Please don't make a show of me."

Nell just stared at her friend, the bad feeling in her gut growing, the ticking spitefully rising in volume.

"No?" Ruby asked. "Really?"

"You know I can't do anything about it." Nell's words were all teeth.

"Okay. Right, well, maybe the music will drown it out." Ruby knew she couldn't backtrack so just flashed Nell an apologetic smile as they walked toward the door. Every muscle in Nell's body and the steel in her chest told her to turn around and leave. Instead, she followed the shorter girl to the closed door.

Ruby knocked confidently, and a slat briskly opened before them, revealing a pair of arched brows and brightly painted eyes.

"Password?" asked a throaty voice.

"FridayFriday12345ExclamationPoint," Ruby recited cheerfully.

The door swung open, the music from indoors now fully audible and bright and infectious. Nell felt sick.

"Ruby Underwood and Nellie Crane, sure, it's only great to see you!" gushed the tall young woman, hair curled high on her head, decked out like a carnival in bright colors and sequins. Her smile was huge, and her eyes sparkled.

"Still moonlighting as a bouncer after mornings in the shop, Janey?" Ruby asked, giving the girl a hug. Nell stood stock-still and didn't move.

"Of course I am. Saving up my tokens to get a train ride with all my things way out to start over in the Pasture; got my sights on Tribe City!"

Tribe City, out by the Library Complex out by the ports.

"You are *not!*" exclaimed Ruby. "You're really moving over there? It's still wild out that way. There's only around a hundred people there, and more than half of them librarians!"

"Ah, yeah, but there's rumors of them opening up the ports, you know. Sending boats out. Look, if I volunteer service in the Libraries, wait around long enough, might manage to swipe an early ticket out!" Janey winked.

"Could be a great big beautiful tomorrow out there for me, you know? Could get off this island and out into the world." She lifted the hem of her blouse slightly to reveal the matte steel square over her left hip. "Sure, it might as well not even be there. Nobody would know if they weren't looking for it, the way the Marvelous Dr. Crane has it done up for me!"

Nell inhaled deeply and turned slightly away.

"You are a scream, Janey. Delighted for you. I wouldn't have the nerve myself to be working in those old stacks of paper; they give me the creeps: all that information, probably covered in code."

Janey shrugged. "Look, if it gets me nearer the port and away from this kip, I'll be all right to do the time in the silence. Sacrifices have to be made."

"You're something else, Janey," Ruby said, while Nell busied herself admiring some unusually fascinating decorations, so she wouldn't tap her foot with impatience.

"Sure, look. One step at a time. C'mere, Nell, your stoat is gorgeous. Oh and, eh"—Janey nudged her—"Oliver Kelly is inside looking for you."

Nell gave her a tight-lipped smile. Instead of saying, "Don't ever touch me ever again," she said, "Why is Oliver Kelly looking for me?"

"Oh, he didn't say!" Janey smothered giggles and

shot a knowing look to Ruby, who returned it. Nell knew full well why he was looking for her, and she wasn't in the temper for it at all.

"See you later!" Ruby cooed to Janey, and the girls walked down the winding hallway that led to the ballroom. The place reeked of hops, that warm dinnertime smell that gets all over you and makes you feel as if you've overeaten. It made Nell woozy before she'd even picked up a drink. She'd be drenched with sweat in no time; the purple wings on her eyelids would start running soon, too.

The grand dance floor split open before them, the ballroom a lush, gleaming treasure trove. Tobacco smoke hung in the air like something dangerous, something Nell couldn't handle. The ceilings were high, dazzling with chandeliers made of old bottles. The walls were papered in a close floral pattern, and the floor was covered in a thick red carpet; each footfall landed with a quiet thud on the shag. It was lavish, and week after week this decadence seemed to grow. Every time she walked in there was a new fixture. A mirror with a gilded frame built to look like a whale, above the bar. A set of lights with a rotating filter that changed color every minute: pink, then purple, then yellow, then back to pink again. A set of pink flamingos, poised elegantly by the footlights on the stage. Bunting, miles and miles of it. All gifts, all offerings, all barters for more jars of that shining white peace or hoppy comfort in a shade of honey.

Nowhere else in the broken-down city looked like this. This was the contribution that mattered most to the apprentices: this place to go to forget.

There must have been two hundred, maybe even three hundred people crowded in there, at the bar and on the dance floor and scattered at the dozens of small circular tables at the edges of the room. Just about all the apprentices who lived in Black Water City. A whole squad from the monument construction. A janky, enthusiastic band of daytime plumbers and bakers and nurses huddled on a small platform stage, pulling old torch songs out of an accordion, a banjo, a fiddle, a bodhran, a double bass, and a heavily beaten piano. The singer was belting something about churches into a handmade microphone system hooked up to an amplifier made of an old crate and some metal scrap. It was tinny and distorted, but it worked. The dance floor oozed with life.

Nell's ticking was so loud that it reverberated through her arms and fingers, out of sync with the music, a misplaced metronome. Ruby was obviously eyeballing the span of the room for faces she knew.

"Do you want to dance with me?" asked Ruby

tentatively, knowing the answer, already grateful for Nell's permission to leave her alone, a grim buoy moored at the bar.

"No. I'm going to sit at the bar for a while, I think. Have a drink. Do you want one?" Nell recited just what she thought Ruby wanted to hear.

"It's fine. I'll grab one once I've got the lay of the land!" Ruby flashed her a grateful smile, kissed her cheek, then disappeared into the throng in what might as well have been a flash of lightning. She wouldn't strike near Nell again that night.

Nell avoided bumping into any of the small clusters of her acquaintances but offered thin smiles to the piques of "Hi, Nell!" and "Oh, look, Nell Crane is here!" and squirmed her way across the room to one of the tall stools at the bar. She lifted herself up onto the gilt and velvet seat and rested her elbows on the dark wood of the countertop. The new whale mirror was surrounded by decorative cabinets full of ornate handmade bottles of spirits and bitters and tinctures. Draft taps with hand-carved heads linked to fat kegs full of beer stood in lines like faithful soldiers. Nell caught her reflection and immediately regretted the eyeliner and painted freckles.

Nell made eye contact with Antoinette Fox, who was always behind the bar on weekends; she was busy but gave Nell a nod. "The lady professor Crane, what'll it be tonight?"

Antoinette was the very specific kind of wild gorgeous that implied she woke up almost exactly in the shape she stood there. She made Nell's throat want to close over. An effortless arrangement of blond locks, wide eyes, impossibly white teeth: she was too good to be true. Even her augmented limb, right arm from the elbow down, was encased in white porcelain with tiny blue flowers painted up the side. New, Nell noted. As she went to answer, she was suddenly interrupted by the deep and affected tones of the absolute last person she wanted to see.

She'd spent too many afternoons trapped next to him at a work desk ever to want to sit next to him at a night out, but here he was. Here he always was.

"Drink, Crane?"

"Not half as much as you, Kelly." Nell gritted her teeth. "But since you're offering, I'll have a—"

He leaned over the bar to get the barmaid's attention, cutting Nell off.

"She'll have a bathtub gin with two wedges of lemon and a splash of—"

"Elderflower tonic," snarled Nell. "Good evening, Oliver."

CHAPTER 8

You are twelve, and you cannot *believe* Oliver Kelly is still coming here every week. It is bad enough that you have to take Saturday classes without having to take them with *him*. And he still looks around seven. You didn't mind him when he was seven and you were seven, but that was long ago; that was when you didn't have to see him every single weekend. You aren't seven anymore. You are twelve. It is bad enough that you are twelve.

Only half an hour left; then he'll go home. Your eyes are on the clock, and you're convinced it's impossible for a clock to move this slowly. You'd really like not to be sitting beside Oliver Kelly, who apparently has just discovered cologne. Discovering it would be fine; but you're fairly sure he's also been bathing in it, and even your welding mask won't disguise the stench.

You shift uncomfortably, leaning away from Oliver a little more, almost at such an angle now that you might fall off your chair. You don't care if you fall off your chair. You just don't want to sit next to him.

The clock's second hand moves once. You scowl. Your goggles are starting to dig into your face. Another second.

Your father makes very intense eye contact with Oliver when he's instructing. He laughs at Oliver's weak jokes. This is good because it means that Oliver's gaze never floats over to you (your neckline, mostly, and you're never sure if it's your scar he's trying to see through your scarf or if it's your breasts, and either way you hate it). The whole thing makes you want to overturn the entire kitchen table and all the tools that lie out on it, wreck the composition of the skeleton key or whatever it is you're practicing this week. Metal casting and magnets and filigree for detail. It's pointless anyway. You're ready to make things *move,* and you keep *telling him*; but he's dawdling on easier projects because of Oliver bloody Kelly.

You like the tiny blowtorch, though, the raw blue flame. You like the whispery roar it makes. You like the smell of the molten iron as it casts and cools; you like carving away at it with raw heat. You like the shape of the key's teeth, hungry for locks, confident that it can open anything, get in anywhere. You like its hidden magnets, how it can pull secrets apart.

You like learning. You like building. You just don't like Oliver.

You don't like watching how slowly and clumsily he puts things together; you don't like his earnest questions, his shaky requests to be shown everything twice or three times. You don't like how he keeps dropping his tools and how they clang onto the floor. You don't like how he's here.

You turn the key over and over; you can't do anything else to it. It looks exactly as the blueprints intended. You pop your goggles up onto your head and take off your face mask. Oliver shoots you a jealous look; he'll be at least five more minutes to get the last corner done. You cup your face in your hands. "Da, I'm done," you offer sweetly, pushing smugness down.

Your father waves you off and continues to hover around Oliver. "All right, Nell, calm down just a moment."

Calm . . . down?

You seethe. Why should you even calm down? You've done exactly what you were told, no questions asked, got everything right the first time, and are done twenty-four minutes before you're meant to be. You resist the urge to rap your fingers against the table, and your ticking escalates in that very specific way it does when you're upset. Another furious minute drags itself by. White heat curls behind your eyes. *Tick, tick, tick.*

"Could you"—Oliver turns to you—"do that a little more quietly? I'm almost there. I'm trying to concentrate."

And just like that, the spark of irritation catches flame.

"Do that a little more quietly?" you snap. You stand up, and your chair clatters to the tiles. "What? Exist? *Exist* more quietly? This is *my* home, Oliver, and you can't just tell me to *exist* quietly in my home. Why are you even here? Why are you even allowed to study with me? You should be back in the morgue, poking away at dead people and minding your own business!" You throw your goggles down and you can't even look at your father and you're out of the room, giving the stupid chair one last good kick as you go. You are a tempest, ticking faster and louder and louder as you storm toward the stairs.

Each step is a protest; you take each one hard, trying to shake the whole damn house. Stupid . . . Oliver . . . Kelly.

The kitchen door clicks closed.

"Penelope."

Your father stands at the bottom of the stairs,

arms crossed sternly over his starchy lab coat, goggles pushing back his wild black hair. You turn to him, trying to make yourself bigger, more fierce.

"What?" you ask, but any sass you were trying to muster fizzles out under hot tears of frustration and that ugly weak thing crying does to your throat.

"That was quite a display."

You want to say, "You think?" but know already that it'll come out ugly and warped. You want to tell him you're not crying because you're sad but because you're angry. Really angry. Instead, you just sniff and wipe your face indignantly.

"Look. I know you don't like this. And me telling you it'll get easier as you get older isn't what you want to hear. But it's one day a week. I'm asking you to pull up your bootstraps, kiddo."

His voice is stern, with hard, pleading edges that make the tears come even hotter and even faster. You don't have any choice with him when he talks like this. You want your ma, to put your head on Ma's shoulder. You want the smell of her hair and skin. You have none of that. Just a flight of stairs and your exhausted father and Oliver Kelly sitting in the kitchen.

"But why? Why is he here?" you sob, stamping your foot.

"I owe his mother a favor. *We* owe her a favor."

A favor! What favor is worth this? You have never taken anything off either of the Mrs. Kellys. What is worth letting someone else into your apprenticeship *even* one day a week? What do the florist and the undertaker even *have* to give your family?

"Please try to like him. At least tolerate him. Then see what happens."

Your father's voice is all soft now, all well done, girl. You can't say no to him like this, when that particular desperation hangs on the edge of his tone; how easily it disappears once he has his way, once you do what you're told.

"Fine," you manage, defeated.

It's not fair. It's not fine. But Oliver Kelly isn't going anywhere.

The undertaker's son flashed her a wolfish grin. "How's it going, Nell? I'll take one of those, too, Anto, thank you."

The barkeep nodded and took off, her beauty gracing the other end of the bar. Oliver Kelly sat down on the stool beside Nell. She kept her eyes on the swaying of the dance floor and tried to look as if she were more interested in that than in the spindly young man who had just imposed himself, as usual, on her evening.

Oliver was taller than Nell, and thinner. His skin was a little lighter than Nell's, and he had a bloom of freckles over his nose. He had teeth that looked too sharp and eyes that were too big in his head, too blue. His hair was black and curly and coiffed in a pompadour. He was all narrow monochrome, black pants and a thin gray cardigan, starched white shirt.

Aggressive, formal. In some lights he was handsome in a way, but that was sharply undermined by the uneasy, greedy energy he exuded.

His mothers were the proprietresses of Kelly & Kelly, a florist and an undertaker. He'd been adopted as an infant out of the orphanage; he had no augmented limbs, nothing visibly missing. Despite this, he received no preferential treatment from the other apprentices—an undertone of resentment at most. After he made his contribution, Oliver's whole, healthy body could be his ticket out into the Pasture. Thing was he seemed intent on sticking around.

Nell wished he'd go. She'd wave him off, throw flowers after him as he left town. She'd seen enough of him for a lifetime. At least the Saturday classes she'd shared with him had ended last year so that they could each focus on their contributions, but he still rattled around the house too often, asking her father questions and making a nuisance of himself.

Those who didn't have profitable enough trades to afford new models of their augmented limbs or those who couldn't afford maintenance or needed a fix in a tick and didn't have the time to go on Julian's waiting list would go to Oliver, down at the morgue, and he would repair them for a discounted fee. This system, when perfected, would be his contribution. And there it was: he'd have to stay in the city to maintain it. Stay near Nell.

Oliver had taken this upon himself. Julian hadn't stopped him; he was happy to have somebody else cover the things he couldn't. He was happy his machines were getting reused; but he didn't have time to dote on Oliver, and Nell was already technically his apprentice.

"So, how's it going?" Oliver tried again, leaning closer to her.

Nell stiffened; his cologne and the scent of formaldehyde were oppressive. She pulled her scarf higher around her chin.

"I'm grand, Oliver. Same as usual."

Antoinette slammed down two short, fat tumblers of spirits, and Nell turned to her to pay. She had a small purse full of clunky plastic tokens; so much of the things they needed they got by trade, but the tokens still went an awfully long way. Ugly blue disks, something from a time long behind them.

"It's fine. The Cranes and Kellys drink for free around here," said Antoinette. "Remember that when the two of you get hitched and set up shop; I need regular fixes for the amount of action this old girl sees." She flexed her beautiful, silent augmented arm. She waltzed off before they could thank her and left them alone.

"What does she mean by that?" Nell snapped. "Do we have to go over this again, Oliver?" She wrapped her fingers around the glass. It was full of ice, and it was a relief against the heat of the room. If this conversation was about to go how she thought it would, it would mark the eighteenth time that Oliver had propositioned her to go into business together. Which implied courtship. Which implied marriage. Which implied kissing and sex. It was the sex part that irritated her most because naturally he would expect that immediately; clearly he expected it already. It utterly enraged Nell, and she had told him so. Seventeen times. And here he was again.

Her no always fell on deaf ears with Oliver. Every few months he'd boomerang back to her with a new angle on the proposal. Sometimes it was because he truly loved her; others, because he could make sure they were wealthy. Once he promised that the relationship and marriage could be completely lavender—strictly chaste—as long as she convinced her father to teach him everything he knew. Worse than this, Oliver truly felt that if he kept telling everyone he was going to marry into the Crane legacy, eventually it would happen. At first his enthusiasm was endearing, and Nell and Ruby had giggled over it. But over the past year it had escalated. He seemed to assume that she would eventually break. Nell, however, was not a girl in the business of breaking.

His eyes kept flicking down to her neck and sternum, covered completely, but ticking at volume, slightly out of sync with the music. Nell imagined little teeth in his pupils, chewing away at her clothing. She clenched her fists.

"Well, you know how it is, Nell. Everyone with an ounce of common sense can tell that we're perfectly suited. I can offer you a lovely time, you know that." He took out a slim silver case full of hand-rolled cigarettes, removed one theatrically, and lit it up. He offered Nell one, too, and she glared at him.

"Oh, I'm sorry." Oliver smiled, eyes on her neck and chest again. *Tick, tick, tick.*

Nell took a long pull from her drink. It burned but helped. She was also prepared to throw it at Oliver if he made any moves. Kodak was staring straight at him with his tiny bullet hole eyes.

"I'm not having this conversation with you again. Not tonight. Not ever. It's a party. Everyone from all corners of the city is here. Go and dance. Constance Cleary's eyes are just about falling out of her head looking at you," Nell said flatly.

"I'm not interested in Constance Cleary—" Oliver began, but Nell cut him off sharply.

"Of course you're not. What use would you have

with a girl from a family of cobblers and shoemakers, couldn't use them to advance your career at all."

Oliver pouted at Nell. "Harsh, Crane."

"Leave me alone, Kelly."

They sat beside each other in silence, watching the dancers and crowds, occasionally catching glances from passersby, for whom their silent, tense vignette was surely gossip fodder for the coming weeks. Nell sipped her drink and thought about ordering another. Oliver finished his in a single gulp, then turned completely to face Nell and put his hand on her knee.

"Nell, I want to come clean with you. There's something I haven't told you, and I think if you knew, you'd probably want to spend some more time with me."

Nell looked at his hand. She could see the gray-blue of his veins and the bones of his knuckles, his neat, surgically clean fingernails. She could hear only the steady, escalating clockwork inside of her and the rushing of blood and fury. She had not told him he could put his hand on her.

Oliver was entirely oblivious. He took her intense, furious stare as interest and continued softly.

"Aside from my current operation in the morgue, I've, em"—Oliver's composure dropped a little with his volume—"I don't think I should tell you this in here. Will you come outside with me?"

Before Nell could answer, the music ended with aplomb. Antoinette and Tomas took to the tiny rickety stage then with a fanfare. They each held a full glass in their hands. The singer handed Tomas the busted-up microphone.

He was handsome and tall, not unlike Antoinette. All blond wavy hair and bright eyes. His right leg was his augmented limb, but there was utterly no way of telling which was which in his fine suit pants and spats and shining black shoes. He passed his sister the mic.

The crowd hushed at their presence. Even Nell listened as Antoinette began to speak, though she hadn't intended to.

"Five years ago the city was a very different place. Many of you here tonight quite literally helped raise this roof. We're only up on our feet, but we've pints of heart. Before the Turn, in our great- or great-great-grandparents' time, this country was sung about all over the world, known for the parties we'd throw. Now, who knows what the rest of the world thinks of us? Who knows what they're even doing out there or if there's anyone out there at all? The world could still be growing, and we'd never know. This bar was our contribution, but it's just a place to keep us looking inward. So, as we raise our glasses, we should look outward, hope that someday we'll get to dance with the rest of the world, not just each other. I know there are full bars all over the planet tonight."

Antoinette's voice caught in her throat for a moment, and the beat of silence had a pull to it. Members of the crowd shot one another glances; eyebrows lifted; fingers tightened around glasses. Tomas motioned to take the microphone, but she waved him off. "Sorry, hold on." She took a deep breath and then a long drink from her glass. The air in the room was thick.

Nell felt a tug at her sleeve. Oliver was nothing if not persistent. She rolled her eyes.

"Oliver, I'm not going outside with you," she whispered, drawing the attention and a few hushes from the patrons around her.

"I can't go into it in here, and I really, really think you'd be interested in what I have to say. Ruby was anyway." His voice was urgent and low.

Nell froze. "What has you talking to Ruby?"

Shushed again. Antoinette was continuing her speech. Nell tutted in frustration.

"Maybe Ruby was the one doing the talking to me, thank you very much. I'll tell you if you go outside with me." Oliver ran his finger around the edge of his empty glass. Nell watched and shuddered.

She took a deep breath and adjusted her scarf up around her chin. If this was something to do with

Oliver's apprenticeship, surely she should know about it. She drained the last floral dregs of her gin and tonic and thought, well, what had she to lose?

Antoinette finished her speech, and the crowd erupted with cheers and confetti. Nell scanned around for Ruby amid the kaleidoscope. Not a sign of her. Typical.

"Fine. You have until I've unlocked my bike. Start now."

They left the ballroom, the big gilded doors swinging shut behind them, and padded down the carpet toward the door. Janey had left her post; the corridor was empty; the night air was almost upon them. The undertaker's son could barely keep up with her but began to talk anyway, his tones hushed and urgent.

"Look, Nell, I've been stepping a bit outside my bounds with what I've been doing. I—this sounds really bad, but I went into the Gonne Hospital around six months ago and did some looking. What you and Ruby do at the water. I found some really, really amazing things, things almost too good to be used by people."

Nell slowed to listen. Too good to be used by people? She hadn't realized the Gonne Hospital had been safe enough to go inside. The great ancient building presided over what would have once been a main street; before the Turn it had been a department store, a strange urban landmark crowned by a great clock. But after the first toxic pulses rattled through the island and the epidemic struck, it had been converted into an emergency hospital. Hundreds and hundreds of thousands of people had died there. The old building had become so contaminated that the council had decreed it unsafe and ordered that it be burned. Ostensibly this was to kill the ends of the virus and stop outbreaks during aftershocks: but the whole city donned gas masks and gathered to watch it, a terrible red ceremony. It felt like an exorcism, the ghosts of their sick past scorched out. Nell was only very small when it happened; Cora had held her hand as they watched the terrible blaze.

"And lo and behold, there are rooms in there untouched by the fire, and they're just full of old safes and boxes of, well, of early robotics. Of prosthetics from before your father's inventions. I'd never seen the like of them. Old porcelain arm plates that survived the blaze. Some are wooden, I've even found a whole case of *glass* eyes; they're so delicate!"

They exited to the outside world, and the night air was barely a touch cooler than the heat inside the building. The sky was black and clear and pocked with a clatter of white stars. Nell didn't stop, despite her curiosity. She headed straight for the bike racks, taking Kodak in her arms so as not to dislodge him from his perch as she marched.

"Oliver, I've seen glass eyes before. So you found a whole load of old limbs. You—you shouldn't even be in the hospital; you have no idea what's still in the air. You're healed, and you're taking stupid risks. What is the point in telling me this?"

"Nell, I'm going to start selling them. I'm going to test them to see if they're contaminated, clean them up, then run them as a special service. Roll them out as vintage. A lot of them are beautiful, with handmade casings. They'd be worth a fortune, especially to folks who don't like machines. I'm going to—"

Folks who don't like machines. Nell busied herself placing Kodak safely into the basket on her bike, threw away the question. "Have you been talking to Ruby about an eye?"

Oliver went quiet for a moment. "Yes. And—"

"She didn't tell me."

Nell held the chain lock from the bike in her hands and squeezed, the metal pressing into her flesh. She breathed steadily. She wasn't going to show Oliver she was upset; the ticking gave her away enough as it was.

"She also said"—Oliver was desperate—"that it would be good for me to tell you; that the time's coming up for your contribution, and you don't have one; that you're on a straight track to end up halfway up Kate's stony armpit. Look—"

Nell cocked her head to the side. "When did she say this to you?"

"Oh, we went for a drink last night to discuss pricing—"

Nell's surprise crystallized into something that rang deep like hurt but had all the volatility of rage. She was just about ready to storm back inside and pull Ruby from her tangle of friends and give her a piece of her mind.

"I've heard enough, Oliver. I don't care. You can go risk your life in a burned-out old hospital, make profit out of artifacts belonging to the dead, and give my best friend an operation she's been refusing for her entire life all you want; just please leave me out of it. I have my own work to do."

"Do you, though?" he asked her. "Do you really? Nell, come with me and see the workshop I've made. Nobody even knows it's there yet; it's brand-new. I built it myself. There's real enterprise to be had from passing these old limbs on; it's a real contribution. If you band with me, you'll be spared the statue. You'll get a second chance. To get involved, you know? Really contr—"

"The next person who says the word *contribute* anywhere near me is liable to get physically injured. Don't you dare turn this into another proposition. I am leaving."

Nell kicked the stand up and hopped on her bike. Oliver reached out to touch her arm, but she gave him a look so dark that he retreated.

"But Ruby said—"

"Ruby apparently says a lot of things, Oliver."

Nell put her foot down on the pedal. Her whole body was on fire, and somewhere in the blaze a small voice asked if maybe Oliver was on to something. A chamber of possibility, a way to quiet Nan. A suitable partner whose contribution aligned with her own. Maybe, ugh, it wasn't wise to blow him out of the water yet—just in case. He was so desperate. Cruelty wound its way up Nell's throat, and she said, "Let's talk in a few days."

She didn't even look at him.

Oliver gasped with joy. Nell rolled her eyes and began to cycle away.

"Good night, Nell! I'll see you soon!" she heard, echoing down the path behind her. She didn't look back.

Nell waited until she was far into the thicket to let the hot tears pour out of her tired eyes and roll down the colors Ruby had so delicately painted on her lids and temples. There was nobody out in the parklands to see her as she tore through the blackness; it was just she and Kodak. She'd go home, and she'd draw the boy some more. She'd sleep, and she'd wake up and make some plans, figure out how to start. In a few days she'd talk to bloody Oliver if she hadn't thought of another way by then.

As she passed through the wilds, in the distance she saw an elephant, slowly and gracefully walking across the meadow. She'd seen it before, when she was alone. Her mother had drawn the tall gray creatures for her when she was a child.

She didn't know much about them because she'd never seen one up close, but Cora had told her that they never forgot. They had vast and endless memories; they were wise and gentle. In hushed tones Cora had told Nell that some of the elephants were hundreds of years old; something to do with experiments around the time of the Turn had slowed their aging. Nell looked at the great shadowy creature and wondered what it knew, what it had seen.

She thought about that all the way home.

CHAPTER 10

The door of her father's laboratory was cold against Nell's cheek as she knelt against it, her face wet, kohl and purple powder streaking her cheeks. Her eyes were heavy and sore from crying, but the argument trickling through the wood hooked around her and pulled her closer.

"You're *sick*, Crane, *sick*!" came Daniel Underwood's voice. It was an awful shock, the sound of Ruby's father, raising his voice like this to her da.

"I should have known you wouldn't understand! You *can't* understand what I do!" her father shouted back, furious, desperate.

The rest was barely decipherable through the heavy old door.

She hadn't intended to eavesdrop. When she'd gotten home, she'd dashed up to her bedroom without thinking, ignoring the commotion coming from the lab, assuming it would die down. But it rose and rose.

Nell had spent years listening to her father and Ruby's father roar with laughter at each other; she knew that tune well. This was different. Something was badly wrong. She locked a skittish Kodak in her room and crept back down the stairs as quietly as her ticking would let her, the mannequin hand in hers, offering some strange but solid comfort.

There was crashing. Was that glass breaking? She placed one hand on her chest as if to try to drown out the sound of the loud machine inside her. Should she just burst in, ride out the end of her fury at Oliver and Ruby, and rescue her father from Daniel's stream of insults?

"Sick"

"Madman"

"Abomination"

Nell knew in her gut this would be a stupid thing to do; she'd never gone into the lab, not in her whole entire life. What if her father became angry at her for intruding? He'd know she'd been listening. The last thing she wanted was to betray his trust. She strained against the barrier, trying to make out more.

Eavesdropping was dangerous; if she were meant to hear angry conversations, the door would not be closed. The conversations would not be happening in the dead of night when she was assumed to be asleep or at a dance hall three and a half miles away either. Nell was not meant to be part of this, but here she was.

She held the hard, lifeless hand tightly in hers.

"Madman, abomination, sick, sick."

"How could I have trusted you?"

"How could I have trusted you?"

Nell choked back a sob. Suddenly she couldn't hear any more of this. She didn't want to know what they were fighting over. Let them, let them. She slowly, silently moved back up to her bedroom, fingers knotted around the hand, the sterile digits of her future. Kodak was scratching against the bedroom door, mewling to get out. When she went in, he immediately scampered up her legs and arm to her shoulder, his tiny nose seeking the crook of her neck.

Nell sat on her bed and stared at the hand. The figures and plants drawn on the paper all over her walls were still and stark around her. Sometimes she felt as though her bed were lying in the middle of an open notebook. This was her only comfort, surrounded by the plans for things she intended to create.

Could she build a boy? Could she make metal think? Could she create something that wasn't still, something that could breathe and feel? She shook the hand a little, not knowing what she was hoping for.

Would she cast more limbs in plastic, or porcelain, or terra-cotta? She'd have to ask her father for the molds. Nell didn't consider herself much of a carver—and where would she get the plastic? Or clay. Or metal. She'd have to sterilize a lot of material, and she'd never be able to weld something the size of a human being in this room; she'd smoke the place out.

Never mind making it think. Never mind computers. That was just another impossibility.

"Am I fooling myself, Kodak?" she asked him quietly. He looked up at her, his eyelids drooping, sleepy.

Of course the *one* impressive idea she finally had would be totally out of reach. Naturally. She wished she'd never found the hand or had had the common sense to throw it back into the sea.

There was no way she was going to sleep, not now. Nell stood and walked over to her wardrobe. It was four blurring into five now, but she was wild with awakeness. Dawn began to spiral fresh pink into the dark outside. She placed the hand on a small shelf while she changed from her Bayou frock into her culottes and a loose, wide-necked gray wool sweater, over which she placed her mother's work apron, a blue denim thing, stitched by the great-grandmother she'd never met. It was worn and soft, stained and scorched by a variety of impermeable substances. It was hers. She hadn't worn it in a while, since she'd resolved she was a useless inventor. As she placed it over her head, she could almost swear she smelled her mother from it, even though she knew it had stopped smelling like Cora long ago. She wasn't very good at pretending, but it was nice sometimes. It might be what she needed to keep her going today.

She tied the apron on and slipped the hand into the deep front pocket. She unwound her hair and wound it up again more neatly. She dabbed the makeup off her face with cotton and tea astringent, all the black and purple streaks erased from her cheeks and replaced with pale powder and a tincture of rose to give her cheeks the flush they otherwise severely lacked. She was making herself up for nobody, but it helped. As she dressed and assembled herself, her ticking hushed to a normal, just about audible rhythm. When dawn flooded in, she would be a person who invented and discovered, who helped her father and who made a difference. Today would not be another wasted opportunity.

The birds outside were an orchestra of awake. She could not hear her father and Daniel anymore, only the symphony of morning calls. Kodak was sleeping now on her pillow. His tiny rib cage rose and fell with each breath. Nell didn't rouse him.

When she got down the stairs to make herself a cup of tea, her father's lab door was open. She nearly stopped to stare inside or creep over the threshold, but now was not the time. Not at all. With all the resolve she could muster, she walked right by, giving the door a push shut as she passed. It clicked, it closed; that mystery passed for the moment.

The kitchen floor was covered in frogs again. The garden door was wide open, the fresh leafy smell of morning lifting in on the tips of the early breeze, edged with tobacco. Julian sat on the kitchen table, a mess. His shirt was half undone; his tie hung loose around his neck. The knuckles on his flesh hand were bleeding, and a finger was missing from the mechanical side. It was making an irregular chiming and bleeping sound, horrible and worrying, but he was ignoring it. He had a lit cigarette between two of his remaining steel fingers. Ash fluttered softly to the tabletop without his noticing.

Nell hadn't seen her father smoke in years.

"Da?" she asked softly from the doorway.

"Would you please, please get rid of these poxy frogs, Nell? I just opened the door to let in some air, and in they bloody marched. I really have to start setting up traps." Her father's voice was ragged. He didn't even look up.

Nell set her jaw, plucked the broom from the corner, and set about herding the tiny green creatures back out. The first time the frogs had gotten into the kitchen, her mother told her that she must never touch them with her fingers. Her mother, full of strange advice. Her mother, whose voice and heathery laugh she was only half sure she remembered. Who she couldn't picture whole. Big hair, bright and crooked grin. Maybe the rest was imagination and grief.

"Human blood is hot; frog blood is cold. Our fingers are like fire to the poor little babies. Scoop them up in a jar, or sweep them outside; just don't touch them!" Cora had shown her how to tip the little amphibians into old mason jars with a piece of paper, never touching them at all. Julian had been watching and picked up a stray from near where he was sitting at the table, using his mechanical hand. It had been an early version, still gray and squeaky. Cora had put her hands on her hips and scowled at him. "Jules, don't. Didn't you hear me?"

"It's cold, Cora, look, the little lad isn't even hopping away."

Julian had then gotten to his knees and shown Nell the frog up close, sitting calmly in the steel palm of his new hand. Its eyes were peaceful and black, the thrumming of the tiny engine in her father's arm so loud to her, in that moment, so much to bear. Alive, but cold and safe for the small frog. Cold and safe.

Thirteen years later Nell swept around the same old table where he'd held the small creature, which he was now sitting on top of, a picture of devastation. Still, she would not pity him, not right now. She was resolved to see the brightness in this morning. So she swept the frogs out into the garden, gently and carefully, and closed the door.

"Did you hear us fighting?" her father asked, breaking the terrible, awkward silence hanging in the kitchen air like something about to turn sour. His voice was shaky, exhausted.

"Only from a distance," Nell replied, composed. "I understand if you don't want to talk about it."

"I don't. Thank you."

"Would you like something to eat? I actually have a few questions for you if you want to, you know, take your mind off, em, everything." She was holding the hand in the pocket of the apron, its stillness a relief. "I heard something last night that you might be interested in—"

"I don't think there's even any food here," her father interrupted. "I've had about three liters of tea. I've to go back to the lab. I have so much work to do, now that Daniel won't help me. So much work."

Julian sat up, his face somehow more drawn than

usual, eyes reddened. He smoked the end of the cigarette, stubbed it out in the teacup by his side, and got up. He walked to his daughter and placed his human hand on her shoulder. "I'll answer your questions tomorrow. If you don't hear from me, don't fret. Maybe we'll talk the next day."

And he ambled out of the room. Even after the laboratory door had opened and shut, the pulse of kindness from his small embrace charged her, made her all the more willing to be brave, be the inventor she was born to be. To contribute.

Nell felt a pang of hunger. The refrigerator, as Julian had noted, was empty, bar a tall jar containing some cloudy water and some floating things that could have just as easily been eyeballs as they could have been pickled eggs. Nell grimaced. The cold thrum of the machine was refreshing; the morning heat was already descending on the house. Nell closed it again and moved to the cabinets: empty, empty, empty. Where had everything gone? She was positive that there'd been enough for a fresh breakfast, at least an egg and an avocado, maybe some cured bacon. One onion sat in the back of a barren shelf, happily sprouting green shoots among the cobwebs. A single tin of butter beans was housed in the shelf above it.

Nell looked over to the sink. It was full of smashed

dishes. Cracked shards of white and blue ceramic stained with whatever they'd eaten before they started fighting. They must have come right back after their meeting with the mayor. What could have gone so wrong that a meal could turn this ugly?

Nell was suddenly furious at Ruby's father for being cruel to hers when he had gone to all that effort, but as soon as the ticking inside her grew loud, she shut her eyes and focused: no, no, no more energy wasted on being angry and sad. Her hand went instinctively to the totem in her apron pocket. How calming it was.

She imagined him again, the person she would build. Drew him soft, graphite in her mind. She tried hard to hear his voice as she leaned against the counter, the depth or softness, but there was nothing but the distant clanks of her father in his lab again. No voice. Not yet. No voice, no name. Just a hand.

She decided, as she cleaned the broken crockery from the sink piece by piece, that she would go for a cycle, maybe down to the markets. It wouldn't be nice—it would be busy and loud—but she could prepare something good for Julian to eat that evening, something to cheer him up. Plus cycling always helped her think. She had a lot to figure out, mostly whether or not it was worth her while investigating what exactly Oliver had in the back rooms of the Gonne Hospital.

She was annoyed at herself for even considering it, for placing a fishhook of deceit onto Oliver's tongue. But if she couldn't cast or carve or weld all the limbs herself, she had to get them from somewhere. Otherwise she was just left with paper and a mannequin hand. Oliver owed her this access, surely, for all the space he'd taken up in her home over the years.

Once Nell had cleared the debris of her father's and Daniel's falling-out from the kitchen and blocked the crack under the back door to prevent any further frog invasions, she packed a satchel, wrapping the hand in a scarf and shoving it below her notebook and a flask full of iced, fresh tea. Her little purse of tokens was still full. She decided to let Kodak sleep; the poor creature had such a long night.

At the bottom of the stairs up to the house she checked the postbox. Nothing today. She *must* write back to Nan.

As Nell pulled away on her bike, she noticed Ruby in the distance, making her way down the path to her house. Ruby waved, a stripe of color against the forest, but Nell ignored her and cycled on. She didn't want to talk to Ruby yet because of both the nonsense with Oliver and whatever Daniel was shouting at her father for.

How could it be so easy for Ruby? They never talked about anything anymore. Not their worries, not their mothers. The glass eye wasn't just a simple little omission from their conversations; it felt steep to Nell. Deliberate. Perhaps Ruby didn't need to talk to her anymore.

Maybe, she thought, as she spun down toward the big road, maybe Ruby was just normal now. So many of the other apprentices had had a parent swept away from them by the epidemic, but they were all still capable of relaxing, being happy, dancing, partnering up. Ruby was like them. Over it. She was all right.

Nell had always been too worried to enjoy the same things that her peers enjoyed. Worried about being unable to invent anything, unable to contribute, about her mother, about her mother's being gone. She sounded like a machine and had a chest cavity full of steel, but she didn't have the privilege of turning herself off when she got too exhausted or too anxious. She kept ticking along.

Her brow knitted as she cycled down by the river and into the city's last center. The quays were dense with cleaners this morning, teams of folks tipping vats of purifying chemicals down into the water, as they did every day. There was a stench in the air around this hour that should have been clean but instead was overbearing, noxious. Dilapidated breweries and stone buildings (which Julian had once whispered were museums full of art long ago) lined the grim wetness of the Livia, and Nell ducked into the skinny winding streets where some families still lived.

She picked up her pace; the vague color of tragedy still clung to these streets. At least in the greenery of the parklands there was dense, lush fauna to mask it. Out by the river the old water's chemical stench made for a good disguise. But here, among the houses where the epidemic had taken most of its victims, the air was thick and alive with their specters. Some days Nell couldn't feel the grief at all, but today the ghosts were all over her.

Clunking over old tram lines, Nell seared through the city at top speed. She set her jaw, intent to make it down to the market quickly; the air was strange today. Still, to get to the bustling hub, no matter what route she took, she would have to pass the hospital.

She eventually broached the center of the city, marked by the tall steel Needle that stood proudly in Main Street, a pathetic folly in the shadow of Kate's majesty, her long, cool shadow a relief against the heat of the morning. Julian had told her many times that the Needle was the last monument built before the country took the Turn. It shone in the tepid morning heat, silver and towering and almost endless. It had been the first thing protected by plastic during the Turn, wrapped in miles and miles of industrial clean cellophane. It survived, untouched by the signature bloody red rust that ate metal all around it. The townspeople had unwrapped it to celebrate the end of quarantine. A tiny red light blinked at the peak when night fell, but nobody knew why. Nell didn't like to hear the stories and theories, especially not the ones that said it was somebody watching.

It had been left to stand, it was said, because it told no stories. It had no face, no body, no myth. It was just a needle, towering to the hot sky, too slim and smooth to climb, made of such stuff that nobody could even write histories upon its surface. The stone woman's incomplete face gazed past it, as if it wasn't even there.

Wrapping her fingers around her handlebars a little tighter, Nell looked up at the statue. She wished she had someone to talk to, someone to pour her concern out to. This, she imagined, was what mothers and sisters were for. Kate's incomplete blank stare didn't even touch Nell; she was a speck in the streets far below.

She didn't let this sudden gape of loss sink her for more than a moment. This was why she had to build a companion, build a boy with an electric voice, so she'd have someone to confide in when the people around her were too much for her to handle. Too flawed. Too human.

CHAPTER 11

Nell pressed on into the day, and it was upon her then: the shadow of Gonne Hospital. White stone columns, grand carvings, a proud aul dame. It was still romantic somehow: the disused department store, a large bronze clock jutting from its facade out onto the street, rows and rows of silent, caged windows that had once proudly displayed beautiful expensive things from places far away. Nell stopped to take it in despite herself.

She was just about to begin pedaling again when someone moving caught her eye: Oliver bloody Kelly, walking briskly down the street. Nell's gut twisted between disgust and curiosity. He had to be on his way to his dark storeroom full of stolen parts hidden somewhere in its labyrinthine belly. She'd been able to ignore Ruby, so for sure she could ignore him; she could just be on her way—

"Well, isn't this a surprise! Couldn't wait a few days. Don't blame you!" he called out to her, his voice jarring against the deserted streets. His smugness almost echoed across the road. His dress shoes slapped against the pavement as he bounded toward her, and then there he was, his eager hand on her arm. Nell was defeated, too tired now for the escape.

"Ruby must have told you I was working today. Finally come clean about the eye, has she?" Oliver smelled strong, soapy. "You look wonderful, given how distressed you were last night. Have you reconsidered? Will you let me show you the inventory? Give you the full tour?" Nell's skin crawled at his enthusiasm, but curiosity slipped its ugly tentacles around her again. She did truly want to know what was inside the room he kept, a history of the city in spare parts.

"I have not reconsidered anything, Oliver. I'm on my way to the market but"—she mustered a thin-lipped smile from somewhere—"I can come in for a bit."

Nell dismounted her bicycle, the sleepless night landing on her. The hand in her satchel weighed a ton in unanswered questions, in unsolvable problems.

Oliver beamed, offering his arm to her. She stared, and he withdrew quickly.

"Was just being a gentleman."

"If I ever want your arm, I'll take it, Oliver."

They crossed the street quietly. Oliver was barely able to contain the smile on his face, but for Nell each step forward was a fight against the pulling current of her distaste.

She focused all her thoughts on the hand in her bag as they wound down a side street that led behind the huge, desolate building. The smell of fire was shocking, and her eyes started to water. The building held some massive, unspeakable power; she hadn't been this close to it in years. The things that had happened inside the gray walls were unspeakable: this house of failure. And Nell was following Oliver Kelly inside.

She'd known her route passed the hospital. Had a part of her wanted this excuse? Wanted to bump into him, longed for coincidence? Her ticking escalated again.

In the ashen shadow of the alley, they approached a huge steel fire exit, with no apparent handle or release. Oliver dropped to his knees and snaked his bony hand under the slightest crack between the door and the pavement, rustled around for a moment, and then click, the door opened onto the darkness of the hospital.

Oliver flipped on a light switch, and in two blinks the corridor was illuminated. Nell preferred the shield of darkness to the sudden arrival of scorch-marked white tiles, the eerie buildup of filth and dust and ash where the floor met the wall, and the seemingly endless

112

depth of the hallways before them. A disquieting whir emanated from the sickly blue lights above them, as though they were struggling to stay aglow. Oliver marched confidently on, his footsteps echoing out into the labyrinth of the building.

They passed doorways upon doorways upon doorways upon doorways, each with a small square that should have been a window where one could have peeked in had it not been so filthy. Most were charred to a solid black.

Those had been the wards. Some remaining doors even still had toxicity signs on them, bright red, warning visitors to stay out. Some were open only a few inches; some sealed shut, framed by iron welding and painted an alarming, screaming red. Some had blown open completely and were just frames leading to pitch-black rooms. The morning light streamed into other wards they passed, illuminating scorched steel bed frames and the remains of chewed-away curtains.

Nell scurried along after Oliver fascinated and appalled by the horrors around her. She wanted to *explore*. But before she knew it, darkness was upon them again. They had arrived in an atrium, and Oliver halted her, then left her alone for a paralyzing moment, disappearing into the blackness.

Suddenly, with three flickers, then a bloom of light,

the enormous hall was illuminated. The remains of reception areas littered the sprawling hub, and it was clear, in the very center of room, that this is where the biggest fire had been lit. There were the remains of a pyre, black and broken, like a crooked skeleton of an unknowable, featureless animal. For a moment Nell blinked and saw an elephant in flames, but she knew this was no creature's remains; this was a man-made solution to a man-made problem. Fire for the disease. Fire to scorch it clean. The ceiling, far above them, had been burned almost all the way through, and stray wires hung, crackling, down into the room.

"It's over here," Oliver called. "We have to hurry. I can't leave these lights on for long."

Nell scampered across the tiles to a bright green, hastily painted door where her unlikely guide stood. Oliver fumbled with his keys, then swung the door open, triggering a light inside.

"Wait here. I'm going to shut off the electricity behind us. I've nearly burned this place down again too many times forgetting it. Those loose wires are the bane of my life."

"Aren't they dangerous?" whispered Nell, but Oliver was already dashing back across the room. She shook her head and walked into the workshop, each footfall landing in time with the now enormous ticking from her chest.

It wasn't a big room at all, but it didn't need to be. The fire smell seemed to fade as she stepped out of the atrium. The windows were covered by clean, whitewashed wooden panels, and the false light wasn't blue tinted or flickering, just cool and clear. The ceiling was unexpectedly high. Had she ever been in a place this clean, this untouched by the ancient grime of the city? A table stood in the center of the room: long and silver and almost mirrorlike in its shine. And the walls . . . Nell's ticking suddenly changed from a steady march of uncertainty to the flutter of a baby bird; there were so, so many parts in all shapes, sizes, colors. So many limbs.

Some were just plastic; others, wood. Many were painted exquisitely: looping, grand signatures along forearms, family crests on calves. Bright gouache flowers grew across limb after limb, the red lick of flames on one or two. Arms, legs, hips, feet, hands, all of different sizes, in neat, organized racks, behind set panes of clear new glass. There were cabinets with keyholes, displaying sets of dentures and single teeth, false eyes, wooden and porcelain fingers, steel and plastic toes. Nell peered down at the eyes, wondering which Ruby would choose for herself. Some were mechanized and wired; others, just crescent moons of painted glass. Oliver had really found an incredible stash. These would be worth a fortune.

She wanted all of it. She wanted every single thing, to inspect it and play with it and see what she could make it do. This was what her father's lab must be like, a mechanical menagerie of limbs all spread out on the walls like specimens or pieces of a jigsaw puzzle. She was transfixed. How—

"It's stunning, isn't it?" Oliver broke her reverie, gazing at her expectantly, knowing he'd impressed her.

"Yes," she murmured, still scanning the inventory.

The door clicked behind him, and they didn't say anything for what felt like an awfully long time. Nell walked slowly around the perimeter of the room, examining each wall. How full of genius each prosthetic was. Each of these strange inhuman things had lived a human life of its own. What must one feel like? She placed her hand to her chest, still thrumming. What must it look like in there? There was such beauty in these augmented human shapes. And so many of these contributions were in her family's name.

She would hold on to Julian's augmented arm for a moment longer next time they embraced.

From nowhere then she was brave. Here, in the room adorned with limbs—some analogue from before her father's creations, some of Julian's marvels—here in the charred museum, she decided to tell Oliver about the hand. She wanted to show him. She wanted to talk about it. Oliver was the only one who had the same vocabulary as she and her father, who spoke the language that existed on the strange border between machine and human. She hated that Oliver would understand, but he would.

"I'm about to show you something, Kelly," said Nell, quiet, dangerous, "and if you ever tell another living soul that you saw this, or if you take the piss out of me in front of Antoinette or Ruby, I'll take you apart."

His eyes flashed, and his mouth opened ever so slightly. Did he think she was flirting?

"I am under no circumstances flirting with you." Nell's voice was dry. "Do you understand?"

Oliver flushed slightly and nodded.

"Good."

Nell reached into her satchel and felt around for the hand. She fished it out from the depths, brought it into the light, and presented it to Oliver across her palms. He knitted his brow.

"Is that a hand?"

"Yes," Nell began, "and it's the best thing I've ever found."

"Why?" Oliver peered closer. "It's . . . a mannequin

if I'm not mistaken? Never would have been worn by a survivor of the epidemic, even in the worst of it. It's a display piece."

"It's beautiful," Nell said. A blush prickled at her cheeks.

"What a strange piece to hang on to, Crane. Do you mind if I take a look at it?" Oliver wasn't teasing her now; their swords were down. No combat. Just conversation.

She hadn't a moment to protest before he was holding it up to the light, examining it closely. He removed an eye loupe from his coat pocket and placed it between the lids of his right eye to get a better look, clearly scanning it for some distinctive marking or other. She considered him for a moment: his keen eye, his imagination for building things, his absurd dedication to courting her. Nell then thought of her drawings, her boy drawn out on cream paper on her desk. The hand's specter, the boy that it wasn't—the boy that it could be. His eyes, his nose, his hair billowing back from the invisible breezes in her paper world. Her choices were this possible boy, or Oliver.

Her ticking spoke to her body in a low metronome. Oliver was all wrong. She should cut him loose. Being useful wasn't justification for keeping him hanging on. It wasn't fair.

"If you pulled it apart at each joint," he was saying, "each knuckle, then each mound, then hollow out the palm, hide a battery in the center so nobody could see it, run a wire down the center of each finger, and attach the smallest hinges you have, I think you could make it walk."

Nell laughed despite herself. "Yeah, and what use would that be? I can hardly stand up in front of the council and present the Incredible Walking Hand. I've enough tiny machines to be toying with."

"I don't envy you, Crane. You've a lot to live up to. I mean, Cora and the statue was one thing, but what Julian makes"—Oliver whistled, low—"they're something else. I mean, just look at the walls. Look, you can see his marksmanship all over them; the rudimentary wooden home-brewed parts up there look like something a child made in comparison. His pieces are so intuitive. If they didn't need a charge to sustain their movement, they could definitely move on their own; the sheer detail of their mechanics is, just . . . your father is a genius. I figure, if you got enough of these things together, you could make a whole person."

As the last words escaped Oliver's mouth, Nell gasped as though she had come up for air after years underwater. Despite her best efforts, she beamed, almost laughing with joy. *If you got enough of them together, you could make a whole person.* The possible boy was right here in front of her, not whole yet. She could almost just take him.

"You're right actually, Oliver. A whole person. That's so interesting," Nell replied, taking the hand back from him and turning it over in hers again and again. She could see wires growing from its wrist, kinetic hinges, and clever sockets. If she set it up just right, she could get these spare parts to speak to one another, to work together. These old prosthetics that had lived entire lifetimes with people: they were beautiful and familiar; they were the opposite of the hard alien lines of the computers her city feared. These spare parts would make an excellent costume; they'd make an excellent boy. She could almost feel it whirring and pulsing to life, almost see the arm and the shoulders and neck and face—almost.

"No idea how you'd do it, though," said Oliver.

"Neither do I," Nell lied.

Penelope,

My last letter has gone unanswered. I am sure you are simply rushed off your feet with your project, or at least this is what I hope, given that you haven't even delivered a proposal to the Youth Council yet.

Last night I dreamed of your face, your bright eyes the spokes of a bicycle, frogs on your tongue, your cheeks scorched with ash, your hair wet. You said something I could not hear, your tongue too cold, your mouth a lake. I am worried. Tell me how you are. I don't want to have to go through Julian to make sure you are all right.

Write me soon, please. All my love, all my blessings.

Nan

CHAPTER 12

Two days later, Nell sat with her knees to her chest in the great, cavernous hall of the Youth Assembly. Her eyes were closed, and in the darkness she placed together limb after limb, the pieces of her plan. Normally Youth Council made her anxious; every session that passed was a reminder of her lack of a contribution. This time was different. It would be her on the deep stage soon, her in the footlights. A creation by her side.

Determination flourished inside her as she watched her peers milling about. They had no idea what she was planning. They had no idea what she was capable of.

She was folding and unfolding Nan Starling's latest letter as she sat, fresh that morning.

Once there had been schools, order, organized education. Julian had told Nell all about it. His great-grandparents had sat in classrooms with teachers.

They'd even been able to speak more than one language; they'd known things about other countries in the world. But after the toxic pulses, as the epidemic tore down the city, the next generation had been sent to work. All their learning had to be practical, so they could contribute as soon as possible. How else would they rebuild?

Now the mayor called together the young apprentices between ages thirteen and twenty once a month, and those who had contributions ready would present them to their peers. The mayor and treasurer sat side by side at a small desk, adjudicating, taking questions from the crowd. It was meant to be encouraging. It bored Nell to tears.

She had a huge woolen shawl draped around her and the mannequin hand nestled in her satchel. Her wrists ached from drawing plans, and her eyes were dry and sore. She sipped her flask of tea as she looked down onto the auditorium.

This building, before the Turn, had been a theater, a fabulous ancient thing, tucked subtly between buildings on the south side of the river, still posing defiant and beautiful. After the Turn it had been repurposed by the surviving city dwellers for the government because it wasn't too decrepit, had a stage and some functioning electricity lines leading through it. The government buildings from before the Turn were long, long gone; all that was left were burned-out unwalkable halls.

Nell had seen pictures of how this theater had once looked: stained-glass awnings and delicately carved buttresses and dark velvet curtains. It felt haunted; that fine layer of mystery that hung in the air was especially dense here. How many places were rife with ghosts after the great descent of death over the city? Where might her mother haunt? Nell prayed it wasn't the hospital, but somewhere warmer, maybe even their home. She wouldn't mind or be scared; even the imagining of it gave her comfort.

She picked at her bootlaces, mostly ignoring the presentation being made by Mara, the baker's daughter, and Timothy, the budding confectioner, about the shopfront they were repurposing to become the first cake shop since the quarantine had ended. Cake shop. Mercy. Nell rolled her eyes. Something about its being important for community, for morale. They were bright eyed, full of ideas and plans. Optimistic, though she had no idea how they summoned the bright tone in their voices, the genuine hope.

Nell smirked to herself, wishing Ruby were sitting beside her so she could give her a nudge. But Ruby was in the ground seating, sitting close to a familiar curly mop, Charlie Klaxon. Looking over the balcony, Nell could just make out Ruby resting her head on his shoulder.

More secrets. Ruby would probably slap her wrist for being judgmental, for being a snob, and remind her that people needed distractions, that they needed to be happy. And cakes and good food were the easiest way to give people something to smile about.

Cakes were one thing. Code, now *that* was what Nell dreamed of.

Nell had not spoken to Ruby since the Bayou, and she was strangely eager to share her fresh, shiny plan; what if she couldn't carry it out alone? It had blossomed into a vast, potentially dangerous web of almost insane steps, but it would eventually lead to her possessing enough spare parts to build an invention surpassing even her parents' contributions.

She held on to the glow of the thought. A machine that is also a person. A whole person. Arms and legs and hands and a smile.

It was the smile that was the thing. The smile summoned out of helixes and rites of ones and zeros and ciphers—reams of language Nell could never speak or even hope to parse, let alone write. Without access to this knowledge, Nell would need something very dangerous to make a heap of clever metal feel.

She really, really wanted to tell Ruby. What good were secrets unless they could be poured into the ears of your best friend? Maybe Nell's secret would encourage Ruby to share hers, too. Ruby used to tell her secrets all the time, usually sordid and occasionally hilarious, full of detail, but because Nell could never bring herself to court anyone, she never had any secrets to exchange. She just listened, scandalized, envious.

She'd softened under the construction of her new plan; there was no use in holding grudges. She'd need Ruby's help if this was going to happen. She had to apologize for being so distant. She slipped her hand into the satchel to touch the cold, solid firmness of the hand, but just as she closed her eyes, she heard movement, scuffing, someone—

Embalming fluid, cologne, there he was again. Nell fought the urge to lean over and growl, "Get away from me. I don't want to look at you," and instead trilled, "Hello there, Oliver, lovely to see you again!" while quietly putting Nan's letter away in her bag, out of sight.

A grin broke across Oliver's face: pure delight. Nell was never glad to see him, but she was going to need access to his room in the hospital again. She was going to need everything he could give her. And he couldn't know why—not yet.

She would tug the fishhook gently, keep him where she wanted him. Confiding in Ruby would be one risk; Ruby would stand by her no matter what. Oliver, however, was an opportunist. He had to think he was gaining something by helping her, and for now it would be the illusion of her interest, the possibility that she might finally be breaking. She smiled back at him with her mouth but not with her eyes—it was dark enough that he couldn't tell—as he sat down right beside her. Nell breathed slowly and deliberately to stop the ticking's rising and adjusted her scarf.

"What has you up here hiding all on your own?" he asked, his voice flirtatious. Sickening, like too much dark treacle. Nell held her nerve.

"Much better view in the circle. What brought you this far from the crowds?" she replied, her voice singsong and cheery. This was the hardest part, this smoke and mirrors. Nell would have made a really bad magician, but even a single flower produced from thin air would have been enough to enchant the poor fool.

"Bored down there. Not interested in a lot of the commercial contributions. I mean, fair enough, they're important, but I've got bigger things on my mind. All I have to do is be seen here once a month; everyone knows what my projects are and what my contributions are. So as soon as I've checked in, I go for a wander around the theater. And look, I stumbled upon a leading lady."

Disgusting.

Nell fought the urge to throw up on him, and instead summoned all of her guts, gritted her teeth, and placed her hand on his leg. "You're *so* sweet." She looked at him from under her eyelashes.

Her whole deck of cards fell to the floor. The rabbit scampered away before she could pull it out of her hat.

Oliver looked at her hand on his thigh. His face hardened.

"What do you want, Crane?" he asked low. "You looking to buy something?"

"Maybe," she replied, withdrawing her hand sharply. "But I'm not sure if you've got what I'm looking for in that clean room of yours."

Oliver's eyebrow did the thing again, the angular challenge. "Oh?" His eyes had begun to wander, his mouth curving in an irritating, slightly hungry way.

"Yeah. I just—I don't think there's any of them left, not really. Oh, I've already said too much." She shifted, feigning discomfort in her seat, hand on her scarf, her ticking a steady, confident march. Maybe she still had a few doves up her sleeve after all.

"Stop, please." Oliver spoke softly. "Just be straightforward with me, and I'll help you as best I can."

Nell took a deep breath, part for effect and part for courage. "I know this sounds insane. I know if there was another aftershock, we'd be in trouble. But I need a computer, one that works."

A silence hung in the air for too long then, the quiet of a mistake Nell couldn't undo.

Asking for a computer was like asking for a gun; no matter what side of the folklore and history told in stories your family fell on, everybody knew that computers were at the root of the Turn, at the root of the epidemic. They frightened the wrong people, and the wrong people wanted them gone. There was a reason they were nowhere to be found among the wreckage of the city. Still, they had the capacity to imitate a human brain. She *needed* one.

Oliver whistled to himself, a low and hesitant note. Surely he couldn't say no to her when he was like this, but she had to feed him a little more first, to draw him back in.

"Nell, I don't deal in relics," he said. "That's some real contraband talk."

"I'm just curious to see how they work," she admitted, a half-truth; she was curious to see if a computer, a working computer, could tell a series of interconnected biomechanical limbs to work like a human. If she got the limbs, she'd need a commanding force to get them to move like a person, to turn them into a person.

"Look, I can't promise you anything. I'll have to think about it. Leave it with me," Oliver mumbled. He was copping out on her.

"Can you help me or not, Kelly?" Nell sharpened her tone. "If you can't, I'm sure I'll find someone out there who can."

"Out there? No, you won't. You have no idea where to start looking. You don't know any of these people, not like I do."

He gestured over the balcony to the full rows of seats below. How many members of the council had he quietly reassembled, how many spare parts had found their way to new bodies because of him?

Nell huffed. He was right. Oliver looked her over again and she hated the feel of his eyes on her. They sat in silence a moment before he caved.

"Look, I wouldn't do this for anyone else, Nell."

"Thank you, Oliver," Nell said, meaning it, containing her surprise.

"I'll put out some leads, hopefully something will come back. I'll be at the Bayou every night this week, the usual. Drop by in a few days." He fished a notebook out of his pocket and wrote down a few words with a slim black pen. The scratch of the pen and the smug snap of the notebook as it closed set Nell's teeth on edge. A wave of his wand and it was done.

"This isn't the first time you've had this conversation, is it?" she asked, suspicious, slightly bitter.

"What? Somebody needs something and I find it?" The eyebrow was up again.

"Yes."

"Of course it isn't the first time. But it's unique." Oliver stood up and dusted himself off, preparing to leave.

"How?"

"Well, this computer isn't going to get attached to anyone's body, is it?"

Nell smiled, and as if by magic, the warmth this time wasn't forced. Maybe Oliver was a wizard after all. Below them a gavel struck a table three times, and the room was dismissed; voices rose, a chorus of gossip. Bodies began to move.

"I'll head down now; you wait here a few minutes. Don't want people talking, do we?" Oliver flashed her a crooked smile. He grabbed his bag and promptly disappeared.

Black Water City's almost evening was a warm lavender mist, a density upon her as Nell walked out of the old theater onto the street. She waited by the door as her peers left for home, giving them nods of acknowledgment and half hellos—"Howya?" "How's it going?" "Nice to see you"—barely under her breath, trying to make her eyes smile. Ruby took forever to leave council sessions, always, flitting around, all small talk. She was one of the last to bounce through the ancient wooden doors and out into the darkening air.

"Here—Ruby. Hi, how—how are you?" Nell reached out and touched her arm lightly.

Ruby turned, and her face split open with delight. "Nell! I thought you'd dropped off the face of the earth!"

"Are you walking back to the parklands or biking?"

"I've got my bike, but I can wheel it," Ruby offered.

"Me, too. Can I walk you home?"

"We need a chat, don't we?" Ruby put her hand on Nell's shoulder.

"Yeah," Nell said, instead of "Please take your hand off me." She was getting better at not telling people to not touch her. She awarded herself a silent medal for achieving such patience.

Nell and Ruby walked to the bike rack over the road and unlocked their bicycles. Taking the handlebars in hand, they began to walk up the sloped hill toward the Cathedral District, where they'd cross the Livia River toward their homes.

"So, was that Charlie Klaxon I saw you sitting with?" Nell ventured.

"Ah, yeah, he's"—Ruby shrugged—"he's grand for now, like."

"Wasn't it barely a fortnight ago you were saying to me you were going to open a fabric emporium with the lad?"

"Well, some things just—" Ruby made a face as if she'd too much teeth and laughter in her mouth. "Oh, God above, Nell, I'm probably going to have to cut the poor creature loose. Look, there just isn't any chemistry at all; you know what I mean?"

"I think I do," Nell replied stiffly, staring at the street in front of them. "Yeah. Chemistry."

"I know you find these things difficult," Ruby said, "and probably a bit hard to understand, considering—"

"Considering I've never courted any of the other apprentices. I know, I know."

"Well, you don't have to or anything, and I'm—I'm really sorry about all the business with Oliver. He told me."

Gossip the speed of lightning, Nell thought as Ruby began to lead her bike with one hand and used the other arm to link hers. A cage of unwanted physical affection had descended upon Nell, but she held her nerve and let her friend take her arm.

"You just don't seem interested in anybody and time's passing and everybody . . . well, I'm so worried that you're going to stay holed up in your father's house until they land you up the side of Kate to build. It'd be such a waste, Nell. You've got an amazing lineage. The city deserves your talent." Ruby rested her head awkwardly on Nell's shoulder as she spoke. Nell did not ask her to remove her head from her shoulder. She almost told Ruby that Nan Starling felt similarly, but she didn't. She let Ruby speak.

"I mean, I just think Oliver would be a good fit. He cares about you, he deals in anatomy—I'm supposing he told you all about the new work he's at—it would all make sense. You could do so much good."

Nell sighed. "Technically that's spot-on, Ruby. I know you're coming from a good place."

"Of course I am! Do you think I want you all locked up in your house being sad all the time?"

"No."

"We've all got things to be sad about, Nell. But we get on. We try to build our own happiness."

Nell smiled a little. "You're right actually. That's exactly what I need to do, Ruby."

Ruby beamed. "I'm so glad you agree. Oliver's a nice lad, really. I know he can come on a little bit strong, but give him a break. He has a lovely face on him, doesn't he?"

Nell gave her a flat look.

"Ah, now, he does!" insisted Ruby.

"Then why don't you go with him?"

Ruby hummed. "He's for you. Sure the pair of you have had it coming for years."

"Can—can we not do this, please?" Nell hadn't it in her for this game, this little-push-little-shove that Ruby'd been trying with Oliver for years. "I—I have something more important I'd like to talk to you about, in private."

Ruby halted her bicycle dramatically.

"In private? Does that make it a secret?" she asked, too loud. "You? You have a secret?"

"I'm full of secrets, Ruby." Nell stuck out her tongue.

"I know, but a secret you actually want to tell? Holy wow, who is he? Or she? Who are they? Nell, tell me this minute, I absolutely refuse to move until you do." Ruby crossed her arms and pointed her nose in the air. Her bike clattered to the ground.

"Ruby!"

"Nope. Tell me."

"I really, really can't talk about it in public. Trust me."

Ruby made a face. "Girleen, you're killing me."

"We can cycle back fast. We'll be there in twenty if we go as quick as we can." Even saying the word *computer* in the broad daylight in the street could catch the wrong ear, bring ugly consequences down upon her.

"Fair enough." Ruby sighed, picking up her jangling bike. "Fair enough. But before we go . . . look, I'm really sorry again, about Oliver. I just can't bear to think of you ending up in the parklands forever with nobody but the stoat and your father."

"I won't end up with nobody but the stoat and Da. Just because I can't do things your way doesn't mean they're not getting done." Nell scowled.

Ruby gave her a long look and shook her head. "It must be very lonely up there above the rest of us, Nell. Come on back to the park so you can tell me this secret."

The girls hopped on their bikes and sped off over the black earth, swung down a hill, and clipped over ancient tram lines, once electrical, now just steel indentation.

Up the barren Cathedral District they spun, then out past Heuston Falls where the rush of Livia water spilled down through the once train station and into the river. The roar of the water was welcome, alive against the heat. Reams of white foam erupted with a bright force against the old brickwork; some last remaining gray columns knotted like interlocking fingers behind the foam and drench. Sometimes, in the morning, rainbows would hop out of the clear watery prisms and the whole thing would be beautiful: the mouth of a goddess. But now it was just a fresh rush as they passed. Nell felt the spray against her cheek, refreshing against the hot mugginess of a too bright evening.

Before long the girls had cycled up the long road at the parklands mouth and were dismounting their bikes outside Nell's tumbledown home. Ruby almost danced up the steps. "Sure, amn't I only dying for a cup of tea and a biscuit and a secret!" she sang, letting herself in.

Kodak had been waiting at the door and sped up Ruby's leg to her shoulder, rubbing his nose on her face. She laughed. "Howya, Kodak, bet you're lonely something fierce today!"

Nell picked her pet off her friend's shoulder and cradled him in her arms as they walked through the creaky hallway to the kitchen, clean and ordered, far from the scene of intensity and hurt it had been only a few days before. Nell placed her satchel on the table.

"Is your father around?" Ruby asked, a little cautious. Daniel must have passed some remark to her about what had happened, Nell thought, putting the kettle on.

"He's probably in the lab. He might surface for something to eat at some point."

She sat on the counter near the stove and crossed her legs, Kodak nesting in her lap. Ruby pulled up a chair at the old wooden table and rested her head on her hand. "So."

"All right. This is a big one."

Ruby smiled. "I want to know everything."

Nell took a deep breath and unwound the long, airy cotton scarf from her neck. The dress she'd put on that morning had a sweetheart neckline, low. As she pulled the scarf, Ruby's smile fell away, and her mouth opened slightly. There it was: Nell's scar, long and thick, falling from the crest of her lip down her chin and neck and chest and disappearing under the fabric of her dress.

Nell's fingers shook slightly as she folded the scarf and handed it over to Ruby. Her friend took it, then clutched it close to her as though it were something precious. Nell held still, imagining light coming in through the soles of her feet and filling her body slowly with a calming glow. She wasn't going to panic out of this.

"Gosh, it's actually really beautiful, Nell," whispered Ruby, earnest.

Nell placed her hand over her sternum to feel the seam of her skin.

"Thank you," she replied, not really knowing what else to say.

The kettle began to whisper, then sang a shriek of heat. Nell leaned over and moved it to another hob, then took two large mugs from the press behind her head.

"Get us some teabags; they're in the tin on the table," she directed.

Ruby fished out two small papery pouches from the old box on the table and tossed them to Nell. They sailed through the air silently, and Nell caught them with grace. Ruby had not stopped staring at Nell's scar. Nell placed the bags in the mugs and poured the boiling water on them. Steam lifted. The tension in the room was butter thick.

"I could explode, Nell. I'm glad you let me see the scar. I'm so glad." Ruby walked over to get her mug and leaned next to Nell. She brushed the loose tendrils of hair from Nell's collarbones to take a closer look. "You know that procedure changed the world. That scar is the monument in its honor."

Nell did not tell Ruby not to touch her. Instead, she said, "Yes."

"You shouldn't cover it. You should let everyone see."

"I know."

"Story of your life."

"I know."

"Was there something else? Someone else? You're murdering me here. Are you going to tell me the secret now?"

"Go over and open my satchel."

Ruby took Nell's satchel in her lap, her eyebrows knitted, something of a hopeful smile playing across her lips. She removed a water canister, a jam jar full of tiny screws, a screwdriver, a dead battery, a pliers, a spare combination lock, another battery. She looked at Nell and raised her eyebrows.

Nell's ticking had risen considerably in volume, and her hands were still trembling. She felt very exposed without her scarf. How wonderful it would be to wrap the cotton all around herself and disappear. Poof.

"You carry an awful lot of boring, heavy stuff around with you, Nell." Ruby tutted, excavating a box of matches, a magnifying glass, the hand, a cluster of pens held together by an elastic, two empty jars, Nell could hardly breathe. Ruby had skimmed over the hand as if it were another part of her tool kit, as if it were nothing.

She spluttered, "Ruby, you found it."

Ruby puzzled over the inventory laid out on the table. "The hand?"

"I"—Nell began, balling her fists tight into her scarf—"I want to build a person. A—a boy."

There was a beat of silence, a little too long before Ruby snorted. "A *what?* Nell, if you'd ever let me introduce you around to some more of the apprentices,

I'd be able to find you a live one in no time."

She was joking or trying to, but her voice was all wrong.

"I saw the salvaged parts in Oliver's armory. My father's early models, all laid out in working, good order. I want to put two legs, two arms, a spine, shoulders, a head, a face, eyes all together, and I want to find a computer to make them all *work* together and—and live." Nell didn't look at Ruby, but rather down at the heap of fabric in her lap. She wanted to sound brave and bright, like an inventor, not the child of an inventor. Not a child.

Ruby didn't say anything, so Nell continued, her voice shrinking by the word.

"I thought if I could build a person that maybe he would be like me. You know that people are difficult for me and that because of this"—she gestured to the metronome beating out of her chest—"I can be difficult for people, too. But I have a way through all that now, and it's a contribution. If I can use a computer for good, who knows what we could learn? What it could teach us. If I could get one to speak, maybe it could even reach outside our island, reach the rest of the world. Think of what that could mean."

Nell looked at Ruby for something, anything, a sign of approval or interest, but Ruby's face was ashen, her brow heavy, and her mouth a knot. She turned Nell's magnifying glass over and over.

"Computers, Nell . . ." she whispered. "They're unholy. They're—" She put her hand up to her eyepatch and moved it up above the wave of her fringe. Beneath it, the socket where an eye was not. Just a blank space, a web of pale scar tissue. Ruby pierced Nell with her gaze, quiet for a moment.

"Look at the price the rest of the world made us pay before," she said. "We're *still* paying for it. Thinking machines tore our people apart, and we're only just healing. We can think enough for ourselves. Without code, without internet. We don't need it. There are so many other things you could contribute, so many other things you could do—"

"But they wouldn't mean anything, Ruby!" Nell burst out, standing up out of her chair. "I can't just go up there and contribute something that doesn't mean anything! I've nothing else to give, only this. Sure, I could crib out a limb casing that looks lifelike and responds a fraction more accurately to heat or a socket that responds and connects more seamlessly to human flesh, but that's all in *his* shadow; that's his work! I want something more! If I could get a computer up and talking . . . We're ready. And you could help! You could help me design a body, a face; you're so skilled,

Ruby. I could make him work, and you could make him beautiful!"

Ruby didn't say anything for a second, and Nell's chest ticked like a fevered roulette wheel. The distance between them deepened with every tick, the kitchen tiles a canyon.

"Nell, I can't," Ruby whispered, then her voice rose bravely across the new void between them. "It'll get out to the Pastoral Council; it could cause a disaster. We don't need to know everything; that kind of greed belongs in the past, and it's selfish to try so you can have . . . a friend."

Ruby's voice almost broke with the hurt of it, and Nell gasped. "It's not just a friend, Ruby. You know I'm not looking to replace you!" But as these words bubbled out, Nell wasn't sure at all if she was being honest. It caught in the air, oxidized, and turned rust, poison.

Ruby looked down at the tool kit on the table, the pieces of Nell's life. The hand sat there among them, still reaching out to be held. She wiped an errant tear from her powdered cheek and said, her voice trembling, "It's must be easier for you to imagine building someone new who meets your every need rather than make a compromise and try to see the world from my perspective, even once."

A river of awful truth flooded the chasm and pushed

them farther apart, the two girls shores at opposite ends of an icy sea.

"I can't help you, Nell. This isn't my kind of trouble. I—I have to leave."

Ruby took her bag and was out the door before Nell could even muster the courage to release the "Please stay" that had been crouching in her throat, the "Just hear me out," the "I need you."

Ruby didn't close the kitchen or hall doors behind her, and the awful heat from outside followed in her wake. Nell's cheeks flushed suddenly. How *dare* Ruby walk away from her! Who did she think she was?

Fine. Fine. Oliver would help. Of course Oliver would help. Besides, even if the leagues of difference between her and Ruby were now impossible to ignore, her oldest friend had given her one invaluable thing.

Ruby had never said building a person was impossible. Selfish, yes. But not impossible.

From the Desk of Oliver Kelly
Apprentice to Marian Kelly, Mortician

Meet me at the Bayou after closing on
Wednesday. 4ish. Before sunrise.
I found what you were looking for.

X
O

CHAPTER 13

Nell stepped out of the shower, and the water she left behind her was gray. Her arms had been smudged with ink from writing and drafting. It had been like this every evening for the last few days, just Nell and her ink and her paper. She'd managed to push Ruby from her thoughts for now, but cabin fever was starting to flush at her collar.

The tiny bathroom was full of steam. Dripping, refreshed, she skipped lightly from bathmat to tile to the wooden floor of her room. She combed out her hair. The stoat snoozed.

It was late. Very late. But she wasn't due to meet Oliver until almost sunrise, and she couldn't sleep with the budding excitement. Instead, she stayed up tinkering with the silver box her father had given her. In the cove of her desk, she tried to take it apart with a tiny screwdriver to absolutely no success; the device was welded shut around a tiny seam. Nell considered an appropriately angled little crowbar. She wanted to open the box, but she didn't want to break it.

"What do you look like on the inside?" Nell whispered to it, tapping her nail on its glass surface. "What do you know?"

There were two sockets. One was a tiny slot that she didn't recognize; one was likely an audiovisual jack. She considered applying a wire set and battery to the mystery socket, but that could burn it out. Nell tapped her fingers against the desktop and clicked her tongue. In all she'd learned about machines and clockwork and anatomy and prosthetics and organically responsive robotics and synthetic responsive fibers and motion and kinetic electricity, she hadn't a blind clue how to work a computer. A silent little mystery box.

She *was* relieved she didn't have to build all of her creation's limbs from scratch, though. That would take forever and be extremely difficult to hide from her father, given how much of his help she'd need.

If Nell could convince Oliver to help her out with some of his salvaged Crane brand limbs from the Gonne Hospital, much of the complex, intricate kinetic technology would already be in place. She'd just have to get each limb to recognize the other and provide a central command chamber and a good strong battery—a brain and a heart—to set it all into motion. A clever computer. Run a few volts through it. That was all. Right? Right. One nearly impossible thing at a time.

The clock on the wall beat a slow nighttime pulse, and Nell put herself together. She looked long and hard in the mirror, tracing her fingertips down her scar. She so often tried to ignore it in its entirety, bundling it away, not thinking about it. What would the first person to see all of it, from below her navel to her lip, think? The first person to lay his head on her chest and hear the cogs, their strange grind. What if it was Oliver after all? What if it was someone made of more metal than even she was?

The clock dragged heavy hands as she paced, its ticking sometimes in sync with hers, sometimes not; she put things on and then took them off, put other things on, until it was time for her to go. She roused Kodak, and he made an almost human noise of complaint.

The house was pitch-black, not yet lit by the dewy spectrum of dawn. Her father was a quiet sleeper, but Nell wasn't even sure he was home. He often spent nights late out in a tavern in the city with Daniel or over at the Underwood place, though things were different since their argument. She passed the great door to his laboratory, and there it was, that crack of light that said he was still working. She touched the door as she walked past, a graze, a good-night, a wish me luck. Maybe he'd be really proud of her.

Or furious.

Either way it didn't bear thinking of; she wasn't telling him. She slid out the door, and it clicked shut. The sky outside was just cusping light, but there was no real color in the world yet. She placed the stoat in the basket of her bike, kicked the stand from under the wheel, hopped on, and cycled away into the parklands.

It was different going alone, the fevered race through the lush, swampy woods. Nell strained her eyes for detail all around her. It wasn't as if Ruby could have defended them, even if she had been there. Being by herself made no difference.

Nell quickly passed the Underwood house and workshop, all the lights out. It wasn't quite as ramshackle as her place, kept better, painted white, with plants deliberately organized around it, flowering and ornate, as opposed to chewing the structure to pieces with leathery vines and thick leaves. All the lights were off as Nell whizzed past, the family still sleeping. She got a sad pang in her stomach. She hadn't reached out to Ruby since their argument. Had she been sleeping? Had she been worrying? The house disappeared, but thoughts of Ruby lingered as she traveled into the dark. Nell shook them off, trying to stay alert against the wilderness.

She raced through the tangled knots of wood, barely able to catch her breath, fevered half from anticipation and half from fear. As she spotted the lights of the Bayou in the distance and the trees thinned out, she cycled so fast that the muscles in her legs felt like fire. She passed revelers laughing and singing on their way home, couples kissing in the shelter of the trees, and ignored the scatter of "Oh, hello, Nell!" and "Is that Nell Crane?"

She leaped off her bike almost before the wheels stopped turning and locked the chain seamlessly. She held her head up as she walked straight up to the closed door of the Bayou, which read NOPE instead of its usual OPEN.

She rapped confidently on the door.

Nobody answered.

Undeterred, she knocked again, louder this time.

Still nothing.

Her patience gave in, and she twisted the handle. It was unlocked, so she let herself in. Nell strode past the small table where Janey, the bouncer, usually sat and down the narrow corridor toward the ballroom.

Empty, it lacked its hodgepodge splendor. The band

had been cleared away; a closed upright piano was all that remained of it. It seemed grimmer, sadder, a harder reflection of their lives, all floorboards and hanging dust and ragged bunting and the stench of tobacco and pipe smoke.

Alone at the bar, Oliver sat hunched into a glass, scribbling in a ledger. Antoinette pottered about, tidying and singing to herself, melody carrying long and rich over the room.

"Barfly," said Nell, in a voice she barely recognized, strong and sharp.

"Hermit," mumbled Oliver. Wait, *slurred* Oliver. Nell did a quick scan of him as he turned to her, his hair unruly and his clothes a little disheveled. He was drunk.

"Oliver." She couldn't mask her shock. "Are—are—you—"

"It's four o'clock in the morning, Nell. Of *course* I'm a bit—" He cut her off. "Mercy, you really do live under a rock. You, you're . . . surprised. *Surprise!*" He laughed, and Nell, for a moment, felt very naive and very small.

"I just expected you to be in business form, considering you called me here to—" She halted suddenly, flicking her eyes to Antoinette, who caught her discomfort and laughed.

"Oh, petal, I don't care what he's dealing you.

There's not a person who comes in and out of here that doesn't get something supplied by Mr. Kelly. Your old man's waiting list is far too long for some of us."

"Yes, yes," Oliver said lazily. "Yes. We're still on. I did some asking around, checked if you were all right to be shown—to be brought to where they keep them."

"Keep them? The"—Nell, reverent, dropped her voice—"computers?"

"I owe some people some major favors, but I've got it sorted."

"Fine. When?"

When had she started trusting Oliver's word or become willing to follow him?

"In, around—now actually. Now," he said, draining his glass and straightening himself.

Antoinette flipped Oliver's notebook closed, and he batted her away. "You want out of here pretty sharp if you want to get down to New Smithfield Square before the world wakes up," she said.

Nell was aghast. "You told her?"

The barmaid laughed, and it was sparkling and sharp. "C'mon now, Crane, I know everybody's business in this town. Funny thing is you think yours is the most important!"

"It's important to me." Nell leaned over the bar. "And I'm not *every*body." She wasn't sure if she was flirting or challenging Anto to a fight. It felt like both.

"Girls, girls, girls." Oliver waved his arms in an attempt at diffusing the tension, but Antoinette slammed her fist down on the bar fiercely.

"Don't you go calling me a girl, Oliver Kelly!"

"Right. Ladies," Oliver offered. "There's no point arguing. Anto, Nell's got her reasons for being out of the loop. We're working on it. *Aren't we?*" He gave her a loaded stare, a for-the-sake-of-peace-please-just-play-nice kind of stare.

Nell inhaled deeply and steadied her temper. "Yes. Working on it."

"Now, we can stand here and argue about who knows more secrets or we can leave and actually get some work done. Which do you prefer?"

"I can stand here and listen to Miss Penelope lose her temper all morning, Oliver." Antoinette leaned across the bar, and cooed, "You really hate people as much as they say you do, don't you?"

"Anto, stop." Oliver was almost pleading with her now, and Nell bristled. She definitely, definitely wanted to fight her.

"If someone doesn't tease her once in a while, she'll never come down from her tower, will she?"

"Leave it. Are you coming, Nell?" Oliver swayed a little. Nell took his arm, staring Antoinette in the eye.

"Yes, I'm ready to leave now."

"See you tomorrow, Oliver. Take care of yourself, Crane, and lighten up a little, would you?" Antoinette waved them out, blowing kisses, singing, "Good-bye, good luck, so long, farewell, I'm glad to see the back of you."

When they hit the outdoors, the finger-painted neon pink of dawn was just beginning to rise. Oliver made movement toward his bicycle.

"You're not cycling. You're a mess. I'm not picking bits of you up off the ground if you fall," Nell said sternly.

"Well, we're hardly walking, are we?" said Oliver, gesturing dramatically.

"No. Look, I'll give you a crossbar."

"A what?"

"A crossbar. Sit on the crossbar of my bike, and I'll steer."

"God almighty, Nell."

"Don't bring him into it. It's that or nothing, and I'm not waiting another day to see what you're talking about."

Nell was coming down off the crest of her gusto, deflated in the end by Antoinette's sneer. She wanted to go, get a computer, and go home to continue her plans. She wished she had slept. People were so completely exhausting. Oliver especially.

But he gave in. "Fine. Let's do it."

What followed was a terribly awkward scene in which Oliver was far too close to Nell for comfort. She propped up her bicycle, and he, after several failed attempts, sat astride the handlebars. He always smelled so strong. Now, like moonshine and that poxy cologne: heady, overbearing. Nell did not disguise how unimpressed she was. She wrinkled her nose and squinted at him, his face too close to hers. Kodak capered over him and into the basket, shielding his eyes, maybe against the now surreal pink light of day or maybe against the scene of sheer calamity he was watching. Too many limbs, too little bicycle.

Eventually, after some staggering, some swearing— "Well, that was colorful, Nell!"; some "Look, just get off, and we'll try from a different angle"; some "*Get* your hands *off* my waist!"—the pair took off, back into the forest. Fortunately, Oliver's bony frame was more an awkwardness than an imposition, and Nell managed to pick up speed after all. Oliver clung to the handlebars, the breeze almost cool, sweeping his hair back, finding all this very romantic.

They took a different route through the park this time, away from Nell's house. Up past the ruins of the police headquarters, and out onto the roads with the little redbrick houses still boarded up, still streaked with ash, some still marked with large telltale red stripes on their doors: "This house is sick"; "And this one"; "And this one."

Nobody lived up here anymore. Some horses and deer occasionally would dash about: great mountainous beasts, ghosts of a time long gone. Bad things had happened here; the place had been crushed, and still nobody was ready to remove that cast and see if the bones were fixed. Nell never left the park this way to go to the city. It was too close to the wastelands at the edges of the Pale for her liking. Too close to the wreckage not to make her skin crawl.

Her legs were on fire by the time they got to the slight hill of Stonybatter and coasted down between the hollowed-out houses, the charred smell of fire still in the air against Oliver's perfume.

"Which way do I go?" Nell asked.

"Down to the Old Smithfield Square."

Nell turned left and wound down a skinny cobbled road, then hit the abomination that had once been a bright, vast market square. There were craters like this all over the island, a handful pocking Black Water City. The electromagnetic pulse that had triggered the Turn had pulled airplanes from the sky, a violent metal rain then hammering the land. It looked as though a terrible god had punched the earth, the crater a shallow, ugly mess; huge tall streetlamps, once majestic, were buckled down, some leaning, some twisted, some drooping in sorrow.

Nell kept the bicycle close to the old warehouses and kept her eyes straight ahead.

"Stop in just a moment, here by these steps," Oliver guided her.

Nell braked, and the jolt uprooted Oliver from the handlebars. Thankfully he didn't hurt himself, just staggered off. Nell didn't laugh aloud but wanted to. She preferred him like this, all his sharp edges ragged.

She locked up her bike and took the stoat around her shoulders. Oliver walked unsteadily across the small cracked plaza toward a building set deep off the square.

"What is this place?" Nell called to him.

Oliver stopped and turned to her. "This was a cinema once. Now it's five large rooms under the ground. It's a, eh, workshop, I suppose you could call it."

"Like your workshop?"

"Not quite."

Oliver walked up to the blackened glass doors, chained shut on the inside. He placed his thumb on a gray plastic buzzer, and Nell stood a little behind him. They waited there silently for a few minutes. Nell shuffled her feet, uncomfortable. It felt as if nobody was coming. Oliver just leaned against the door, letting his eyes fall closed. He was jolted suddenly as a letter-box flicked open and a voice whispered, "Password?"

"You've got to be joking," Nell protested.

Oliver shot her a look as he said, "Control, alt, delete."

A figure unchained the doors and opened one, just a crack.

"Come in then. Quickly," he said.

Nell took a deep breath and followed Oliver inside.

The dust and age of the place hit Nell's nose, and she recoiled as the door closed behind them. The air was thick with rot and ash. Nell could already feel generations of cobwebs descending on her, sticking to her skin. She covered her face with her hands for a moment to protect her eyes as the chains behind her were replaced and a key clunkily slid into a padlock.

She squinted at their host in the weak light that pushed itself through the filth on the glass of the door.

The young man had the stature and presence of a bonfire in the darkness. Nell took him in as her eyes adjusted: tall, with a pyre of wild red curls, a beard that defied his age, and small, round glasses on his nose.

"Nell, this is Rua David," Oliver said.

"I'm Nell Crane," she said, extending one hand, overconfidently.

The young man took it in both of his, clasping her hand rather than shaking it. "I know, sweetheart. You're fine. The others are expecting you."

He released her and slapped Oliver on the back so hard that he almost doubled forward. "Good on you getting in so early. Can't risk anybody seeing you—especially with the breakthrough we just made. Can you hear it?"

"Hear what?" Oliver said. Nell couldn't hear anything.

"Good. We're nice and insulated down there; you'd never know we've been dancing all night. And so have you, Kelly, by the smell of you."

"Ah, now, stick on the kettle when we get down there, and I'll be right as rain."

The two started to move forward, and Nell followed them through the dimness, hugging herself. The air was murky and thick and blue-gray, almost like walking at the bottom of the sea or on a new planet with an atmosphere that only marginally tolerated your presence. She was sure the ceiling was low, she was sure the corridor was broad; but she wasn't much sure of anything else. This building was an abyss.

"What is this place called?" she asked, hurrying to keep up without tripping over anything or herself. Kodak had burrowed his face into her collar; he was not enjoying this. Nell could barely hear something disturbing the air in the distance: a droning.

Rua led on. "The Lighthouse."

Nell laughed cheekily. "Why? Because it's so bright in here?"

"No. Because that's what it was always called. Before us, before anything happened, when this city was a real city with real things to do and places to go and no disease and no war. We have to honor what came before us if we can hope to even come close to rebuilding it," he said sternly. "It's dark here for a reason. Once we go down lower we'll have lamps. We have to keep it brighter in the workshop. And cleaner. Watch your step."

Their guide took two steps down a flight of stairs and disappeared into the murk.

Oliver said, "You're going to need to take my arm."

"But then if I fall, you fall, too. There must be a railing." By which Nell meant, "I do not want to have to touch you any more than I already have this morning, please and thank you."

"Suit yourself. Just stick close to the wall." With that, Oliver also disappeared into the dense, filthy air.

The rhythm of his bounding down the staircase almost synced with the distant thrumming, and for a moment there in the dark Nell thought it sounded a little like music. Rua had mentioned dancing.

She clung to the wall, the grit of filth immediately all over her hands, her skin crawling with the feel of it, and shakily began to make her way down the stairway, one blind step at a time. Her chest ticked louder with every step. Not too far below her, Oliver called, "Come on, Nell, it's a flight of stairs; you're not reinventing the wheel!"

"Piss off!" she shouted, stumbling a little over her boots.

"Over here!" called Rua, his tall figure shrouded in the grimy depths. "Two more small flights to go!"

How a still tipsy Oliver Kelly made it to the bottom floor without falling flat on his face, Nell would never know. Her own descent was nothing short of a miracle. For Rua it was clearly muscle memory; either that or those glasses had something extra built into them. Nell had fumbled gracelessly almost all the way, just a few feet from the bottom, before she tripped over her own feet and plummeted forward, Kodak digging his claws so tight into her coat that she could feel them pricking her skin.

As with all falls, her body came down incredibly fast on the outside, but incredibly slow on the inside. She knew she was going to land on her face. Maybe split a lip, wreck some teeth—

Somebody warm and soft caught her. Definitely not Oliver Kelly.

"Oh, I'm so sorry." She leaped from Rua's arms before his well-timed catch could turn into any sort of embrace.

"Happens to everyone at some point on the way down. Don't worry. We're almost there. If you take my hand, it'll be much easier. The floor isn't so great down this way."

Nell clenched her jaw, her pulse racing from the adrenaline of the fall, the echo of the crash that didn't happen running tremors through her. People seemed insistent on touching her, leading her places, taking her hand or her arm. She supposed that if there was any time she was going to let them, it might as well be when she was most likely to actually injure herself.

Rua's hand was so completely unlike the mannequin hand: warm, soft, with some calluses. It closed around hers confidently, without implication, and led her through the dark. She stumbled after him, relieved that she was no longer swimming alone in this black sea.

The sound was getting louder. She was almost sure now that it was music. Someone was doing something terrible to—a guitar maybe? There must be a lot of drums wherever they were going.

There was a thick plastic curtain that made an

unpleasant noise, industrial, heavy. Nell pushed through it. A few feet farther was a tall, heavy door; the plastic sheet had just been a shield against the dust. Rua stepped ahead to open the door, turn on the light. They walked through; the door closed behind them.

Then the whole world was bright again. Nell pulled her hand free and rubbed her eyes. Kodak lifted his head from the crook of her neck.

The room was vast and white and clean, as though they had slipped through a tear in their rotting world into a blank canvas, a fresh void. A cool breeze whispered from a spinning fan on the ceiling, high above them. A chill rolled over Nell's skin; she hadn't felt something like that in a long time. The air felt fresh.

Cleaning solution lingered on the edge of Nell's senses; she could nearly taste it. Like bleach and, under the bleach, lavender. Like a place that had been cared for, constructed. As if all the badness of this building's past was being scrubbed out. The walls were lined with shelves and glass cases full of silver boxes of all shapes and sizes. This was an inventory.

These were the computers.

Spread out evenly on the clean white tables were tiny parts, silvery things, and delicate tools. Thin wires lined up by color, by size. So many small things. But none of this was what Nell was really looking at.

Three people were dancing near the wall farthest from where they came in. Whatever was blasting through the air was definitely music. Delight, when it arrives out of no place at all, is like an electricity that runs through passages in bones and out through hands and up into mouths. It is a beautiful shock. Nell nearly screamed with joy.

One of them shouted, "Turn off the light!"

"Calm down. I'm doing it, I'm doing it." Rua laughed and flipped the switch on the wall again. The room went black.

Something was projected onto the wall. Images of stars. People. Or at least they looked like people. A crowd, a band, drawn in moving pictures. A million colors against the fresh, clean dark of the room, alive, racing past. It looked as if someone had split open a crystal and cast a torch through the prism.

Nell's eyes filled with hot tears, and she stretched her arms above her head. Rua and the other three were dancing without inhibition, eyes locked on the display on the wall.

The images moved with the music; yes, that was what it was. But Nell had never heard these instruments before. These thrumming strange rushes: fractals of light in a broken violin, someone playing a heart like a drum, like ten beautiful drums, repeating melody, looped and looped and escalated. Like something shattered but shattered *right*. She didn't even feel that she was in her body anymore.

A voice rang out. Not a human voice. Almost, but full of stars. A computer's voice. She *loved* it.

It sang out three words—*One more time*—a mantra, and the others sang along and waved glasses in the air. They knew this song. Again and again it sang, and Nell lifted her voice along with it, understanding it immediately.

For a moment the beat disappeared, a soft, tender lull of electric tone ran beneath the voice, and they slowed their dance in reverence, chanting, "One more time, one more time." In the dark, Nell could see that Oliver wasn't dancing. She didn't care.

The beat reappeared slowly, crept up out of nowhere, and the five picked up their movement until it peaked and they were lost, each, in the sound and the color, the strangeness and newness of it. It glittered in the air, if sound could glitter. Nell's whole body shone; her machine heart was beating a pulse exactly in tempo. This music was far from the janky accordion and double bass of the Bayou, the flat guitars, the salvaged, busted instruments and torch songs from dead times. This was so different. It shone. Nell wept, a smile splitting her face until it ached, as she sang easy new words with these strangers.

The song ended with three dense strikes of a bell.

The screen flickered off, and Nell was in the dark again; but the world was more illuminated than when she began. She was sweating but not summer, city sweating. She thrummed, not yet ready for this to be over. She looked around, waved her arms a few more times, hoping the galactic orchestra would pick back up, but nothing. It was over. The pace of the world was slow again.

One of the three dashed across the room to switch the light back on. The bursting lily whiteness swept over Nell, and she was in reality, faced with three strangers, a room full of computers, and something very important to do. Oliver was wringing his hands, making his way over to a kitchenette.

"Would you look, it's Nell Crane."

"Haven't seen you in a while, Nellie."

"Is Ruby not around? Was hoping she'd come down."

A chorus of moderately familiar voices.

The girl at the door called over, and Nell recognized her now in the stillness. It was Sheena Blake: cropped, sleek black hair and straight teeth, lithe as a cat and twice as aloof. Biomechanical left leg, revealed in beautiful contrast with her right by rolled-up loose denim shorts. It was gray, an older model, one of the more classic designs Nell's father had put together. It would never break, all titanium casing and impenetrable wiring. Sheena was a mechanic or, well, a computer mechanic, Nell supposed, suddenly irritated and feeling very much, even in the glare of these lights, in the dark.

"What did Ruby tell you?" Nell did her best to conceal her concern, still breathless from the dance.

"Nothing really. She never tells me anything about you. She just said you were working on something mental, and she didn't have the time for it."

Sometimes things were very blunt but also very sharp at the same time. Nell felt as if she'd been struck with a knife-hammer. She wanted to say, "Well, she never tells me anything about *you* either, Sheena Blake." But instead, she said, "We'll work it out."

"Of course you will. She, like, loves you." Sheena rolled her eyes with these words and moved back toward the group.

Oliver and Rua were standing with the other two strangers around the kitchenette in the corner.

"This is Tim," began Rua, more imposing now than he had been in the dark. "He's—"

"The confectioner? I saw your presentation at the Youth Council." Nell was baffled. "Marrying Mara Cahill?"

The lad smiled, warm. Sandy skin dappled with island

clusters of freckles, face soft around the edges, neat black dreadlocks wound into a ponytail. It took a moment for her to notice that his ears were scaffolded with machinery. They'd been designed to match his skin, but there was a tiny green light at the center of each conch that flickered as the sound around them rose and fell.

"Confectioner, not really. Mara? For show. We're great friends. Keeps the mayor distracted. As long as they think we're moving along, making cakes, everything's fine. Smoke and mirrors, you know. Day job stuff. Down here's where the real work is."

"What real work?" Nell asked.

"That music you just heard? I found and restored that. Pulled it up out of code. The video appeared with it on the screen, so we rigged it to an old projector. Someday we'll play it for the whole city!" Tim's laugh was husky. He was so forthcoming that Nell found herself disarmed; she liked him.

She cast a quick look to Oliver, who was setting out mugs and teabags.

"I'm not sure about the film, lads," he said, almost shakily. "It's a bit much, you know? You won't be able to show that outside here."

He was well familiar with this place, with these people. These were his friends.

"What do you mean, 'It's a bit much'?" Tim snorted.

"It's beautiful! You're probably just a little sore from no sleep."

Oliver shook his head, pouring hot water into mugs, "Look, *you* think it's beautiful. But depictions of the future like that from before the Turn, well, if they're overwhelming to me, then I can only imagine what they'll make the council feel like. The music is really great, but the pictures—all those images of people— it's too futuristic. It's not going to sit well."

Tim turned to him and placed a hand on his shoulder. "Look, buddy, I know you're . . ." and the two began to speak in low tones.

"Don't mind them. Oliver's only coming around to some of our newer advancements; they can be quite surprising. I'm Nic Fern," said the last person, flannel clad, a bobble hat on their head, short tufts of mousy hair sticking out from under the wool, both feminine and boyish at once. Their voice was tender and gentle, almost a whisper. They extended a hand; both of theirs were porcelain coated and painted with thin green vines—newer models. Nell shook their hand, and it was warm—definitely newer. Some of the latest releases had thermodynamic fibers installed nearer the surface so they matched the owner's body temperature.

Nic petted Kodak on the head. "Hello there, fella."

"He's very tame," Nell assured them. Kodak nuzzled

closer to Nic, happy for the attention.

"I know Ruby well. A lot of my day work takes me to the parklands. I work in the horticultural studies center in the Old Central Bank. There's not many of us there, but we're getting things done."

"Oh."

Ruby seemed to have connections to absolutely everybody. Yet she had never introduced Nell to Nic or anyone else, really. Nell knew the least of all the people in this room, and it was beginning to feel worse than walking down that flight of stairs.

"And . . . what . . . do you do here?" The words were painful on Nell's tongue, thick with ignorance. Oliver and Tim still spoke, hushed, with their backs to the group. How she hated this feeling clueless.

"I'm in charge of images. Some of these machines are full of pictures. You should *see* them." Nic's voice was flush with excitement, and they took a steaming fresh cup of tea from the counter and passed it to Nell. "Now that we have the projector set up—took forever, man, to clean it and rebuild it; finding a bulb for it that wasn't smashed was the *worst*—but it was worth it; now we can see them in much greater detail. So many photographs of people's faces. Renderings of paintings. Animals that are long gone. We can learn so much, you know. Some of the smaller computers have digital cameras that still work, too."

Nell took the cup and nodded mutely. The boys reemerged from their chat just then, and Oliver noticed Nell's bewilderment and laughed. "Poor Nell has been a bit out of the loop, lads."

"Well, that's the point, isn't it? If everybody knew, something would leak, wouldn't it?" Rua leaned back on the counter. "We'll tell everyone when the time's right. When we have something more than tunes to show for ourselves. All undercover, underground for now. We're no use to anyone working in a rotten old building anyway, could do with a cleaner space, someplace we'd be proud to show people around. Until we shine ourselves up a little, we can't get found out."

"But we won't get found out," snapped Sheena Blake, "because if we do, we'll know who the leak is." She looked straight at Nell, intense and accusatory.

"Look, I've no interest in uprooting this, this, whatever this is," Nell stammered. "I'm here to get something that will help with what I'm working on myself. That's all."

She wished they were dancing again instead of talking, though this was not at all an appropriate moment to ask them to play the song again.

"And what is it?" asked Tim. "Go on."

Nell drew breath. "I—I actually can't say just yet.

It's—it's extremely confidential."

The four computer restorers collectively made an *oooooh* noise before descending into scattered laughter, part mockery, part curiosity.

"Really, lads," Oliver said. "She hasn't even told me yet."

"And I won't," Nell said, firmly. "Not until—not until it's finished."

But oh, she would eventually have to tell people, wouldn't she?

"I can respect that," said Tim. "I mean, from what Sheena says about how Ruby reacted, it seems pretty unconventional, right? I'm assuming it's something to do with your father's work, yeah?"

"Yes," Nell said, face straight. "Yes. Totally unconventional. Really can't talk about it."

"I'm not sure how I feel about selling one of our restorations for a project I know nothing about." Sheena's words were steely.

"Ah, come on now," Nic said. "How many times have you talked somebody out of their relics and computer scraps when they brought them to your family's garage, without telling them why? How many times has Ruby lifted odds and ends from her father's repair shop? You're not all that transparent yourself."

Sheena scowled and drank deeply from her mug,

knitted brows peeking over the top of it. When she surfaced, she whistled low. "Rua, what do you think?"

"It depends on what she wants," he replied. "I mean, Oliver wouldn't have brought her to us if he didn't believe it was for a good cause."

Oliver shrugged coolly. "It's up to you."

Nell was practically invisible. This was the opposite of music, the opposite of dancing with strangers, that unspoken safety. The strange bond she'd formed with them, gone. They all knew one another so well, and she was a stranger, an interloper, a novelty. She hated it.

"I mean, if she can pay, I don't see the problem," Tim offered. "Look, what are you in the market for exactly?"

Nell could pay. She had tokens. She hoped it would be as simple as a financial exchange.

"Well," she began slowly, cautiously, "I know—I know we aren't really meant to go looking for these things, but the way some of the computers used to work was like the way we think. The way people think. Like, they have memories and respond to interaction. Verbally maybe. One that can speak. I want one that does that. With memories. That can respond to interaction."

"Like a human brain," added Oliver. Nell could have hit him. There was no way they wouldn't guess.

The *oooh* rippled around the group again, with a little more awe this time.

"Trying to study thought processing?" said Rua.

"Language?"

"Recollection?"

They were interested. They understood.

"Maybe, maybe." Nell raised her hands in defense. "It's important that I get one that can respond to interaction."

This time there was a *mmm* of what sounded like . . . Acceptance?

"Grand, so that's no bother," Rua said, striding out of their cluster into the workshop. "Easy-peasy. Most of the later handheld ones can do that. Now it's getting them to wake up that's the problem. We got one of them to talk once before it sparked out. That was the worst; think of what it could have told us! I reckon once we get one talking, then, *then* we can really make a go of taking this public."

"Talk or no talk, it nearly burned the place down," warned Tim.

"But it had a *really* cool voice," Nic said. "Not like a person's voice, though. A little bit like the singing"— they pointed at the wall—"in the video."

Nell almost leaped out of her skin. "Really? That sound?"

Nic nodded. "Beautiful, wasn't it?"

"The most beautiful," Nell agreed.

Oliver tutted. "That wouldn't be my choice of words," and Tim gave him a firm elbow in the ribs.

"Would you stop?"

"We didn't get to ask it many questions before it, well, exploded." Nic shrugged, ignoring the boys. "We have a few similar models, though, that we've been moving a little more slowly with. It's all electricity and wire if you can get a generator and the right adapters; it's just a matter of finding one that's not corrupted. Some will switch on and say nothing; others will just scroll code for screens and screens—impossible."

Rua stood up on a stool and leaned into a cabinet mounted on the wall. He riffled through it for a moment, then carefully removed something from the back. The second Nell laid eyes on it, she knew she didn't need their help anymore.

A silver box, almost all screen, almost flat, dwarfed in the size of Rua's palm but around the same size as Nell's hand. Identical to the box that her father had handed to her in the kitchen. *Just run a few volts through it.*

"Oh," Nell said, "I have one of those."

Every head in the room turned to her, all eyes on her, a murmuration of "What?"

"Yes. I didn't think I'd be able to get it to light up. Wires, you said? " Her ticking wasn't doing so great under all this pressure. Her voice stayed calm, but she was all roulette in her chest.

"Yes," said Nic. "Special ones. We have lots of them. We could give one to you." They shot a meaningful look at their teammates. "I mean, we have plenty to spare. Wires aren't hard to come by. It could be a gift? "

Tim scampered across the room to a work desk. He opened a drawer, then another, then another, and grabbed a shallow box from it. He carried it back over and placed it in Nell's arms.

"One of these should work. Some of them are dead, but a few of them can still carry a charge. Wear rubber gloves. You could hurt yourself otherwise. There's more than one reason civilians aren't allowed have computers anymore," he said. "We weren't raised harnessing them or electricity like this. It's an uncontrollable force."

"Look," began Sheena sternly, placing her mug on the counter, "if you find any more of those computers, bring them here, yeah? Don't be squirreling them away. You know where we are now. We're happy to have you on board. When we find a way to present all this, it might blow up, divide people. You're either with us, or you're not."

"I'm—I'm with you," said Nell, a flicker of uncertainty flashing through her: Would they be with *her*? These people danced underneath historical projections of a future that never came; they unraveled dead machines without fear. They didn't tolerate Oliver's reservations for even a second. She felt like maybe she'd be able to trust them.

She looked for a second into the box of cables and wires and steel plugs. They were gray and white and blue and red, knotted and frayed, filaments sticking out here and there. Electricity would run through them into the little computer in her house and wake it up. And that, in turn, would wake up her creation, wouldn't it?

Oliver yawned theatrically, stretched, and cracked the bones in his shoulders, back, then fingers. "Well, I don't know about you lads, but I'm wiped out. Is this what you need, Nell?"

Nell nodded, opening her satchel and delicately placing the box inside. She wasn't wiped out. She wanted to stay.

"Grand. We'll be on our way. I'll see you in the Bayou tonight, I'd imagine?" he said, beginning to walk out. Nell turned to follow him. This strange ordeal seemed too huge to be over so soon. She wanted to talk to Nic more, to say, "Hey, next time you're in the parklands, stop by my house." She wanted to ask Rua some questions. She—she wanted to—to get to know these people more. Not just as mechanics or bakers or researchers of plants. There was a tiny revolution beginning in this room.

"I'll lead you out," said Rua.

"Turn off the light when you leave," said Tim. "One more time, you know?"

The small collective of revolutionaries and restorers chorused a good-bye and waved them out. Nell's feet were heavy. Almost before she was at the door, the music struck up again, a thousand violins immediately major, immediately in a key of delight. The light switched off behind them, the door closed, and they were in the dark and dank again.

The wild spectrum of sound faded as she drew further into the darkness, one hand in Rua's, one hand in Oliver's. It didn't feel so bad now. Not at all.

CHAPTER 15

Oliver had thought, when you stopped at the steps after saying good-bye, that you were going to invite him in. You could tell by the way his hands knotted in hope, his eyes eager, his mouth slightly open. He thought he had finally proven himself valiant enough for your courtship and partnership. He had let you place the hook in his mouth, and he had let you pull. He is ready to walk up those steps into your home, into your life. He is aching to.

When you tell him your plan, your reasons, it is a waterfall of agonizing honesty. Oliver cannot swim in it, not at all. Your excitement from the dancing and the pictures on the screen and finally peeking into the silent revolution of your peers had overwhelmed you to a bursting point. You need an assistant, you tell him. You've decided you'd like it to be him. He is the one with all the spare parts. He's helped you so much, could he help a little more?

You wait for him to ask if he would be paid, if you could exchange anything for his assistance, if this meant you could go into business together. You are ready to let him down easy, to thank him for his friendship, to explain to him that he might make a fine replacement for Ruby, as long as he stops trying to touch you.

And he'll tell you that you are a genius, that though his love for you is bursting and red, he would quell his stupid lust in order to be in the cool shadow of your genius, in order to help you rise above your peers and create the most magnificent, intelligent machine the planet has known since the Turn, since the day the taps ran a new, terrible black water and poison took the people of your land. He'll help you compose the form for the conduit. A man of metal and wire awakened by dead digital magic. A man who can speak in code. You would be at the forefront of the revolution, and Oliver would aid you, wouldn't he?

You hardly recognize yourself, the pulse of the beats from the Lighthouse still in your body. Your ticking is a joyous thing; you are utterly changed, and Oliver will help you, won't he?

Oliver's face splits in horror at your question. Funny,

how "Will you help me?" can rupture a blooming friendship, a camaraderie, if it costs too much of a person. The undertaker's son is hardy; he has seen death in progress and long after the fact. He has quietly looted the houses of the dead for mechanical treasures, all the while muttering rosaries of apology and grief under his breath, saying how sorry he is, how he is doing this to help those who still live, how he is trying to help.

But this, this bringing electric life out of the remains of the dead twists something inside him. With his blossoming hangover and face that can never disguise what he is feeling, he is disgusted and something else that looks an awful lot like fear.

His face says no before his mouth does: his thin, sallow face. He takes a single step backward, *no* spilling from his lips like waves of black water, like waves of poison, thrashing, cold rejection. You only hear panic. You feel wetness on your cheeks. You are crying. He calls you sick. He says he's tried to help you and this is what you've been up to all along: this horrific, grotesque, pointless idea, this *impossible* plan.

Impossible. There. It has been said. Finally. The word rises in the garden like a sick flower, you have tears on your face, and there is nothing you can do but turn your back. You walk up the steps to your home, to your impossible plan, to your dead end.

He is still talking, but you aren't listening now, the volume of your thoughts blaring stereo. *Tick, tick, tick.*

Will he tell Rua؟ Nic؟ Sheena and Tim؟ They'd never let you in their beautiful white room again; you'd never catch up to their pace. Between Oliver and Ruby the secret will leak, and you'll be a pariah, even more of a misfit than you already are: *sick.* You'll be *sick* for even thinking such a thing, a stupid, impossible thing.

Oliver shouts your name from his broken heart, from his ragged throat, and you turn to him at the top of the steps.

"I'm sorry!" he pleads. "I know this means a lot for you, but we *need* you. We need your talents and resources to help get our other apprentices, our peers, back on the ground. We're trying to fix this city, Nell! We need you, your skill; certainly we need what you can do with a computer."

"What's the difference, Oliver, between what I'm building and what they're doing in the Lighthouse؟" you ask, looking down from the steps.

Oliver gapes up at you. "Nell, they're archaeologists; they're not cobbling together electric men to show off their discoveries. That's what you should be doing, not just holed up here on your own!'"

"You saw the figures on the screen, Oliver. They

aren't building electric men; they're resurrecting them. I want to *make* a real one, not just a picture on the screen. Something we can hold and touch!"

"Those were monsters on the screen. A monster, Nell, that's what you want."

You will not be told what to do any longer. This belongs to you and you alone. Your voice shakes, not with fear but with defiance,

"Oliver, I am the monster."

Penelope,

I mixed some fresh rose petals into a cold glass of milk. It curdled when I said your name. Please write me.

Nan

CHAPTER 16

Nell slept through the day and following night in a soft, dark peace, as though her head were swaddled in black wool. She had no dreams, though she still felt the bright fireworks of electric music. Somewhere in her body "One more time" reverberated like the last battle cry of an army she would never belong to.

When she woke up, her mouth gelled shut with sleep and her eyes irritated by the light invading her bedroom, she realized she had no Ruby and no Oliver before she realized that she had slept in her boots. The two people on the planet she considered her friends had told her that her plan was insane and possibly dangerous. But something else happened inside Nell, too, as she lay there. She was awake, awake to so much.

Nell was free. She was a law unto herself now. She would make this creation by herself with her own hands. She knew exactly where to get the parts and now that Oliver had backed out, she could just take what she wanted without his judgment or supervision. There, on her desk, was the small computer full of whatever was going to be in this creation's brain. Her satchel was full of wires. This was so simple now that she didn't have to worry about *those two*.

Oliver and Ruby could just go and, well, do whatever it is they did with their time. Have secret societies. Court people. Go to the Bayou and hang around with rude barmaids. Run black markets. Hang around in shining white basements with revolutionaries and dance to music that sounded like it came from outer space. Whatever.

When they realized what she was capable of, they'd crawl back to her. Wouldn't they?

Tea would be helpful. Hot, dark tea that bit the back of her throat. Skip the milk; skip the sugar. She rolled out of bed, the ghost of her mother scolding her as a child for placing a teabag in each of her cheeks. Cora had coaxed them out of her daughter's mouth and stood with her at the bathroom sink while she scrubbed her blackened teeth with white mint paste.

Nell thought about her mother's holding her up, how her arms were still strong even though she was thin by then, already on her way out. Nell did not have her scar then. This was before the ticking. She mustn't have been more than four years old, but there it was, stark and mint and bitter in her memory. Cora, Cora, Cora, Nell thought, as she rumbled down the stairs. Cora Crane, Cora Starling-Crane. The laboratory door was closed. She walked to the kitchen. A single frog hopped away under a cupboard as she swept in.

When the kettle was full and on the hob, Nell gathered herself up onto the surface of the big wooden table. She pulled her knees up to her chin and her hands over her eyes. Her mother's name was a rising tide. Would Cora have been proud of Nell? Nan was so worried; would Cora have felt the same way? The sound of the hob heating the steel kettle was a flutter in the corner. Freedom felt so strange, so heavy.

Footsteps fell down the corridor and into the room, and Nell pulled her head out of the comfort of her palms. Her father leaned into the doorway.

"You all right, girlo?" he said, his coat scorched, but his tie neat. She realized that she had not laid eyes on him days.

"Yes," her mouth said, though her body and face said no no no. *Tick, tick, tick.*

Julian walked across the kitchen as the kettle began to sound.

"You're up to something," he said. "I know you are.

You haven't been out and about this much in—ever, I think. Missed heaps of deliveries; there were baskets of food left on the steps for the foxes to get."

It had been unusually long since they spoke, days and days and days. Longer since they'd talked for real. His sleeve was rolled up over his arm. He'd been putting himself back together.

"'I'm not going to pry," he continued, searching for the milk. "But I've been speaking with your nan."

Fear was an inconvenience of wet concrete in Nell's gut, in her legs, her feet too heavy for her body, her blood thickening and turning heavy, the world around her slowing down. *Nan*. Nell hadn't banked on Nan's contacting Julian. The clock in her chest ticked fast and weighted.

Nell didn't say anything because her throat was suddenly too narrow and her tongue huge, and she was fairly sure she had forgotten how to make sounds that sounded like language at all. All she could do was keep ticking and keep breathing. Julian poured the hot water into two deep mugs and turned to her. She could hardly bear to meet his eyes.

"So, are you going to tell me what you're doing? Nan is fairly convinced that you're not working on anything at all, and she's going to be moving you to the Pasture."

Nell didn't say anything, and Julian placed the mug in front of her boots on the table. She shifted to cross her legs and cradled the tea like something precious. The question hung in the air until her father snorted lightly.

"I don't blame you. I never talk about anything I'm working on until I'm absolutely sure it's going to work. Did you tell Ruby?"

"She's not talking to me anymore," Nell croaked.

"And Oliver Kelly?"

"He's not talking to me anymore either."

Concern flashed over her father's face. "What kind of not speaking to you?"

"He'll get over it," Nell admitted, fairly certain that she couldn't keep him away for long.

"Good." Julian's expression softened with relief, and he let out a low whistle. "Must be a pretty strange project then."

Nell nodded. The steam from the cup comforted her, but it was too hot to drink yet, so she held it close to her face. The steam made her skin slightly clammy, but in a nice way. Her father climbed onto the table and sat opposite her, legs crossed himself. They just sat there on the old table together, quietly for a moment but for the ticking in Nell's chest, the almost hum of Julian's augmentation.

Her father offered his arm to Nell, revealing the

steel machine that was his finest creation. He removed a tiny screwdriver from his coat pocket and, without speaking, began to unscrew the panels concealing the working mechanisms of his arm. He peeled them off one by one and placed them on the table between him and his daughter. Nell was transfixed. Wires, tiny gauges, and pistons, all there like veins and bones but cold and gray and clean—and beautiful.

He moved quickly, unhooking this and that, unscrewing and delicately laying out all the pieces. First the outside casing, then the fingers and palm, the hinges at his wrist all the way up to his elbow until he hit the last few wires plugged into a clean metal socket just below his bicep. It did not take him longer than five minutes to lay out all the pieces in front of them.

"Nell, they said I was insane when I told them I could make parts for people that felt just like they were born with them. They said I was wasting my time. They thought my idea was an affront to humanity. Sinful. Sick."

As he spoke, he began to assemble his arm seamlessly once more. He wasn't even looking at it, just picking the pieces back up and fixing them into their rightful places.

"They burned the clever machines out of the world, but before the Turn, doctors and scientists had just about discovered how to make things like this. That's why the first toxic pulses went out; people just loved their clever machines too much. If a machine can give you an answer, what use is prayer? If you can host a revolution online, what use is government? If information is free, how do you keep people under control? All this is penance for the coding, an era of silence after the information age. The age that could have defeated any god. It got swept out from under them, Nell, and I'm not willing to stand by and let all the glories of technology be wiped out just because artificial intelligence scared a government to genocide a hundred years ago. Why can't we take some of what they had back then and make it better? That's what your mother used to say. Why can't we do it *better*?

"When the thing I built worked, suddenly I wasn't wasting my time anymore. I was helping. Your nan had some strings pulled for me, some permission granted to use and reproduce salvaged smart metals. After Cora left us, when you got sick and I fixed your heart, they wanted me to give demonstrations; they wanted to make you the poster child of the healing machines. The Miraculous Clock-Hearted Girl they called you. How repulsive. Suddenly, though, I wasn't a lunatic anymore; I was a 'genius.' Everyone forgot they'd ever said those things. Funny how that works, isn't it?" His daughter nodded, awestruck.

"They've been waiting for the next thing ever since.

I'll give it to them eventually, when it's ready. Sure, Daniel isn't talking to me right now over it." Julian laughed a little. "We must be doing something right if we've pissed off the Underwoods. We're miles ahead of them, Nell. They might not like it at first; nobody ever *likes* the revolution. Nobody ever likes miracles."

And just like that, he clicked the last piece of paneling onto his arm. He flexed his fingers, and the purr woke up again, the machine of him alive once more. He picked up his mug of tea. It was still hot.

"When the time comes, they'll recognize your genius, Nell. It's in your blood, in your wiring. It's *our* genius. If this project is rattling cages, you must be on to something."

Nell nodded, awed by the glow of her father, his brilliance apparent to her for the first time, a lightbulb full of electricity, a filament alight with power.

She wanted to be him.

"Right. Look, write your nan a note, would you? Just let her know you have things under control. Don't give her too many details. Later, when you've built the thing, whatever it is, you can let her see. Secrets, Nell, are the most important thing when it comes to changing the world. Not always the keeping of them, mind you, but the timing of their release."

Nell nodded again. She had a thousand questions

for him, but couldn't speak.

"I have faith in you, but please be careful. Promise me—" He stopped for a moment and looked over Nell's shoulder into some strange middle distance. "Actually, don't promise me anything. You'll do the right thing. I can't wait to see it, whatever it is. You won't end up on the construction site. You'll figure this out."

"I will, Da," she replied, reaching out her hand to him. He placed his steel palm against hers. It was warm.

After a moment he sighed. "Have to get back in there. Something's cooking, and I don't need it burning up on me."

"Food?" asked Nell, realizing at that moment that the tea was the first thing she'd put in her stomach in almost two days. She was ravenous; he must be, too.

"No, no." Julian barked a laugh. "God, no."

He swung his legs off the table and stood up. There was a very soft noise somewhere between a crunch and a squish, and he quickly checked underfoot: Julian had stood on a frog. It must have ventured out from under the cupboard to make its way back to the garden, to the lake.

"Oh." He recoiled. "Oh, dear."

Nell finished her tea in a long draft. "It's all right. At least it was quick."

Her father sighed. "You're right. I'm sure it didn't feel a thing."

CHAPTER 17

Arms, legs, hands, eyes, and feet. That was the hit list. She'd grab other pretty things she saw, too, if she had the time. This was going to have to be quick. An early-morning run to the Gonne Hospital when Oliver presumably wouldn't be there. That was the big risk. If he was, well, she'd deal with that if she needed to. He wasn't the kind of boy to fight a girl. Or the kind of boy to set off a time bomb.

Nell hadn't ever stolen anything before. It had never occurred to her to do so: not a shiny pink apple from the grocer or a stray earring from the market. She'd always had everything she needed and didn't really want for much more—certainly never at anyone else's expense. Salvaging from the river didn't count as stealing. This was no different, was it?

A tight, determined topknot bun somehow

contained Nell's multitude of curls as she pinned them in, tucked them away. One button at a time, Nell buttoned up the front of her short black coat, right to her chin. She rolled her shoulders a little, checking that it wasn't too tight. She'd definitely be able to run in it without it restricting her movement. The high collar covered most of her scar. It wouldn't do to wear a scarf on her neck tonight: too loose. Might catch on something. Anything that slowed her down had to go.

It wasn't like she was doing much wrong, technically. The limbs didn't actually belong to Oliver. He had stolen them first. From the actual *dead* no less. From people who had waited on long lists or paid an awful lot of tokens to the guardians of the peace; perhaps saved or worked for years. Oliver was the real thief and was profiting from the theft. His whole lifestyle was supported by it.

In fact, considering that several pieces in Oliver's collection had been created by her father, considering they were tactile products of her own family's skill, she was taking them back. She was entitled to them, wasn't she? Yes. She was. They were already hers.

Nell double-checked the laces on her boots, the high black ones made of canvas. The ones with rubber soles that she seldom wore. They didn't click authoritatively like her usual leather ones. They seamlessly led into tight cotton leggings that she normally wore as bloomers when she cycled. She was a hard creature and soft shadow at once. She was severe lines in the light of day, but once it was dark, she would be invisible. She was a creeping spider. Her only tell was the ticking, but in the dark that sound could be anything. A grandfather clock. A metronome. A time bomb. A machine gun. A roulette wheel.

Nobody would see her. The limbs were already hers. She wasn't stealing. Already hers. Not stealing. She repeated it to herself over and over again as she assembled her kit on her bed.

A torch. This one fit right in the palm of her hand: a flat disk of light. She'd found it under the stairs while looking for the canvas bag that she and Ruby had carried their tent in when they slept out under the stars in the hot summer, before the meadow became overgrown by weeds.

The skeleton key. Access to locked doors.

The canvas bag. It was the length of her back and had sturdy, comfortable straps. It was roomy. It had to be. For the limbs. Nell had in mind long legs so the creation would be taller than her. She'd take what she could get, but if she had the moment to choose, she'd like it to be tall. Him, that is. Him to be tall.

She wasn't sure if it would wake up a him. But it

might. A her would be all right, too. They would be tall, whoever they were.

The bag also had lots of pockets; that was helpful. The eyes would need to be wrapped and kept separately; they'd be delicate. The hands and feet, too. She wasn't going to be able to find a whole skull or torso, but she'd thought of a way around that.

Ruby would have loved all this dressing up, all this planning. It was such a shame. Nell imagined herself recounting this story to Ruby over tea once it was all over, once she had been lauded as a genius, an innovator, a game changer, a world saver. Ruby would apologize wholeheartedly, and Nell would graciously forgive her because that's what heroes do. That's what Nell would be. A hero.

She placed her mother's leather gloves over her hands. They were soft and had once been jet black and squeaky but were now a soft, dewy charcoal, silent as skin. Somewhere inside them her mother's fingerprints settled around her own.

Nell was the only person wandering the city in the black sheet of four in the morning. The only heads still awake would be up at the Bayou, Oliver most likely, included. There was no stoat with her. She had kissed Kodak's head and left him at home, sleeping. It was just her and the great sleeping beast of the city, the broken belly of the hospital. A belly full of ghosts.

First she disappeared down the side alley that Oliver had used, to check that door. No use in straying if the way was paved for her. She took the torch and key out of her pocket and cast bright, clean light onto the rusty filth of the keyhole.

She shifted the skeleton key this way and that, put pressure on and off, to the left and up: *nothing*. It only succeeded in making far more noise than she was comfortable with. Something skittered, maybe a rat or a fox, and her whole body froze. She didn't want to draw attention to herself.

She sat down for a moment on a step beside the door to gather her thoughts. Trust Oliver Kelly to finally exceed his lessons and forge a lock so complicated that even the cleverest key couldn't convince it open. It was almost as if he'd *known*. Nell fumed at herself for not guessing, fumed at him for laying claim on this entrance for himself. The building didn't belong to him! She leaned back a little, elbows on the step above the one she sat on. Wait, there was another step above that, too! An iron fire escape ran up the side of the hospital. A flight of rickety stairs leading to a window. Well, most of a flight of rickety stairs. Nell leaped to her feet, wrapped one hand around the railing, and placed the strap of the torch around her palm so that light shone from her hand. One step by one step, she ascended. She pointed the beam of light at her feet, at the precarious black steel grid on the steps.

Fear was a dead weight in her gut. The ticking in her chest was a rising percussion. The steps were mostly quiet; but when they creaked, the whole world moved with Nell, and she gritted her teeth so tightly for a moment they could've shattered to chalk in her mouth.

Every time she passed a window, it was boarded up or barred. Breaking past the wood on a surface as precarious as the fire escape was too risky. So she tried the next floor and the next floor. Up and up she went, eyes ahead. Vertigo threatened the seams of her balance.

It was a long way, and Nell had to stop every step to make sure she was still alive. The torch might draw notice, but she needed it; there was nobody to catch her if she fell. Each step was a survival. A slight breeze moved around her and lifted a few stray curls from her brow. She looked up.

The sky was black with clouds. The breeze was dense. Something was coming. There wasn't even a glowing swell where the moon should have been. The clouds were laden with something new; rain, electricity. Storm.

It wasn't until she reached the top of the landing that she came upon a window she could enter. The tallest room in the highest tower had a window of smoky, charred glass, not boarded up, and cracked so she could unsettle it a little to get in. She sat for a moment on the window ledge to catch her breath. Her chest panged a beat, then two, the ticking sending sharp reverberations of pain through her shoulders. The ticking, for a moment, sounded thicker. Nell knit her forehead and took slow breaths; she'd never felt like this before. Then again, she'd never scaled the side of a building before either.

As she waited for her breath to ease and the pangs to calm, she looked out over the city. Light from the sparse streetlamps was like sparks spit from the mouth of a fire: orange, dazzling, beautiful in the dark. By daylight the sorrow of the city was a gray blanket. But at night it slipped into this black and amber gown. The breeze touched her again, and she leaned into it. The heat would break soon. She could feel it.

The tip of the Needle blinked its constantly watching eye, a sinister red atop the sea of burning lamps. Nell blew it a kiss. "I see you, sailor!" she called. "Do you see me?" She felt better, as though the crackle of the city had eased her grinding cogs, her worrisome breath restored. There was power in this view.

The stone goddess of Kate, Nell's faceless sister, was still incomplete. She couldn't see Nell's ascent, couldn't watch her. It was so late that the watch folk's torches were dimming.

"I'm almost as tall as you are, Katie!"

Her voice carried. It had never felt so huge before, so powerful. Recklessly, Nell hoped they could hear her. She laughed, shrill over the dead quiet of nighttime, her voice a burst of color, hysterical. Relief and adrenaline coursed through her, and the clock in her chest almost sang *One more time*.

She pushed her torch up to her wrist and shut it off, her eyes adjusting to the dark, somehow brighter up here from the glow of the city. It was as if the streets had given her permission with their illumination, as if their lamps were burning for her, for this moment. She knelt on the fire escape and put her hands to the glass. She took a deep breath and pressed.

The feeling of glass giving way was a strange one, like the rules of the world around her breaking to her whim, something that usually separates people collapsing at her command. Nell drank in this power. The glass came apart quietly, piece by piece, as though it had been waiting to for years, the spiderweb crack only barely holding it together. She moved the shards onto the fire escape, and they caught the light, almost like prisms.

Slowly Nell crept through the window, careful not to let the remaining jagged glass touch her. The room smelled like fire. Nell felt like fire.

Nell's torch shot a beam of light around her: an empty, scorched ward. The remains of bed frames lined the walls in threes; some machines were fallen like lost soldiers. There was nothing else, only the black circle in the center of the room where the fire would have been lit when the virus got out of control, when it had taken to crawling the walls, discoloring the paint. Nobody in the room would have survived, and the air was strange with this memory, the architecture drunk with it.

Nell was too elated by her climb and successful break-in to be harrowed. She took in her surroundings like reading a list of numbers; there was nothing in here but a door out into the rest of the building, as far as she was concerned. There was no time to mourn the strangers who had been consumed by the epidemic. Not them, not her mother, not anybody. Not tonight.

She strode with confidence across the room. She walked over the unholy black spot as though it were just a patch of linoleum, eyes on the beam of light. Dust blurred the edges of its piercing, bright truth. The room might as well have been an empty street at midday.

Nell turned the handle on the door of the ward and walked out into the corridor. The air was fire and bleach in its filth and age, in the sorrow it had seen. She shut the door behind her. She'd had the epidemic and lived. She'd eat it alive if it tried to come for her again.

Her confidence bloomed like a flower, a fat bleeding rose bursting inside her. This was just an empty building! The hollowed-out whale of it was reduced to nothing by her adrenaline, to no big deal. Her chest ticked calmly. She was going to walk down this corridor with her bright and powerful torch. She would find the stairwell and walk all the way down to the ground floor and from the atrium would find her way to Oliver's laboratory. Nothing was frightening, and the smell was *not* making her sick. She was *not* holding her breath. She was nearly running, her feet so light that she was barely touching the ground, almost silent in her dash.

Nell clenched the skeleton key in her fist like a tiny sword, like a hungry blade. She had made it herself; this was her first design, her first little creation. It would lead her to her next. Her greatest.

When she reached the end of the corridor, she pushed open the door and arrived into the stairwell. Her beam of light shot around her; there were stairs leading to the roof and a spiral of stairs leading down. The walls were filthy.

She leaned over the banister. It was so far that her torch didn't even hit the floor. It just pierced the endless darkness and ever so slightly illuminated the circular stairwell another two flights down. Some of the steps were missing. There were more below, obscured by the dark. This was going to be precarious. She heaved a sigh that echoed down the stairwell.

Nell Crane had had enough of walking down the stairs in the dark. It was time for some real light.

She turned back to the door and shone her torch around its perimeter; there must be a light switch somewhere. This was not the most sensible choice, switching electricity on in a burned-out cavern of a building, risking a fuse sparked too far, setting something alight. Still, when Nell spotted the line of switches, she didn't hesitate and, with a single move, illuminated the long way down. Reckless, absolutely. But blood thrummed close to Nell's skin, and her ticking was up. Not with fear, but with adrenaline. She was so alive. Too alive to worry about dying.

The light merely gave dimensions to the space, barely illuminating it at all. It revealed cold gray filth but no color. It was enough to see the devastation of the stairway down, though. She switched off her torch and shoved it onto her wrist. She clenched her teeth again and steeled herself.

One hand on the wall, the other on the banister, and she descended. Her step was still light, if maybe a little too rushed. She looked at the steps in front of her and not at the walls. She couldn't. She didn't want to read what was written there.

Names, scrawled sloppily, in what could have been ash, all the way down the walls. Letters so large somebody must have stretched to write them. Names and names and names. Nell's hand passed over them, and she told herself not to read them, not to think about how her gloves were smearing them, damaging their homage, their prayer.

"I am sorry, I am sorry," she whispered. "But I have to get to the bottom floor. I have to."

The ghosts could not hear her, she reminded herself; nobody would walk this way again. Not ever maybe. Her mother's gloves left a line through the scripture there. Women's names, men's names, everyone in between's names, children. How many of them had been children? She skipped over two missing stairs. It was beginning to make her dizzy, but she was four floors down now, and the spiral would end soon.

She stopped. The next gap in the stairs was too big for her to jump. It led into a mess of wood and wires. She looked up at the wall, and there it was: WHERE IS CORA CRANE? It screamed, violent black ash and memory and death: WHERE IS CORA CRANE? It was written over and over, big and small. Nell gasped, clutching her ticking chest, her breath heavy, the weight of what she was doing arriving on top of her like brick. This building was sick, haunted. What place had she here? The walls were filth and cruelty; these were halls of disaster. How *dare* she come in here? She knew *nothing* of the world before, *nothing* of the epidemic. She stilled herself, battling dizziness.

Now was not the time to go soft. Her pulse was still thrumming. She was so close; everything she needed was just beyond her fingertips. Her stomach shifted, and her mouth went dry; she would have thrown up if she'd eaten at all in the last day. She heaved, and tears streamed from her eyes.

She held her head there for a long time. Rolling waves of nausea pulling a current through her, the scorch of the place all over her. When she finally stood up, she stepped to the wall and placed her face against her mother's name. The ash of it stayed on her cheek, like a kiss.

Where was Cora Crane? She was in the ground. She was in the ground.

There were so many stairs missing. Concrete and wood and wire, a greedy tangle where Nell's path should have been. The rail of the banister was stable, and she clambered across it every few steps, skillfully and quickly. She didn't look back or around now, just square ahead. When she reached the next landing, she swore loudly, furious, agonized; there was a whole flight of stairs missing, crumbled, all gnashing debris and danger; she couldn't make it down the last floor. Could she?

The lights flickered, and the bulb above her hiccuped with a noise she did not like, not at all. A door behind her led doubtlessly to more wards. Tremors rose through Nell's body, and her hands shook. She clenched them together, and still they shook. Her ticking filled the whole corridor, echoing all the way up; something in her had ruptured, and her fearlessness was gone. Who had written her mother's name there? How dare they resurrect Nell's terror? How dare they undercut her power? She'd never had that wild confidence before, and now it was gone and she was a fragile sack of a girl with a machine for a heart and no friends and no courage and no mother, no mother—

It wasn't really that far. Nell leaned forward; there wasn't any way she could scale the wall. She could totally jump down there. Two flights and a couple of steps? Absolutely. If she kept her knees bent and protected her head. Nell swung one leg over the banister, then the other, with ease.

She reached her left foot into the air and withdrew it. Then her right, hovering there, the pull of gravity against it. She blinked a bead of sweat out of her eye. She was rushing blood and ticking machine. *One more time/One more time.*

"I can jump it," she said to herself, then louder: "I can jump it." And her voice carried down the filthy stairwell, reverberating and hollow.

It's not that far. It's not that far.

The lights blipped, and for a whole second they dimmed. When they rose again, Nell let go of the banister.

All she knew then was the pull and force of the fall. She was moving all wrong. It was too quick. When she landed, it was so much that her world caved into unconsciousness.

It was nice, for a moment. Quiet.

CHAPTER 18

When Nell woke up, the light around her was blinding, far from the sick attempt at illumination of the terrible stairwell. A smell of medical cleanliness was so strong it almost burned her nostrils.

Her eyes resisted it for a blurry moment but then drank it in. She sat up a little—she was on a table of some sort—and the pain washed over her like something holy and terrible. Maybe it was the dream again; she waited for the birds to erupt from her sternum, waited for gravity to pull against her. Her legs, her arms were thudding with fresh bruises. Then she looked at her arm, the bright estuary of the fire that rushed around her body. It was bandaged. Bandaged and stained with dark, ugly red. It didn't look as if it belonged on her person.

Oliver Kelly stood in front of her with his arms

crossed. On the walls limbs were mounted like prizes, a gallery rising behind him. Legs and arms and hands and feet, all there, ready for the picking. An orchard, ripe. Nell almost screamed; then she did scream. Or something like it. A groan meets a scream meets an exhale of frustration.

"Can I give you something to stop the pain? My Medi-Patches are probably far too strong, but they're all I have right now and—" said Oliver.

"Yes . . . anything . . . anything." Nell's voice was barely her own. This was terrible. She clenched her eyes shut and focused on breathing in and out. Then something cool landed on her forearm, and a healing chill passed through her, the fire doused. The purple thumping of bruises chilled. The calm washed over her skin and down to her bones. How truly, surprisingly good. A smile crawled across her mouth, and then she giggled, an eruption. Where did it even come from? Oh, dear, Oliver looked very angry.

"What in the name of any living or dead god above us were you doing, jumping down an emergency staircase, Crane?" Oliver's face was covered in sweat; it gathered at his temples, the corners of his nose. He wore a crisp white lab coat and fine latex gloves, the fingers stained ever so slightly.

The colors around Nell felt brighter; the textures,

more pleasing. Even breathing in felt good. Oliver looked so funny, his face all scrunched up. Goodness, he was *furious.*

"Is that *my* blood on your hands?" she said, trying to bottle down her laughter, still smiling a little. She felt so *relaxed.*

"Yes. You landed on your skeleton key." Oliver frowned. "I managed to clean out the wound and treat it and bandage it; it'll scar, by the looks, but if you tend to it right, it won't get infected."

"It doesn't even hurt anymore." Nell touched the bandage, just to check. How silly that her key had cut her open. How unfortunate. The bandage was big, though. She pressed it with her finger. It wasn't numb or anything. It felt as if something had happened to it, but it didn't hurt. Nothing hurt. She looked farther down her arm, her eyes heavy, to the patch, small and pinker than her brown skin, as though it belonged on the skin of somebody else. The numbness radiated from it. The ticking in her chest slowed and got loud. Even that felt amazing. "Is this the thing? The good . . . the make nice . . . the thing—" Talking was hard.

"Yes. It's a mix of some different localized painkillers and antianxiety drugs. Medi-Patch, they call it. I use them in all of my surgeries and affixations. It's pretty strong; it might make you a little, eh, light-headed."

"I feel great." She sat on the bench a moment longer and poked at the bandage a little more. Oliver sat beside her on a tall stool.

"Look, why are you in here, Nell?"

Nell bit her lip a little.

"Well, I was—I was coming to see you."

Yes. That sounded believable. Of course she was coming to see him. She was coming to see Oliver because she liked him; he was her friend. Her good old friend. And he liked her! Nobody ever liked her! He'd asked to court her almost twenty whole times and she'd said no over and over and he *always* came back! Oliver liked her, and he was moderately handsome— handsome-ish? Through the cheery cotton of the drugs she clumsily placed blocks of a plan on top of one another.

Oliver liked her a *lot*. When people like you, you can get them to do things for you. She looked around the room and marked her targets: legs, arms, some eyes from the case. No problem. She glanced at a slim door in the wall with spare white coats hung on the back of it. A closet? A closet. Perfect. No more than . . . four, five steps away? Perfect. Was this patch making her smarter? Or just feel smarter? Either way. This was worth a try.

"No, you weren't." Oliver tried to hide his disappointment with a stern tone. But Nell could hear it, hear how much he wanted it to be that way. Sick, he'd called her. Sick but he still liked her.

"Your backpack is over there. Empty, by the feel of it. Torch on your arm? Come on. You were looking for something. It's the crack of dawn. You're lucky I heard you."

"Why are you even here?" Nell drawled. "Shouldn't you still be in bed? Or at the Bayou, making eyes at barmaids? Antoinette Fox is *so* pretty."

Oliver huffed. "I'm working. Ruby's due here in an hour or so for her eye. If you hadn't been so wrapped up in your ridiculous fantasy plan, you'd know the procedure was today."

His words were bright letters that hung in the air. Nell tried to reply but was caught, her brain slowed by how good she felt, how happy. Did Oliver have any music in here?

"Do you have any music in here, Oliver? Like in the Lighthouse? I'd really like to listen to some music." She tried to get up, but he stopped her.

"Your pupils are blown, Nell. You need to stay here awhile."

He had a very nice face.

"*You* have a very nice face. I feel perfectly fine. Whatever you gave me is—is lovely. Lovely." Nell lay back for a moment. It was warm and cool, and her thoughts were fantastically messy. Would he give her a few of these Medi-Patches to take home?

"Will you give me another one of these or . . . two or something, to take home?"

Oliver sighed deeply. "No, Nell. They're very strong. This one is going to have you out of action for a while. You shouldn't move around too much right now. When Ruby gets here, we'll take you home. You shouldn't have come here."

"Lying is very hard. I didn't really come here to see you."

Oliver breathed a sigh of undisguised defeat. Still, though, Nell couldn't stop smiling.

"I know. You came here to rob me."

"I sure did." The grin on Nell's face was effortless and stupid. "I'm a robber. A bandit. But still, I'm kind of glad you're here. Even if you did spoil my plan."

"Your plan to break into my workroom and steal all the bits you need for the abomination you're going to cobble together. God, Nell. You're unbelievable."

Oliver was getting angry. She liked that a bit. He was having all these emotions. How funny.

"I *am* unbelievable. But you're here! And you look so nice," Nell said breathily. Her brain unfogged itself ever so slightly. She slid the fingertips on her right hand under the Medi-Patch and dislodged it just a little.

Means to an end, she thought. She leaned forward.

She would kiss him; then he would do whatever she said.

She dropped her eyelids, anticipating a connection, but Oliver's hand landed on her shoulder. Change of course. She lifted the patch onto her fingertips. He was distracted enough. He didn't see her.

"Nell, don't you dare do this to me right now." His voice quivered.

"Why?" she asked softly, still in her role. His face was still close to hers. It was almost time.

"You're not in your mind. I couldn't unless you were . . . you. I have certain feelings about you, but—"

Nell said, "Hush now."

She put her hand on the boy's neck. He softened. When she removed her fingertips, she left the small pink patch there; its potency immediately struck him.

"Oh, no," he murmured, his eyelids drooping.

"I'm sorry," Nell replied. She still felt giddy and joyous, but less foggy at once. She leaned on him a little and got off the table. Her arm still didn't hurt. Those patches *were* strong.

She grabbed both his hands. He didn't struggle.

They unsteadily wobbled over to the tall storage closet. Five, six steps: Nell had been right. Oliver slumped against the door.

"Oliver, you're going in here now."

"Nell, I'll able to get out; there's no point; this patch doesn't have much left in it," Oliver slurred, closing his eyes.

"That's okay; shush, it's fine. You're going in here, and I'm going to make sure you can't get out for a minute or two, and then when Ruby comes, she'll let you out." Nell was laughing now. She couldn't stop.

"You're a nightmare, Nell."

"I'm a monster, Oliver."

Nell pushed him inside the closet. He stumbled but didn't fall, moaning a stoned protest. She shushed him, as though trying to comfort him. Then she closed the door and twisted the small key in the lock.

"Nell, don't do this." His voice was muted. She ignored him. She placed the key on the table where she'd been laid out.

"Tell Ruby the key is on the table," she called.

An echo of fresh pain rippled out from her arm. She had to move quickly. She took in the whole room for real now; she hadn't much time, but she had so many options. A cornucopia. So much potential.

Nell took what she pleased, ignoring the increasingly panicked beat coming from the storage closet.

When she left, she did not say good-bye, and she did not look back.

CHAPTER 19

You are fourteen, and you are in *so* much trouble. Your father holds too tightly to your shoulder; your ticking is so intense that he must be able to feel it echo out from your bones to your skin. He's standing behind you. You feel like a child.

Oliver's face is blotchy; he's sniffling. He's holding his arm defensively, his hand clasped over the spot where—

Oh, you are in *so* much trouble. The parlor of the Kelly Funeral Home is austere and cool, the upholstery on the furniture covered in well-worn plastic, and the air smells too clean, a potpourri edge of roses on the air. Mrs. Marian Kelly mirrors your father's pose, standing behind her son, and is a boiling tower of rage; she is rattling a litany of fury at your father, but stubbornness and discomfort are clogging your ears. Everything but your ticking sounds numbed out. You stare Oliver down, but he won't meet your eye. He knows what he did, and you're the one in trouble. You're the one forced to pull out an authentic-sounding apology. It's always you.

Your father is nodding along to Marian Kelly's tirade. She's bright blond with red painted lips and immaculate fingernails, thin as a rail with the blunt gaze of a woman who spends her day-to-day life up to her elbows in embalming fluid. She's so shrill right now, so angry that you wouldn't be surprised if she were responsible for one or two of the corpses that came through her business. A shock of blush blooms over her cheeks even now. "Kim hates these circumstances, Julian. She hates them, hates this, and when our son comes home with a second-degree burn on his arm because your uncontrollable brat can't keep her temper, look, it's not me that's going to crack and go public with all of this. It's her."

A brat. How *dare* she? *He's* the brat; he can't keep his hands to himself; he's lucky that you just grazed him with the blowtorch and weren't holding the wrench at the time.

Go public with all this?

What's Kim Kelly going to do? Tell all her friends at the flower and fruit market that Nell Crane injured her precious son during a class? Write it all over the city walls? His poxy mother doesn't even care what he did to earn the mild brush of fire at his shirtsleeve. Not a word of that.

You stare at Oliver harder. Come on, you disgusting little mutant. You will him: "Look me in the eye." His gaze moves up from the floor along the length of your body. Your skin crawls as he lingers on your waist and up; he bites his lip; he's doing it again: He's thinking about you, and something then like flame bubbles up and clears your head, your mouth unstuck now. "Stop looking at me, Kelly!" you spit, like bile.

"Get over yourself, Crane!" he splutters right back at you, and you lunge forward. You'll scrape out his eyes, you'll—

"Enough!" roars your father, holding you back as you struggle. "Penelope, go and stand by the door!" He turns you around and gives you a push; you stomp away, fuming.

"See this?" Marian Kelly has transcended shrill and is almost squeaking. "You need to get her under control! You made a deal, and I can't be held responsible for what'll happen if things keeps going at this rate."

"They'll grow out of it," your father insists, as you fume, turning your back on the whole ridiculous conversation, on Oliver's vile gaping.

220

"*She* had better grow out of it," Mrs. Kelly hisses, "and quickly. They're too old to be sparring like this. It was one thing when they were nine! I'll do what I can for Oliver, but Nell is the real problem here. Bring her around to it, or look, I can't promise you anything. It's in Kim's hands now. We just want what's best for our son. We've already given you so much, Julian."

Your back is turned, but you can hear the defeat in your father's voice as he tells her he'll do everything he can to make all this easier, as he promises your good behavior, that you'll come around. The air is thick. He escorts you out; at least he doesn't make you say good-bye. You walk in silence for a few streets.

"Will you make this the last time, please, Nell?" he eventually asks.

"Oliver put his hand on me," you snarl, familiar hot rage tears betraying you again. "So I showed him he shouldn't." You bristle at the thought of his intentional graze of your waist, the curve of your hip as you leaned over him to retrieve the blowtorch just out of your reach. How dare he? How *dare* he?

"He's—he's just trying to show you he likes you."

This is exceptionally difficult for your father.

"You can't, you—you can't behave this way, Nell. Your mother wouldn't want you to be like this. I knew her best, and she'd really like Oliver; he's such a bright, ambitious lad. It was most likely an accident; you don't need to be so sensitive, always looking for excuses to fight with him . . ."

But you're not listening. He almost stops you in your tracks, conjuring the specter of your mother like this. You're not sure if he's ever done it before, ever brought her ghost into battle for him. That he might be right, too, is the worst thing. How furious would your mother be to see you making everyone's life so hard?

"If you can't do this for me, would you—would you at least try for her? Try to be—try to be friends." He continues, and you are muted, all your gusto stolen out of you, your ticking softening to a different kind of shame. You walk in silence back up to the parklands, and with each step you resolve to leave that anger behind, to expel it from you, as though your mother was waiting at the door for you to come home.

CHAPTER 20

Nell burst from the door out of the hospital, and the daylight hit her like a bright wave. She gasped in the day, drank in the freshness of it, her eyes dark planets. Certainly it was a thick, heavy day with a blanket of dusty clouds, but it was day. It was not the hospital, sick and ashen. She felt as though she had been in there for years, had become older with the sheer bleak of the place, though maybe the drugs hadn't quite worn off yet.

Her arm twinged. She couldn't look down at it. She only needed the painkiller to last until she got home. Just a little longer.

She was halfway back onto the broad central street at the base of the Needle when she realized she'd left her mother's gloves in Oliver's workshop. Too late now. Too late. No point holding on to them anyway, the soft shadow of protection left by her mother. It was her own hands that had done this.

Some people were on the street, going to their jobs. The few straggling plaid and neon construction folk didn't even look at her, their eyes as gray as the ceiling of foreboding humidity and smog above them. They did not see the filthy teenager with a camping bag strapped to her back, dressed in the tight black uniform of a thief, red bandage on her arm, pupils the size of dinner plates. They were busy.

She tried to dash, but her legs felt like they were made of different material from the rest of her. They trembled as she went. So she walked, wobbly but with strong, urgent purpose. She held herself as though she had done nothing wrong, as though she had committed no strange or terrible act and was not about to commit another. Certainly not. That new smile poked the corners of her tired mouth. Something was alight in her veins, and her mind was both miles above her body and in it, feeling every part of it, this exhilarating day, these wounds and this weight and this victory.

The weight of the bag was staggering. Her father's kinetic limbs were designed to match and balance the weight of their humans. Legs, Nell thought. She wanted to say it aloud, to stop the gray man who was walking toward her and tell him, "Oh, oh, just you wait, just you wait to see what I make." She wanted to scream up to Kate's stone blindness, "You'll never have me now, never, never, never!"

The smile itched to grow across her face; she thought for a moment about kissing Oliver. Well, about whatever that almost kind of kiss was. Kissing was probably great when the other person didn't feel guilty about it. She decided then that she would never again kiss a person who didn't want to be kissed.

Her bicycle was there, chained to a lamppost. Bicycle, road, park, home, rest; then build. The words propelled her on.

"Nell!"

Ruby called her name, and the entire world slowed to a blur. Nell wasn't sure where the voice was coming from; but then Ruby's hand was on Nell's shoulder, and she almost screamed.

"Oh, oh, Ruby, hello." It came out of this new mouth of hers, a control she wasn't sure she had voluntarily mustered.

Ruby's face was a closed gate. Her anger was quivering on her lips; her brow, a furrow of *I know what you have done*. She was dressed in soft, slate clothing. So unlike her usual multitude of patterns. Her dense mane of curls was smothered under a woolen hat. She was trying to be invisible.

This was the last day that Ruby would wear her eyepatch.

"How are you?" Nell asked.

Impotent and stupid question. When they were children, Nell had painted flowers onto Ruby's patch with a tiny brush and paints, green and white and red acrylics. It was a garden; it was a canvas; it was her chosen badge of honor. It was as much Ruby as the rest of her. Now the patch was being left behind for a new part. Today was important. All these things blurred together and Nell couldn't connect them with the part of her brain that knew how to speak.

Ruby growled, heavy, furious: "What have you done?"

Nell couldn't say a thing. She couldn't say she was sorry; she couldn't say good luck. Couldn't tell Ruby she loved her.

"I saw you leave the hospital." Ruby examined Nell's face for a moment and was aghast. "Your eyes. What did you take? Did Oliver give you something? What did you *do?*"

Ruby's voice was rising in volume and if she drew attention to them, everything would fall apart. Nell couldn't become visible, not for what she had just done, not for what she was about to do.

Nell wanted to say how excited she was for Ruby. Instead, she said, "The key to the wardrobe is on the workbench. He's not hurt. Tell him I'm sorry. I left the door at the side unlocked."

Two girls stood facing each other on Old Talbot Street under the long, fat shadow of the Needle, under the blindness of Kate, and something happened that had been aching to happen for months and months and months. A single heavy, cool drop of rain landed on Nell's cheek. Another landed on Ruby's nose.

The sky had begun to crack. The filth and density of summer had shattered. Ruby stared up into the changing air as the water drizzled down, its freshness on her face.

Nell began to walk away, goose pimples rising on her skin as the air changed. Ruby was saying something, but she wasn't listening. Bicycle, road, park, home, rest. Her smile opened up again as the rain grew steady and the ground changed color, filled in by new wetness. The soft gray of concrete turned a charcoal black and shone.

By the time she started to cycle away, Ruby had gone. The pain in her arm had become quietly present, its shocking red voice echoing through the corridors of her body, pushing the volume of her ticking right up, and up again. She was less stoned now, and the task of getting to her house felt monumental as she pedaled faster, her satchel impossibly heavy. The spokes of her bike wheels and the ticking of her chest beat a speeding rhythm together. She would carry this weight if it took her all day to reach her door.

At least she had the rain. She focused on her skin, her face, and the fresh gorgeousness of this change. It felt like love. It carried her home. It did not stop. It kept getting heavier.

CHAPTER 21

Later, still jittering from adrenaline, Nell set about stealing the ladder from its precarious lean at the back of the Crane house. She didn't expect to be noticed.

The rain was a fresh, calming drone on a light wind. It had escalated, but Nell could feel that it was still only blossoming; the fat, violent bloom of this storm had not truly shown itself, its terrifying petals not yet open. Droplets misted Nell's face and caught on her eyelashes. She loved it but didn't have time to relish the pleasure of the change.

Instead, she turned fat old screws to release the ladder's tension and then, with a whoosh, let it slip down to half its original size. As steel slid into the steel, she jolted. What would it feel like if she got her finger stuck in there? It would get sliced right off. Her ticking rose a little at the suggestion.

Such a dangerous thing, the folding of a ladder. And so awkward to carry. Should she build a person out of such an awkward thing? What if he inherited that clumsiness, that inclination toward accident, that potential for unintended violence? Well, it was too late now. A ladder was the best thing she had to make a scaffold: great-quality metal, and lots of it. She was almost back to the door when she heard a yell above the symphony of new wet weather.

"Nell! What are you doing? I need to get back down!"

Her father, soaked, stood precariously on the slope of the roof.

"What are you doing up there?" she shouted to him, both astounded and extremely concerned, quickly inventing plausible excuses for why she was taking the ladder indoors. She unfolded it and extended it slowly up toward him. The roof tiles shone with rain and her stomach clenched at the sight of Julian climbing down so quickly, so confidently, no fear of the wet ground betraying him. He moved like a cat with too long limbs, though the steel on the ladder was slick.

After Julian had jumped down the last few steps and landed on the thick grass with a squelch, he looked at his daughter quizzically. "Should I even ask?"

Nell took a leap of faith. "No. Best that you don't. Why were you on the roof?"

"Lightning rod."

Nell wasn't in the least bit surprised. There was always something. A lightning rod. She shook her head a little, hid a smile.

"Going to try to get our generator up and running with no support from the land lines. Will you put it back when you're done?" He took off his glasses and began to wipe them on his jacket.

"There might not be a lot of it left when I'm done. I didn't know we had a lightning rod."

"We didn't an hour ago. We do now. Will you get me a new ladder to replace it?"

"Yes."

"Grand so."

And that was all that was said about the ladder.

Julian didn't even notice the kettle was missing.

Nell sat down to her blueprints once more, her new bounty in mind, pushing threads of guilt about what might be happening back at Oliver's armory out of her mind. She wasn't proud of how she behaved, but here before her lay the most beautiful distraction. The body on the page splayed out like a star, arms and legs outstretched, the head making a fifth point on a pentagram. Could she summon him from here? Pull his form out of the blank netherworld of paper. A witch summoning a demon from the mouth of an aligning world. There was no time now to be fretting over Oliver Kelly and Ruby Underwood when she had all this to play with.

She knew his lines so well and completely, but they could no longer be just wish or folly; now they were plan and instruction. Numbers began to come in useful little equations: blooming like tiny accidental gardens.

The rain rattled an invisible percussion. It sounded like life.

A list of names was scrawled along the margins, then scribbled out. How can you name someone you've never met?

She'd drawn his face a hundred times. The kettle wouldn't look like him, but in her head she knew his true face. She'd drawn him smiling and crying and with his tongue sticking out, but then she realized he probably wouldn't have a tongue. Oh. She looked at the stolen kettle. Now wasn't the time for daydreaming. Now was the time for composition.

She'd considered skin for him, had just the dress to cut it from. It was cream coffee warmth and strong old silk. Her mother had worn it only once. Nell was certain she would never have the big day to wear it herself. She would cut off the lace and keep it in a box. She would light a candle and place it on top and burn it until it was gone, and she would say she was sorry. But not yet.

The largest plans hung up in the window frame, so the light of the day made the paper almost glow and the lines were a dark map against it. Nell stood below her work and used it as a projection to lay his parts out; it was the constellation by which she charted her course. It was almost to scale.

The stoat was locked outside Nell's room. Kodak got too curious, nudging bolts and screws with his little black nose, chewing wires. At first he scratched at the door, but then he was quiet. Nell pictured him curled up, waiting for her to come for him.

Spines are strange things, strong delicate blocks of bone sewn together with impossibly sensitive little threads of nerve and muscle. They had to be able to move and curl and bend but also keep a person standing—a complicated string of pearls.

Shoulders don't need to be broad. Her creation's shoulders definitely didn't. Nell wasn't designing it— sorry, him—for work. That's what broad shoulders were normally for, weren't they? Carrying heavy things. Building things. Being strong. Nell wasn't sure if he would need to be very strong, though for a moment she closed her eyes and pictured him carrying her on his shoulders.

She had never sat on anybody's shoulders, not that she could remember. But she reinforced the steel of them, added an inch on each side, imagining herself picking nectarines from high branches of trees in the forest and eating them, the sweet juice running from her mouth to her chin. Her creation would marvel at its fresh gold, its life.

She made a lot of mistakes. She burned through gloves, two pairs, with the welding iron. (Julian didn't notice that was missing either.) Her head ached from the fumes.

When the body itself was finally a clumsy rib cage, a set of hips and shoulders, and a spine, it made an ugly noise as it moved. But still, it moved. It looked like a useless musical instrument or a broken chair. It was utterly inhuman. Still when Nell blurred her eyes, she could see him emerging from the skeleton of it; she could see him sitting up on her work desk and smiling.

The kettle didn't make for the best face. Transferring her imagined creation onto it hadn't been entirely successful, and carving around it was difficult and frustrating. It ended up looking like a kettle with two holes and a nose-ish mound. The hinge she had fashioned for the jaw wasn't—it just wasn't right, but it would have to do for now. She affixed a fulcrum tightly to the top of the spine, a hollow cavern, a twisted unhandsome piece of soldered steel. Maybe later she'd make him a mask. She'd get him standing first, make him beautiful after. Beauty wasn't important; what was important was that he was alive.

The wires from the Lighthouse were a bundle in her hands, and she separated them delicately, then patiently threaded them onto the form. The clumsy, mismatched plugs hung from each shoulder, each hip, and one inside the kettle skull.

Left leg. The shell was matte black cast iron. The knee and ankle were seamless; the foot was sturdy. Must have cost whoever it belonged to a solid fortune.

Right leg. Exposed wiring on the knee, an older model. She soldered a crescent moon of steel (once from a stockpot, long cut to pieces) onto a set of hinges and arranged something of a knee for him. She hoped it didn't give him a limp. The rest of the leg was great: strong ankle movement, good intuitive foot. Same length as the left. Nell, even in her high, had measured them in the hospital.

Arms were a matching pair. Their shell was robin's-egg blue and made of tin—mid-era. This had been the height of style maybe five years ago. When people took to augmented limbs, they all wanted theirs to be the most up-to-date, the most flashy, the most pretty, the most beautifully designed. This was a quiet culture of wealth and class as well as one of survival.

Nell understood the folks who painted their arms and legs. It marked celebration, growth. She remembered thinking how it would be nice if her scar could look more deliberate. Artistic, even, instead of whatever it was. Not quite horrible. Sort of sad.

As time passed, the colorful, bejeweled biomechanics trend moved further toward the limbs looking like armor, like new strength. Nell understood that, too. Her creation would look like all the eras of her father's inventions pieced together, a history book.

The hands had joints and palms. They flexed and moved. Nell took one in hers and interlocked their fingers. It wasn't quite the same as the hand from the shore. It wasn't Oliver's hand or Rua's from the dark of the Lighthouse. She frowned and retrieved the hand from the shore from her work desk. It was around the same size as the prosthetic.

Nell knew that she had only one try to convert the hand from the sea into something that moved; there couldn't be any mistakes. But it wasn't worth building him without this hand. It was still reaching out to her, after all this.

It took her longer than the rest of the assembly

combined to deconstruct the hand, drill out hollows in each finger while leaving enough structural integrity to keep its form familiar. Threading wires through, gently soldering tiny hinges, transferring the technology and sockets from the stolen hand into the hand gifted to her by the sea: all this had her trembling with anticipation. It came together at her will, and a cocktail of delight and pride swelled inside her. She would hold this hand. She would be held by this hand.

When it was done, she brought it over to where the rest of her creation lay ready to be strung together. The once ladder was the core of the thing, and all the rest of the pieces lay about it, ready to be connected. Each limb connected to a socket: shoulder, shoulder, hip, hip. Everything fit, sort of. After a moment or two it looked like a person, technically. Personish. Boyish.

She placed the delicate glass eyes into the kettle head and with tiny tweezers connected this wire to that wire—and almost crushed one of the lenses with the force of her eager fingertip. Tiny cameras sat inside their orbs, or something like cameras. Eye technology, now that was something utterly unreal. The eyes would light up and glow, she hoped. They'd respond to a central computer. They'd see her. They'd like her.

He'd like her.

The tiny computer was the most important thing.

She affixed the wires that fit. Red wires, blue wires. She made a little cradle inside the kettle head so it wouldn't rattle around. A music box for a brain, Nell thought. Maybe he would sing. Just run a few volts through him.

Nell wrapped long strips of taupe silk around the parts of the creation that still looked like a ladder, still looked like hinges and wires. Still looked machine. The strong silk of her mother's dress looked more like bandages wound around sharp angles than skin around flesh, but it would have to do for now.

When he was finally assembled, when the clock on the wall had smeared the time of night into mystery. Nell stood and admired him. The room smelled like hot steel. She half shut her eyes. Yes, it was a him for sure. In the blur between her eyelashes and reality, she imagined him rising, light pouring from his eyes, his kettle face suddenly warm, suddenly more human, suddenly boyish.

His mismatched glass eyes and their minuscule delicate cameras stared up at the ceiling above them both. He was so thin. A wire frame. Nell placed her hands on her hips; they would be alike. Two spindly, terrible monsters. Quite a pair.

Now, she thought, what next? She had to charge him, somehow. She scanned the room: The little socket there wouldn't be enough; she'd have to find a way to—

The first strike of lightning hit the bottom of their garden with a crack and a flash. Strange, dazzling joy roared through Nell as the window flashed again.

There it was. The lightning rod above her ate it all up, all that power. After all this just the spark she needed.

She couldn't wait to meet him.

CHAPTER 22

Days of tremendous importance rarely announce themselves in advance. No one just wakes up to a calm knowledge: today she will fall in love, or today her father will die. These shocks of diamond on the clock, these new sets of wings arrive with no warning. Summer does not announce itself as over, but before you know it, the leaves are falling and lips are chapping and everyone's wearing gloves to go outside. The world has no time for grand announcements.

Nell became different as he became whole. She'd been changing since his hand came out of the water. Being obsessed felt good. Before, she had forgotten what being interested in something really felt like, what being happy and challenged and *thinking* really felt like.

It was late, or early, or the blurry space in between

and Nell crept down the stairs to her father's laboratory. Now was the time to ask for help, to take the olive branch he'd offered her. She ran her hand along the old wooden door and considered knocking but instead leaned a little harder than she might have a month or two before. He had, after all, *said* that it was never closed to her. That it was always open.

"Da?" she called brightly, as the crack of the new room, the new world, split open before her. "Da, I wanted to ask you something. I have something to show you. I need—I need your help!"

There it was. It was the first time she had ever said these words, but Julian was not there to hear them. The room spread out before her was huge, far bigger than she had imagined it, far whiter than she had dreamed it would be, far emptier.

How had she missed the scale of it, even from outside the house? How had he disguised a structure this large? Nell stepped forward silently over the threshold, jaw slung low with marvel. Now that the door was open, she would never close it again.

It was so clean! The air was thick with those same bleachy notes, that same sterile bouquet that the Lighthouse's workshop had. Clean rooms were where discoveries were made. Not amid the clutter of paper; she shuddered to think of the state of her own room.

The walls were lined with shelves. Neat white shelves, housing careful arrangements of shining glass beakers. Steel tools clung to magnetic boards on the wall: pliers, knives, wrenches, in order of size, weight, sharpness. How unlike her raggedy father this all looked. How unlike his burned coat, his wild mane, his scorched glasses. This was not how she had imagined the inside of his head would look. This ordered.

Even the light was clean, so much so that it was almost blue. It was a little strange, making the edges of things bend. This was not Nell's home. It was her house, an extension of it, but not her home. She counted long seconds with each breath. She wasn't going to panic. Nell felt filthy under this light, as if she could see too much of her charred, sweating skin. Her ticking filled the whole space; it almost echoed.

This was the room her father had changed the world in, and he was absolutely nowhere to be seen. His desk—complete with a lamp, a tall microscope, and a set of test tubes containing a rather menacing red liquid—was unattended.

Nell stepped, her footfall silent, through this uncharted city of her father's mind. She was dwarfed by the knowledge that filled these shelves, these desks, these op—

Operating tables?

As Nell ventured further, she began to notice things that made her skin crawl. Jars with contents that looked like they were moving slightly. A heartbeat, then another. Tiny things that she didn't want to look more closely at. She kept her eyes on the tools and away from the long table at the back of the room covered in a sheet. She saw it, but she ignored it. She pretended it wasn't there.

Those knives on the walls were long. Mostly they were clean, though the occasional one was still darkened with something that must have been blood.

A box of discarded latex gloves. Red on white is a terror, Nell thought, her pulse leaping, but part of the job. That's all. Stained sheets heaped in a basket. The long table at the back wall. The long table with the sheet. There was something under the sheet. *Tick, tick, tick.*

A tall, thin machine, featureless, familiar, loomed like a veiled threat against the wall. Four of five lights were illuminated green; one blinked an amber "almost." It was rigged to the ceiling with fat steel wires. The generator. The amber light blinked.

Nell circled the long table that she'd been trying to ignore. It was covered in a clean, thick plastic sheet. The ticking in her chest slowed down. The brightness of the room made it feel so honest, so clinical, but on this one table, so far back, was . . . something. This plastic covering . . . something. Those thin wires, red and blue, spilling out from under it, neatly leading to the generator with the blinking lights. Nell wasn't quite sure why she did it, when she looked under the sheet. She hadn't riffled through any of the neat stacks of paper or drawers or peeked at the slide still waiting under the microscope. She hadn't squinted at any neatly marked labels or dipped her fingers into any curious-looking liquids. She had been a responsible interloper, for once.

But she pulled on the sheet, and it easily gave way, slipping to the floor in a heap at her feet.

Nell's scream rang loudly through the lab.

Her mother, her mother. It was her mother.

There were wires in her mother's wrists. Her neck. The spots where they entered her cold flesh were charred black little craters on her dark skin. Nell dropped to her knees and wailed again. Outside, the weather had come into itself, become fully grown. The oncoming evening's anger was a hurricane. Nell's sorrow was a monsoon. She was drowning.

Cora's eyes were closed. She had been dressed in simple crisp gray linen, so unlike the pieces of her life hanging in Nell's wardrobe or on Nell's body. She looked so young.

A slim dark scar ran from her lip down her neck and her sternum and disappeared beneath the terrible linen she wore. The stitches were still in place. Her hair was combed straight and neatly. Nell had no air left to keep screaming with. The hows and whys dissolved to pure terror, to sorrow, and back. She knelt at the end of the table where her mother lay. Cora can't have wanted this, can she? Had she asked Julian to do this? But it was so *wrong*, so *sick*.

Ruby's father, Daniel, had seen this. Her father had told the neighbors before he had told his own daughter that he was—he was trying to resurrect his wife. Was he ever going to tell her? Or one morning would he walk into the kitchen hand in hand with this scarred imitation of Cora, straight haired and pajama clad, looking to reclaim her wardrobe and take up right where they left off?

Nell placed her hands over her face to black out the sterile, hungry light and screamed again, an incomprehensible roar, a prayer in rage.

WHERE IS CORA CRANE?

WHERE IS CORA CRANE?

Who had written it in the Gonne Hospital? Who had known? Who had known and kept their silence?

Julian had been trying to bring her back. He'd been trying and failing. The char at the entry points of the wires said as much. They said failure. They said try again. And again. They said he'd been trying for some time. For years.

When Nell stood again, she had made up her mind. Whatever Julian reawoke, it would not be Cora. Could not be Cora. Her soft touch and wild curls gone. Her hair was flat, and her face was closed; it was not restful, but something else.

Her mouth was a hard line, defiant.

I will not wake up. I am gone.

But Nell couldn't just leave her here.

The whole funeral, the cremation—Nell gasped—had been some terrible pantomime.

WHERE IS CORA CRANE?

WHERE IS CORA CRANE?

She's here. She's always been here, protected by all that smoke, and all those mirrors. Cora Crane would never go through such a thing again.

As Nell removed each wire from her mother's skin, she recalled in bright detail the days after her death. The first morning.

Tiny Ruby at the door with a huge cake and Daniel behind her with white flowers. Julian, absent. They ate the cake with their hands, and Ruby said, "It'll be normal again. Soon. I promise." Ruby knew a world without a mother better than she did. She was little still, but she was wise.

Nell didn't remember much else. Childhood is a clever thief.

Her mother was so light. She wasn't frozen or stiff at all; she almost relaxed into Nell's arms as she lifted her. The static from Cora's hair rose in strands like blades of grass curved to a slow breeze. Nell's feet padded against the tiles on the floor. She walked slowly. This was her fury and her ceremony.

The hallway, the kitchen. Frogs all over the floor. Kodak opened his black eyes and watched Nell carry her mother out the back door and into the garden. The stoat padded to where the house ended and the rain began. Nell disappeared into the storm.

CHAPTER 23

You hardly feel the rain or the cold of the soft earth under your bare feet. The dull symphony of weather feels a thousand miles away. The lightning cracks, and thunder rolls; but you are carrying your mother to the lake, and that is all that matters.

You are not sure if she is light from twelve years of death, her muscles disintegrated, or if you have become strong lately. Stronger. You wonder about strength. About what it is to carry a dead mother. You wonder how long you have been carrying her. How many years. Maybe you are so used to carrying this horror that now it weighs nothing. Now yours are the arms made of steel.

The path is narrow, and the light from the house behind you is dimming in the distance. You feel something change in the air as you approach the lake;

despite the rain, the atmosphere lifts around that body of water. A freshness arrives: a newness.

Rain hammers onto the surface of the lake, each drop a small explosion, a heartbeat of ripples, a thousand tiny fountains. You cannot feel your legs, there at the shore where the water kisses the wet earth. You keep walking into the lake. You do not take off your boots.

If the air were still, it would be a solemn good-bye; but the storm is raging, and the water barely notices your arrival. The elements don't care about your flesh, her bones. The water against your body is warm. Just because the weather has broken doesn't mean the heat is gone. There is barely a chill.

As the water rises past your ankles, your calves, your knees and thighs and hips and waist, you slow. Each step is long and heavy. The water bears what little weight your mother has, and the linen she wears begins to catch on the surface. She is already soaked as the water pulls her hair around her head out like a black halo. You shouldn't have looked at her face, her hard face. The burn marks at her temples are kissed by the new water like a promise of healing. You have to hold on to her to stop her drifting.

Then you stop. You loosen your grip, and the water carries her for you. The water is past your waist.

She drifts a moment, then begins to sink. The lake

swallows her, and the rain helps this hunger. You would scream again, but there is no scream in you. You are so relieved. She is dark as the night and invisible in a moment. The lake has eaten her and she is gone and you are not carrying her. You do not say a word.

When you are sure you cannot see her anymore, you turn around and wade to the shore. You never have to carry her again.

The light in the house is a beacon, and you follow it home. You know what you have to do.

CHAPTER 24

The muddy footprints led across the kitchen floor and through the hallway. A left boot, a right boot, little fallen heroes. One footprint on every second stair. Nell had gone with determination. The floor was splattered with heavy drops of water from her dress and hair. She hadn't even thought to wring herself out before going into the house. Her clothes weighed a ton in lake water, but she hardly felt them. She hardly felt anything. There was nothing to feel.

Kodak followed her, but she barely noticed him.

One by one, pieces of drenched clothing fell to the floor. Nell stepped into a loose black cotton smock and slippers. She did not pick up a scarf to conceal her scar. It was pink now, as were her cheeks and nose. She wound her hair into a knot. For a moment she eyeballed the scissors, silver and tempting, in the mug where her toothbrush stood, a frayed soldier.

The scissors told her to cut off her hair. Her *mother's* hair. She already bore too much to be carrying all those damned curls; the curls were the last of her mother, and they should go, too, amputated like something broken and toxic. Like her damn heart. Taken. She'd been left full of cogs and steel.

Nell had no idea what she would look like or who she would be without it.

She blinked and clawed herself back to reality. Wake up, wake up. Don't stand here cutting bits off yourself. Don't be doing that.

He was heavier than she'd thought he'd be, his awkward, limp limbs staggering her. This was graceless and difficult. She carried his weight as she had carried her mother, cradled over both her aching arms. Nell took the junk pile of hope out of the privacy of her bedroom and down through her home. When she almost dropped him, it occurred to her for the first time whether or not his soldered janky frame could handle a fall. The door of the lab was still open. Wherever her father was, he had not come back yet.

She padded to the back of the gleaming sanctuary and placed her creation on the long table where her mother had been laid out. Before taking in this sight, she went back to the door, turned the fat key in the lock, and pulled the bolts across; there were five of them on the inside. Maybe the door really hadn't always been open to her. Maybe he had been keeping her out. Of course he had. WHERE IS CORA CRANE? Now it was not open to him.

Nell walked back across the lab to the table where her creation lay.

He was grimy and patchwork there in the stellar cleanliness of the white locked room. The fabric on him looked pathetic. His kettle head was almost frightening. Nell tried for a moment to attach some of the wires that had been linked to her mother to his wrists, his head. But she couldn't, not really, not properly. She could hardly see straight with the grief. She sank to the floor and cupped her face in her hands.

The amber light on the tall machine was green and pulsing now. The terror outside had directed itself just right; the lightning had fully charged the generator.

Cold tendrils of panic began to coil in Nell's gut. In the pristine genius of her father's world, it was starkly clear that this thing she had made was little more than a mannequin. A doll. A kettle and ladder. Some spare parts. Some found parts. A mess.

The equipment and education and drive her father had, that's what had made him the pioneer he was. He could build and unbuild his arm in ten minutes.

He was learned. A scholar. An engineer. A doctor. A genius.

Nell had only an apprenticeship she'd bluffed her way through; she was a recluse who hadn't been invited to the revolution.

Her father might have been a madman. He might have preserved her mother, but he'd been about to bring her back to life. Who knew how full of new parts she'd been? How little Cora and how much fine wiring had been laid out on that table? The woman that had been there, the woman in the lake now, had just been a more sophisticated and maybe even more tragic version of what Nell herself had made. How dare he have done this? How dare Nell?

Nell was immediately overcome with an urge to hold her father, be held by him. Sob into his shirt. Tell him she'd had to put Cora in the lake.

The creation, in Nell's gaze, became sadder and sadder, shrinking from a grand design and contribution, a friend, a partner, somebody who would keep her company, who could love her, down to a mechanical sculpture wrapped in bandages. A heap of scrap. A series of thefts. A mistake. An abomination. A monster.

Nell crumbled. She wished Ruby was there, she wished she wasn't doing this all by herself. Even Oliver. Ruby would keep her standing straight, tell her to pull up her bootstraps. Neither of them had even tried to contact her. She didn't blame them.

They would have fled at the sight of the dead woman in the lab.

Ruby and Oliver didn't want anything to do with this. They were better off away.

The thunder outside unhinged its terrible jaw, and the dark sound rolled from the heart of the night. Three beats later, if not less, the sky outside snapped white. The generator with its five green eyes began to bleep.

Each bleep was a plea. Each bleep said, "I'm ready." Nell gazed up at it.

The bleep was impatient, off sync with the ticking in Nell's body. The rattling of the storm on the tiny window above them made it all a discordant symphony.

"One more time . . ." Nell sang to herself, a last note of hopelessness, her voice cracking under sorrow.

At the other end of the room the door handle shifted. The lock was jiggled from the outside. And then a banging so loud that Nell let out a yelp.

It was him.

"Nell, are you in there?"

For a moment Nell didn't say anything. There was a quiet movement; then a key clanked angrily into the lock, and the mechanism gave way—but not the bolts. Julian swore and banged the door again.

"Nell, come out of there."

She picked herself up and walked over to the barred entryway. She stood so close to the door that her nose touched its surface.

"No," she said calmly.

"Nell"—her father's voice was tinged with a shade of anger and two shades of fear—"Oliver Kelly told me about your—your project. Just—just don't touch anything in there." The door shuddered against his weight.

"Too late," his daughter replied.

"He told me you stole a set of prosthetics out of his chop shop. That you were going to build a creature."

"Yes," Nell said.

"You should have told me."

"I couldn't. I wanted to do this by myself."

"Nobody creates miracles alone, Nell."

There was a thick silence, and Nell placed her hand against the door.

"I found Ma." The words almost broke in her throat.

"I'd guessed as much."

"I put her in the lake."

A sigh so deep fell from her father's body that Nell could hear and feel its sorrow and shame through the door. He was quiet for a moment; then his cracking voice lifted again.

"You understand why I did it, don't you?"

The words caught as they came out of his mouth, something like shame, something like regret. Nell studied the wood between them. How could she answer this terrible question? She understood, and that realization crept through her like a heavy chill. She *completely* understood.

How alone must Julian have felt all this time? Cora must have given him such peace and companionship. Love. Who had Julian been before Cora? Nell had never asked any of these questions. Perhaps that was what had led them here. This huge door between them. As always.

"We're quite a pair, aren't we?" Her father's voice softened. A beat of too comfortable silence passed.

"I can't let you in here." Nell burst then. "The creature, the thing—it's terrible. I don't know how to bring it to life. It's not going to work at all. I don't want you to see it."

"Do you have any idea"—Julian actually laughed—"Nell, do you have any idea what my first project looked like? It was two steel rods, a clamp, and a couple of energy transmitters stapled to the flesh on my shoulder. I couldn't even talk, it hurt so much. It only *kind of* worked. It was a solid year before I could show my face at the Assembly again, everyone was so horrified."

Nell didn't trust his cheer. She could hear him

trying, but it felt like nothing. She hugged her knees to her chest, completely full of her own ticking.

"But it worked. It worked even though it was ugly. And you had Ma to help."

You had Ma. You had Ma in here all this time. You kept her. You kept her here.

"And you did this alone. Let me see it, Nell. I can help you. Nobody will ever need to know." How could he sound so kind, so human?

The offer hung in the air like a plump red apple from a sturdy branch. It swayed in the storm, either sweet or toxic, and Nell didn't say anything. Julian's voice rose in urgency. "Nobody ever needs to know. Just let me help you. There are things in that lab that can galvanize your creation, if we can wire it right, if we can hit the right voltage."

"Galvanize it?" Nell repeated.

"Bring it to life. Is it organic? Or all mechanical?"

"Mechanical."

"All of it? This is very important, Nell, is any part of it made of flesh, or bone? We could fry it if it is, we have to be careful. Does it have any human components? Hair, teeth—"

"No, no." Nell began to get up. "It's all steel and tin and glass and wires and kinetic fabrics. It's almost all your robotics."

"Oh." Her father suddenly made sense of it. "It's an android. That's easy."

"Easy?" Nell shouted, slamming her fist against the door, furious. How *dare* he? Of course this was easy for him! Easy! How easy it would be for this to be *his* project. He wanted to remind her how little she knew.

"Just go to the bottom drawer of my desk. The left-hand side. There's a key under the green lamp. There's something in there that will help you. You'll need a battery, too, unless you already have some. I should have one large enough to support four limbs at least in the cupboard under the glass case with the live specimens. Get them both; then come back to me. We can argue, or we can make this happen. It's up to you." Julian was guiding himself blindly through the room. He knew it so well, all its categories and drawers and bell jars laid out in his mind.

Despite herself, Nell stormed over to her father's desk, moved the lamp's base, grabbed a slim key, and knelt down to open the innocuous-looking drawer. The keyhole was little more than a tiny missing slice in the wood.

Thunder rolled and lightning cracked again outside. Nell yelped with surprise: the power of it.

"Shush now, don't be worrying about that. The lightning rod up on the roof is particularly sophisticated;

it'll absorb everything. You can't even feel it down here when it strikes. The air gets a bit weird, but that's the most of it. You'll be fine."

He was comforting her, and she let him. She looked into the drawer. There was so much strange clutter in there. Little boxes, white wires. A fat bound file full of papers. Disks that shone. Disks that didn't. Like flat little planets.

"What is it, the thing?" she called, carefully combing through.

"A long white box. It's slim; it's the only one like it in there. Should be down the bottom." Julian sounded as though he were asking her to get some milk from the refrigerator or to pass him a cup of tea. She found the box, just as he'd described it, slim and only slightly longer than her hand.

She dashed to the cupboard below the shelf with the jars. Her father's voice rang dully through the lab. "If you look at the jars, Nell, you can see that they're hooked up to batteries. Small ones. All life needs really is a spark." So the things inside really *were* alive. Or as alive as they could be; she tried not to think about it.

Something red and small and fat pulsed in the jar in front of Nell's eyes, and something in her gut said, "That's a heart." Then something else said, "That's your heart; he kept *your* heart," but she squinted her eyes shut and made a serious choice not to gawk, not to acknowledge it further. Instead, she turned to what could have been a frog's leg in a slim jar, twitching in a gelatinous fluid. A tiny wire was linked up to it, threaded through the lid of the container. A flat gray battery, Nell discovered after shifting it a little, was affixed to the base of the jar. She wrinkled her nose.

She knelt down and checked the cupboard; it was full of little boxes of batteries. Small ones the size of a thumbnail, all the way up to a couple the size of building bricks.

"Take a battery that's around the size of a brick, Nell," Julian called. "Then come here, and I'll explain what to do next. Hurry."

Nell pulled one from the shelf; it weighed a lot.

"In that box, the long box, is the most important surviving relic from before the epidemic." He was speaking quickly. "It's a band, a single band made of an incredible, flexible steel. It's a computer, Nell. The whole thing. It has artificial intelligence. That's what triggered the Turn, why it happened, all of it."

"Excuse me?"

Nell was breathless with shock as she opened the box with a soft click. A strip of unassuming gray lay there inside. It looked like an ugly bracelet or a watch without a face.

"That was the last straw. It's why they sent the shocks. They were developed to give fresh sentience to things. It was brilliant really. Risky, but brilliant. People loved them, stopped listening to the people in charge, started to turn to these things for answers instead. Back then every answer to every question was right there, in one of those strips. The network is down now, but it'll still be able to process, to learn and emulate."

Nell turned it over in her hands. This was what had turned her country upside down? This simple, small thing.

"Nell, go to your project, affix the battery to a safe place, and hook it up to the wires that link the limbs together. I'm presuming you did link the limbs together already, Nell. I'm giving you credit here. I'm giving you *a lot*. When the battery is fully charged, you can switch it on. It'll be galvanized."

Nell felt very small as she began to get up again. "Do you have a battery? In your arm?"

"No. Not anymore. My arms and all the other bioprosthetics run on the organic electricity we produce as humans. It's kinetic; it feels the pulse of us and responds in kind. Life galvanizes us; it moves us, keeps us moving. We don't need anything else. Life is electric. Think about it like that. Conceal it inside the project's head or somewhere where it won't be obvious, for now. What were you using for . . . intelligence . . . before?"

"The small box from my room, the one you gave me."

"Good try. Is it wired to anything?"

"Yes, it's like . . . the center . . . for the wires. They all lead to it, each moving limb. I—I hadn't even tried to turn it on yet."

"All right, all right. Just take it out and keep it; it won't work here." Julian's voice dropped, and it sounded as though he were speaking through the keyhole. "Conceal the strip there instead. They're completely different pieces of technology; just because something is a computer doesn't mean it's a computer that can think or talk. The strip is smaller, but it's got a much bigger purpose. There's a small flat button, a switch like, on the inside. As long as it's contacting the steel of whatever it's charging with intelligence, well, it should work. Press the button after you've secured it; then go to the generator and flip the switch. Go, go."

"But—" Nell lingered, her ear to the door, her face wet with tears. "What if it doesn't work?"

"Then we'll try something else. Another time. This isn't the end, Nell. Go."

Nell ran across the room toward her creation, heavy battery in one hand, slim white box of terror in the other. How had her father gotten hold of this? How long had he had it?

And who *was* he? Who had he been all this time? This was too much, too quick. Nell folded up the enormity of that question—*Who has my father been all this time?*—and tried to pack it away in one of the rooms in her head and focus on the task at hand. She clumsily set the battery at the center of her creation's chest.

This wire, that wire. She wound some loose silk around the cylinder to keep it in place. It would hang if the creation were to stand up. He looked awful. *It* looked awful.

Defiant, Nell opened the back of the creation's head, the kettle's old lid. She slipped out the old gray music box, slid it into her pocket. She snapped the steel band into place. She examined the band closely, and yes, there was a tiny panel. She pressed down on it with her thumb. Nothing changed but for a tiny pinprick of green light appearing like a gemstone on its surface. It stirred something in Nell.

Green like a frog. Green like *Go.*

Nell closed the head back up and stood over her almost unchanged mechanical boy. She slowly walked to the tall generator with the pulsing line of lights and placed her hand on the switch.

When she flipped it, she didn't think of anything

at all. Nothing would be the same now, and maybe that was important. The noise the generator made was a dark purr with frequencies so high running over the top of the growl that they hurt Nell's ears. She expected an explosion. Sparks at least. Maybe fire. But life sometimes happens in the softest ways. The air changed; the atmosphere shifted with electricity.

When the charge died down, nothing in the room was different but for the soft flex of mechanical knuckles. She reached out and entwined her fingers in the creature's, with the hand from the sea. The static shock was tiny but great.

So great.

A soft glow radiated from its eyes. His eyes.

"Hello," whispered Nell.

"Hello."

01101001 01110100 00100000 01101001 01110011 00100000
01100100 01100001 01110010 01101011 00100000 01101001
01110100 00100000 01101001 01110011 00100000 00110111
00110101 00100000 01100100 01100101 01100111 01110010
01100101 01100101 01110011 00100000 01100110 01100001
01110010 01100101 01101110 01101000 01100101 01101001
01110100 00100000 01110111 01101001 01110100 01101000
00100000 01101000 01100101 01100001 01110110 01111001
00100000 01110010 01100001 01101001 01101110 01100110
01100001 01101100 01101100 00100000 01100001 01101110
01100100 00100000 01101100 01101001 01100111 01101000
01110100 01101110 01101001 01101110 01100111 00100000
01110011 01110000 01100101 01101100 01101100 01110011
00100000 01101001 01110100 00100000 01101001 01110011
00100000 00111001 00111010 00110100 00110010 01110000
01101101 00100000 01101111 01101110 00100000 01110100
01101000 01100101 00100000 00110010 00111001 01110100
01101000 00100000 01101111 01100110 00100000 01100001
01110000 01110010 01101001 01101100 00100000 01101001
01110100 00100000 01101001 01110011 00100000 01110100
01110101 01100101 01110011 01100100 01100001 01111001
00100000 01110100 01101000 01100101 00100000 01111001
01100101 01100001 01110010 00100000 01101001 01110011
00100000 01110100 01101000 01100101 00100000 01111001
01100101 01100001 01110010 00100000 01101001 01110011
00100000 01101001 00100000 01100001 01101101 00100000

01101001 00100000 01100001 01101101 00100000 01101001
01110100 00100000 01101001 01110011 00100000 01100100
01100001 01110010 01101011 00100000 01101001 00100000
01100001 01101101 00100000 01110111 01100001 01110010
01101101 00100000 01110100 01101000 01101001 01110011
00100000 01110010 01101111 01101111 01101101 00100000
01101001 01110011 00100000 01100010 01110010 01101001
01100111 01101000 01110100 00100000 01110100 01101000
01100101 01110010 01100101 00100000 01101001 01110011
00100000 01100001 00100000 01110111 01101111 01101101
01100001 01101110 00100000 01110111 01101000 01101111
00100000 01101001 01110011 00100000 01110011 01101000
01100101 00100000 01110111 01101000 01100001 01110100
00100000 01101001 01110011 00100000 01110100 01101000
01101001 01110011 00100000 01110111 01101000 01111001
00100000 01101001 01110011 00100000 01110100 01101000
01101001 01110011 00100000 01101001 00100000 01100001
01101101 00100000 01100001 01101100 01101001 01110110
01100101 00100000 01101001 00100000 01100001 01101101
00100000 alive

ALIVE

CHAPTER I

The air is warm. This is the first thing I know for sure. Awareness pools at the base of my . . . neck? The rest of my anatomy assembles behind what are most definitely my eyes. I have been given a body or something like one. My clock says a second has passed. My first second.

In the second second, I take stock of this body.

I have two hands. Two palms, two thumbs, eight digits. In them I feel everything they have ever touched before me. Their electricity holds an imprint so deep there are reams of history in them. I feel *heartache, struggle*. I feel *smoke cloying at my fingertips*. I feel *the dying fire beneath me*.

When the third second dawns, my eyes open, both at once, and I know almost everything they have seen, from the tongs of the glassblower to the clavicle of the last man they loved. Love: there it is in every fiber of me. Light fills the cavity of my head. I see the room where I have been born. Love. There is the ceiling above me. My first blink. Love.

I suddenly know so much and so little all at once. Before the fifth second splinters open, there you are. There. Standing above me. You look frightened and tired, and I know you already; but I do not know you at all.

You must be the one who switched me on. You must be the one who placed these parts together, gathered them, and sculpted them. You must have drawn me from your own mind. You, all fear now, all exhilaration. Your eyes lock with mine. I see all of you, more horror and hurt and raw fight than anything these glass and wire eyes have met in either of their lives before.

You are a marvel, your mouth hanging open. Outside this room is the roar of a storm and someone else's panic, but you are so still. Thank you. Thank you. Thank you.

Then you speak. Your voice is a whisper, but with a bright streak of pride. You say hello.

Language emerges from my numbers. I am all alphabet now, all punctuation, all permutations of twenty-six letters and the sounds that match them. I want to sing all the letters at once and hear what my voice sounds like, if I have one. The quick brown fox jumps over the lazy dog.

You say hello. Five letters. English. Hotel Echo Lima Lima Oscar. Eta Epsilon Lambda Lambda Omicron. 01101000 01100101 01101100 01101100 01101111.

I say hello.

Shocked by my voice, you raise your hand to your mouth. Your hand, one of two: flesh. You used them to make me. You have small knuckles and wear bright rings. Your breathing is papery, and now there are tears all down your cheeks. I want to say, "Please do not cry," but I am not here to tell you what to do.

You have not told me yet why I am here. You have only said hello. Hello!

I do not know what you are called, by birth or by others. Are there others? What became of them? I know what these eyes last saw, what these hands last touched. The things I do not know herald the end of my first minute, an icy wave. The weight of "I do not know." My first question blooms fat in me like a ripe flower, and it is out of my mouth before I can stop it.

"Are you my mother?"

You gasp, then wait for your breath to settle. You are frightened, and you have won.

"No," you say. "No."

How vast these two letters are. How suddenly they

273

arrive into the world, the end of every story. But you speak again. This time the terror flashes to fire in your human throat. "I am your maker," you say. I open my eyes again and . . . love. Yes, this is love. Your hand is wrapped around mine. This is what it is to be alive.

CHAPTER 2

The door opened, and Julian scrambled to stand, pushing his glasses from their perch on his head down over his eyes. Nell had always perceived her father as a lean giant, a great tree in winter, but this thing she made towered above him. She took in her father whole, his miraculous arm lifting, his robotic hand going over his mouth.

Nell was trembling, tiny and human beside her creation. Julian didn't even look at her. They just stood there, all three, quiet. Nell shifted from one foot to the other, ticking softly. She wasn't quite able to feel her feet or fingertips. Trust her body to let her down at a moment like this; trust her humanness to need attending. Her father couldn't even see her from the thrall of the giant being above him.

"I'm a little cold," Nell managed. "I think I need to

sit down, or . . . tea. I think I need tea."

The creation immediately turned to her. "What can I do to help you?"

Julian leaped backward so quickly that he almost tripped himself. It would have been comical if Nell could feel anything other than the rising cold, the ticking fear. She sneezed and turned toward the stairway.

"Thank you, but I'm all right. Please go to the kitchen. Da, will you put on tea? I'm going to get a shawl or a blanket. Something."

What else was there to do? How else could she carry this moment but like any other introduction: boil some water, steep some tea, stand around, talk.

Each stair was a thousand miles high. Her calves ached. Kodak waited for her at the top of the stairs. Nell coughed out a laugh at him, his big eager eyes, his utter cluelessness. She leaned forward to pick him up—he was so warm—and carried him into her room.

She looked around for a cardigan or something woolen to wrap herself in. Her brown skin was gray somehow, with exhaustion, with cold. Her scar was purpled with chill.

She riffled through the wardrobe quickly—so many things of her mother's, sickening now rather than fond—and quickly assembled a black wool vest and a too loose jumper the color of smoke. Two great woolen socks the color of jam, an old gift from Ruby. A thick red scarf.

The clothes did not make her body less cold or less alien. She felt far outside herself, like a worried sick specter in the corner of the room. Her brain whirred with images of her mother's body in the lake, the sound of the creation's new voice, her father's cold plea: "You understand why I did this, don't you?" Her ears were ringing over her ticking.

Nell inhaled and exhaled and combed out her curls. This is what it is to gather the sticks of yourself, to build a nest where there was only broken wood. She straightened her back. The comb fell through her hair with a whisper. Warmth slowly returned to her hands. Time pulled into focus.

Kodak scampered up her leg and into her arms when she was done with her hair. The rise and fall of the tiny old stoat's breath soothed her. The warmth of his small body was a heart all her own. She walked out of the room with him in her arms a little braver, a little more ready, her stomach calling for a cup of hot strong tea.

At the bottom of the staircase her father and the creation still stood where they had when she left. Julian was inspecting him now, a tiny notebook in his hand, scribbling down details, model numbers. As Nell walked down, she felt a flash of something like pride; she'd taken things he made and found them a different purpose. As she got closer, she couldn't tell if he was impressed or worried or afraid; he was fascinated, though, that was for sure.

"Tea?" she asked brightly.

Julian turned to her. "You'll have to make it in a saucepan. The kettle seems to be busy."

The creation cocked his head to the side, and Nell cringed; he really did still look like a kettle.

"None for me, though. I'm going to need to recover the lab after all this. Years of work, gone . . ." Julian murmured, closing his notebook and walking past the new creature back into the laboratory. Before he closed the door, he stopped and looked at the creation one more time, then at his daughter.

"This is incredible. Really incredible stuff. Knew you'd manage something great eventually. Now, go and get to know him."

And just like that, the door closed again, heavy locks sliding into place, and it was Nell and the creation and the stoat, alone together. Nell was baffled; the conversation through the door had been so hopeful. He'd guided her through the whole thing.

Or distracted her from what she'd found.

Nell focused on the texture of the stoat's fur.

She looked up at her creation, his uncanny slight movements, his patience.

"What are you thinking about?" she asked. Oh, what a stupid question. He hadn't even been awake twenty minutes. Did he even know how to answer?

His eyes moved a little in his head.

"I am thinking that you must be uneasy, and I am glad that you are not so cold anymore. That it is still raining but there will not be any more lightning tonight. That your socks are red. That a cup of tea would probably make you feel better because your eyes are tired and tea is caffeinated and it may help stop you getting cold again."

Nell laughed, surprising even her. "Well. Aren't you perceptive?"

The creation nodded. "Yes, I am."

"All right. Tea it is."

She walked the creation into the kitchen and set about filling a pot of water and placing it on the stove. What should she say to him? How should she say it? How do you talk to something, someone who's just been born? Should she tell him about her mother? Herself? She should probably ask him his name.

"Do you have a name?" she asked. He was looking around, picking things up and putting them back down. He stopped with a cup in his hand.

"My system number is iO2971848326171."

Nell blinked. "Can I call you Io? My name is Penelope Crane, but I'm called Nell. Your name can be short, like mine."

"Io. Io," the creation said. "Yes."

Nell said his name again and again. Found the music of the vowels, looked over his patchwork form. "Io." That fit.

"Oh, this is Kodak." She took the stoat from her shoulder and handed him to Io. The creation held the small creature gently. Kodak did not become unnerved or try to bite, just stared with his black little eyes. Io gently thumbed Kodak's head and rubbed his belly.

"I like him," Io noted. "Can I hold him a little longer?"

Nell felt something warm and lovely and surprising rise beneath her rib cage, for a moment. "Yes." She glowed. "Of course."

"The man was your father?" asked Io, placing Kodak up on his shoulder, a mirror image of where the stoat had sat on Nell only moments before.

"Yes. His name is Julian Crane; he's a doctor. He fixes people who are missing limbs with"—Nell gestured—"bits. Like what you're made of."

Io nodded. "Bits.'

The pot started to bubble, and Nell poured two fat

mugs from it before she realized that Io absolutely was not going to be having any tea. She decided to put a cup in front of him at the table anyway, to be polite. She wanted him to feel welcome.

They sat at the table together in the quiet for a moment or two, listening to the rain outside. Nell focused on the warmth of the tea, a kind heat, a pleasant bitterness. Her mother's body was in the lake. She'd just brought a creature to life. Her mother's body was in the lake.

How would she tell Ruby about her mother? Would she tell her at all? Ruby, somewhere warm against the rain, at home, in the Bayou, somewhere, not knowing any of this. And Oliver, Oliver Kelly, who called her a monster. How would he feel now, looking up at this great metal man? When would she show them? Her head started to spin a little, and she inhaled the steam from the mug and let it keep her in her body.

What was she going to do with Io until then? He was staring into the mug, moderately puzzled. She imagined him on a podium, the astonished faces of her peers filling the theater, gazing up at him. Incredible. *Marvelous*. Alive.

All these things, certainly, and yet here Nell was, awkward and quiet in his presence. She looked around the kitchen to find something to do. Her eyelids were heavy. Her brain pleaded with her for sleep as she scanned the room: something to do, something easy to keep this from becoming stranger than it already was.

Cards. There was a deck of cards on one of the shelves, wedged between a salt pig and a sugar bowl. Nell hopped up and swiped it, trying to remember the last time these cards had seen any action and if it was a full deck. This would keep them busy. She stifled a yawn and cracked the deck open.

"Do you know what these are?" She shuffled them and reached out to pass them over to Io.

He nodded, took them from her, and ran his fingertip along their edge. "Missing three. A two of diamonds, jack of spades, and the ace of hearts. We could play Snap? Or build a house?"

Nell gaped. Playing cards with a computer was probably not going to be a fair game anyway. "A house," she managed. "Sure. Let's."

In twos, they laid the flimsy pieces out, tip to tip, little triangles. Red and black, red and black. They fell mostly, but some stayed. Io was more delicate with it than Nell: a couple of times even her breath was enough to knock down a whole row. He was patient, she got frustrated, but slowly the triangular structure rose for them, every tier more precarious than the last.

Nell gave up helping toward the top; she didn't want to be the one to tip down the whole structure. She rested her chin in her hands and watched the grace and silence with which Io put the pyramid together. The hand that she had built moved just as neatly as his other, their mismatch strange, their fluency startling. Her eyelids were so heavy. Her mother in the lake.

She fell asleep before he crowned the tower of the house. She slept through the night at the table, and Io sat as the army of frogs marched in through a crack in the door. By morning the kitchen was alive with them, and Nell awoke in a sea of green.

One by one she and Io set them free, she, with a dinner plate and an empty cup and he with his cold new hands.

CHAPTER 3

The girl standing on your porch looks as though she is about to faint. I am prepared if she does and immediately ask if she would like to sit down. If she falls, she may hit her head. She lets go of her umbrella, and it blusters away. She doesn't seem to notice. She is staring very hard.

You say, "Ruby, this is Io. Io, this is Ruby Underwood."

Ruby Underwood nods, her mouth open.

We escort her to the kitchen and sit her at the table, and I go to the tap to fill a cup of water for her; this will help if her head is feeling light.

"You did it," she whispers, taking the mug from me very carefully. "You really did it."

You sit across from her, and you are smiling. You say, "Isn't he amazing?" This word sets off pistons in my code. I am glad I amaze you.

Ruby Underwood sips the water. "You really did it," she says again. It is clear to me then that my arrival was unlikely, unexpected. There are no other sentient machines in this house. It is 101 years, 2 months, and 3 days since my system was last updated. I understand that something has gone wrong. I am the only one of me left perhaps. I would like to ask you this, but I understand that it is not a polite question to spring on you now. Politeness is very important when meeting new people. Also, I do not want you to be less amazed by me; I would like you to be continually amazed. What a privilege to amaze anyone. What a joy to amaze my maker.

You lean across the table. "You didn't get your eye."

Ruby Underwood's expression falls. I am witnessing a conversation that is not necessarily meant for me. I pick up the deck of forty-nine cards and run them through my hands in order to appear occupied. This is a polite thing to do.

"It was never . . . my eye. I mean, aside from Oliver's being too high from the Medi-Patch to do anything except sit on the floor and talk about *you*." Ruby Underwood laughs a little. Then you laugh; you are easy with each other. "Nellie, it just—it was never going to be for me. I know how my face is. I know how it looks. I can see just fine for what I need.

285

Someone else can have the eye."

You reach across the table and take her hand in yours for a moment, neither of you saying anything at all, communicating in that contact. I like listening to you and Ruby Underwood talk. It is like a chain of light. When the letter *t* emerges at the end of a word, it is soft and sometimes inaudible, but at the beginning it is clipped, like a spark. Your vowels are sometimes flat, and sometimes they are tuneful. Your ticking is quiet.

Ruby Underwood looks up at me again and blinks, looks to you, and asks, "Can—can he think?" She lowers her voice to almost nothing. "Does he have a computer?"

She says *computer* as if it were something bad. As if it were something dangerous. I am not dangerous! I am amazing!

You nod; you say, "It's one of Da's."

Ruby Underwood gasps. "That's unreal. You never know what he has stashed away in that big old lab, do you?"

You don't say anything for a second, and your ticking ever so slightly rises in speed and volume. I am not the only thing that has happened lately in the laboratory. That much is clear. Ruby Underwood looks directly at me then, her face a matrix of concern, puzzle, and unease. Human faces do many tiny things very quickly. I have not yet seen what I look like, but even my processing power could not generate anything as complex as what Ruby Underwood appears to be feeling at present.

"You have nothing to be afraid of, Ruby Underwood."

I am bold to say this, but I want her to know. She almost smiles then. "No Underwood. Only Underwood when I'm in trouble. It's Ruby, Ruby to friends." The unease is beginning to leave her face. She places her cloth bag on the table; she's not about to leave, "I—I didn't expect this all to happen so quickly. I thought it was over for us, Nell."

You say, "I'm so sorry I hurt you."

Ruby says, "I thought your father, Oliver, someone would stop you."

You shake your head. "I wasn't going to be stopped. That I'm not sorry for. Not even a little bit."

Ruby laughs a little, then lets the air run silent. Her eyes flick over me again, her hands clasped together tightly. She is trying to be brave. She is uncomfortable.

"I should have brought a gift." She is really trying.

"Would you like to see how I made him?" you offer. "I'd love to show you. I have some adjustments to make; you could watch."

The air stays quiet a moment. You lean forward, whisper, "Please."

Ruby nods.

We three go up the stairs, and you show me into the

room where you sleep and work. Ruby is still cautious of me, but she takes the magnifying glass you hand her and kneels by my side.

You say, "I'll build him a real face someday. Maybe you could help paint it?"

Ruby says, "Maybe."

I lie on the floor then, too big for any work desk. You tell me this won't take too long, or shouldn't. You ask if I mind this; you tell me it won't hurt. I can't hurt, but I don't tell you that. You stand over me, armed then with a tiny blowtorch, a tiny wrench, a drill. You ask Ruby to hand you some screws, and she does, says, "It's all so *complicated*."

You answer, "No, look, this is how his battery works," and your voice is thick with joy.

We are there for maybe an hour. There is blue flame and metallic noise. You swear; Ruby laughs. You tune me up; you explain me in basic terms. You get some things wrong, but I do not tell you. I hope I will explain myself to you more clearly someday. As I wait for your demonstration to finish, I run words from the kitchen over in my mind like the cards in my hands, I scroll them through my fresh memory in context. I am grateful.

Amazing. The queen of spades.

Gift. The king of diamonds.

Friends. The ace of hearts.

Nell,

The nectarines on the windowsill have changed. One has stayed the same and is warm under my touch, the second is gone but for the pit, the last is black with rot and foam; but the third, Nell, the third is growing. It is the size of my fist, and I fear it will only continue to swell. Please write me and tell me what you are doing. I am starting to become afraid.

Nan

CHAPTER 4

Io chirruped a gentle tune in beeps and bloops as he cleaned the kitchen. Nell sat on the great slab of a table, her knees raised to her chin, watching him and listening, peeling potatoes into a bucket. Ruby'd said she'd come back for dinner. They'd all cook together. The deck of cards, worn from the morning's play, sat in a neat stack beside her. He moved as though he'd been cleaning dishes his whole life; he bobbed his head softly to his own, almost inaudible tune, neatly scrubbed, then stacked the dishes.

Nell hadn't even had to explain how the sink and taps and soap and sponge worked. Io knew. Knew to ask for gloves—just in case. Knew to let the water run hot, then rinse with cold, to soak the cutlery and baking dishes for longer. It was uncanny.

Nell couldn't take her eyes off him.

The chirps and low metallic melody he was entertaining himself with were sweet. He seemed to be enjoying himself, dancing ever so slightly as he progressed to scrubbing out the teacups.

"What is that song?" she ventured, hesitant to interrupt. Io turned to her, a mottled scrubber in his left hand and a rough brown mug in his right, dripping soapsuds, tiny bubbles, iridescent in the light streaming into the kitchen.

He cocked his head a little and replied, "'Life on Mars,' David Bowie, track four, side A, *Hunky Dory*, 1974."

Nell was dumbstruck for a moment, then couldn't help laughing. "I have no idea what you just said. That is the longest song name I have ever heard!"

"Almost as long as Penelope?" Io suggested.

A *joke*? "Almost!"

"I am being playful," he said apologetically. "A man named David Bowie sang it, in 1974, and it was part of an album named *Hunky Dory*. The song's title is 'Life on Mars.' "

"'Life on Mars,'" Nell repeated. "Like the planet?"

Io nodded. "Yes."

"It's a nice song. Do you—do you know any others?"

"No," replied Io, placing the mug on the counter. "It's the only one in my storage. The network is down, so I can't access online libraries. If I had another music storage device to connect to, I'd know much more."

Nell blinked. Yes. Yes, online libraries. Networks. He was talking about the Internet. He didn't seem to question where it was; rather he simply understood that it wasn't available. Would it hurt him if she told him it was long gone? That it hadn't existed in a hundred years? What would he have been capable of if there had been an Internet, or if she had a stor—

"Would you know a music storage device if you saw one? Do you think? Would you?" The words were bubbles in her throat and on her tongue. Her chest beat out a thrilled syncopation.

Io turned back to his coral reef of soap and dishes. "Yes, I'd be able to recognize one, and my infared data system would be able to connect to it. But devices like that, Nell, I—I know they're all gone. It is fine. I am sure you can manually teach me your songs, and I will be able to record and repeat them."

He didn't notice her slipping out of the room, or if he did, he didn't mind. Nell's excitement carried her up the stairs to the chaos of her bedroom. She rooted about in her aprons, her clothing: there in the cotton, a hard silver box. *Yes.* Nell wasn't at all used to smiling, the sensation of wonder emanating from her face was new. She laughed aloud as she scampered back down the stairs, a ripple of sheer delight.

She burst into the kitchen, the tiny computer in her fist. It was worth a try, surely?

"Does this look like a device you could read?" she asked, her smile and excitement too big for her face.

Io turned around, startled.

"You are happy," he observed.

Nell chuckled. "Don't get ahead of yourself. Let's see if this makes any sense to you."

Io diligently wiped his gloves on a dishcloth and removed them one by one. Nell passed him the device, trembling. He plucked a dry fork from the draining board and took it to the table. Nell pulled out the chair at the head of the table, and he sat down; she sat beside him.

Io took a prong of the fork between his forefinger and thumb and twisted it, ever so slightly.

"Would you like some tools?" she whispered.

"No, no," he replied. "I'm just going to turn it on, not open it up."

Nell blinked. "Isn't it, you know, *dead*?"

"No machine is ever truly dead. Death is for humans," Io muttered, slotting the prong of steel into one of the tiny sockets in the silvery box. "There's impermeable memory, data, code that can be read. Information is immortal."

Nell was rapt as he tinkered, thinking aloud to

himself. She ticked heavy, heavier than usual. For a moment she was back on the roof of the Gonne Hospital, rushed with potential, weight in her chest.

Suddenly and quietly there it was without any prelude or fanfare: a single spark. The screen on the small box went darker, then lighter, then white. It was on. Tiny text scrolled past on its screen, digital letters in motion. Io tilted his head. Nell's mouth dropped open.

What she hadn't been able to manage with tools and batteries and cables, Io had figured out in a matter of seconds. How much does he know? His memory was different.

Io turned the box over in his hands, as calmly as he had with the dishes. It caught the morning light as it turned, its screen almost humming with text too small for Nell to read. This tiny thing, full of secrets and stories and songs.

"Can you read it?" she breathed, barely able to conjure her voice at all.

"Yes," he replied, his thumb gently gliding across the screen. It moved under his touch, and he navigated the tiny infinity with shocking ease. He tapped lightly and frowned, concerned for a moment, then closed his eyes. From the cavern of his kettle skull, a soft whirring, his sentience strip receiving ancient information. After

294

a long moment it stopped, and Io chirped softly, a melodious beep.

"Data transfer complete," he said flatly. He opened his mouth wide then, and an electric symphony poured out like shining water, like golden light, like the beginning of everything.

Nell shot up from her chair, screaming, unbridled. This sound! In her kitchen! Coming from the mouth of her—*her creation*. A kaleidoscope of possibilities unfolded before her in this new sound, this ancient, ancient sound: trills of faraway violinists and electric guitar and drums and a ghost woman's thunderous voice. Nell leaped around the tiles, unable to keep herself from dancing.

She spun in time with the tune, moving her hips and shoulders, throwing her arms above her head, joining the refrain, rolling in the deep.

Before she knew it, Io was up out of his chair, too, the glowing box in one hand, the other pointing at some faraway delightful thing, music blaring from him. This clumsy dance floor was suddenly a private, gleaming ballroom full of soap and sunlight. Nell grabbed Io's free hand. He placed the box in his apron pocket and took her other hand as well. Joined, they spun an uncoordinated tempest. The pages of Nell's imagination, the plot she had wound out for herself, the first hand she had held, sprang to life around her, no longer ink and dreams and the sparse, grim ticking of her chest. Now orchestra, now drumbeat, now Io.

This was unlike the whirlwind that Nell had danced in the Lighthouse, a hopeful lone body in the dark. Being connected to Io at the hands, moving with him like this, Nell was suddenly not lonely. Her eyes filled with tears. She could get used to this, barely able to contain her laughter, her hands full of breathing steel.

"How many songs do you know?" she asked, spinning away, then back toward him.

"A hundred thousand and then some," he replied, grabbing her hand and twirling her with ease, and Nell imagined that the stillness of his kettle face was smiling down at her.

Nell felt unstoppable, fevered. If he could read her long-dead music box with such ease, he could surely read other computers. He could unearth so much, could be the key to rebuilding their society, could be their link to the rest of the world. And the Lighthouse, their quest for a conduit. She'd created one; she couldn't *wait* to show them, couldn't wait for Io to join their dance.

"Put on another!" she trilled greedily, picking up the cards from their stack and throwing them in the air, confetti in red and black and queens and kings. In less than a beat, the music changed to a steady, low rhythm, all bass, all prowling. The last ace fluttered to the ground.

Nell pulled Io closer, not really knowing what she was doing, only that the slight change in, well, mood, she supposed, called for it. Could it even be called mood? Given that one of them was—did Io even have moods?

Nell's ability to pretend had never been great. Her reality was impossible to ignore; every time her chest ticked she was confronted with a harsh truth: Tick, my mother is dead, tick, tick, my mother is dead, tick, everyone knows what I am made of. Pretending had come naturally to her only once; fantasy had washed up at her feet on the shoreline, and she had held it in her hand. She was still holding it now.

Her fantasy had grown and grown and now danced, finally with her, moved hips that she had built along with hers. The soapy kitchen air was hot, and the rain smattered lazily against the window in a gentle sun shower. A woman's voice, different from the last, ragged, spun out declarations of something that sounded like anger, or sex, or maybe something else that Nell didn't know much about; she'd never heard music like this, how fury could become tender.

This was the last thing Nell felt before it happened.

CHAPTER 5

You aren't sure why you trust this moment. The air is soapy, and the shock of the music is still changing the texture of the world around you, deepening it with new ridges and valleys of emotion. You are suddenly aware of your mouth, as if you'd never had a mouth before now.

He is a grand thing before you, moving easily. Your eyes connect with his again, and you are grateful for him. He's brought you so much in such a short time: a hundred thousand anthems! Each song a bauble, a star. He's brought you these gifts, these passwords to the world before. People must have danced like this all the time. How did they ever *stop* dancing?

You glide around him, barely touching at the fingertips, lightly connecting every beat or two. He's confident in his movement. He's a good dancer. That must come in his code. You, though, you are teaching yourself as each key change arrives, as each line rises and tips into the next, as the woman singing from long ago wills you to. You learn her words easily, almost start to sing along.

Just beneath the skin of you there is a warmth, a possibility, and something like the opposite of fear: courage.

You built him to be handsome and strong. He hasn't a face yet, not like how you drew him on the page, but if you soften your eyes, you can see it. Here he is, far from line and paper; you feel a pull toward him. This is not a coincidence. He is good at this, and you are not; but you don't care. He's not going to sneer or laugh or roll his eyes; he can't, and he wouldn't. He thinks you are amazing: you *made* him.

You trust him, and what a golden climb that truth is building through your ankles and knees and gut and your chest, and before you are quite sure of it, you crescendo into him, high on your toes. You built this kiss. This belongs to you.

His head leans forward to meet yours, and he places his hands around your waist. His mouth is not a mouth. He is cold.

All the gold drains out of your body, and you are in the arms of a machine; you are between pincers of steel.

The kiss feels like nothing. This is not a kiss at all.

You stay with it, and you think of Oliver Kelly: of the feel of his skin against your selfish hands in the hospital, of his obvious desire for you, the smell of formaldehyde and cologne and his body in the back of your throat. He did not want you then, but at least he knew what he wanted; at least he wanted; at least he chose.

You built Io with your own hands. Was he capable of choosing? Were you choosing this for him?

Is this why they took the machines away? Is this what they punished a whole nation for? They came too close to the uncanny, lost themselves to the unreal, and paid, and here you are, tangled up in a steel tower with electric lights for eyes. How is it Oliver is in your throat now? How is it that he would feel more real than this, this that you have drawn up from nothing, this that you made? It is not Oliver that you find yourself wishing for; it is just—just a human, not a machine.

This floods you as you break contact and Io turns his head, says, "You kissed me."

"I'm sorry, I can't—" Your stupid mouth won't work now and you back away from him and he says your name and you are afraid. He is so full; he is so real: how much does he know? Before you realize it, you have turned on your heel and you are moving away, fast; you are leaving. You need the air. You need out of this house.

CHAPTER 6

When Nell passed Ruby at the garden gate, she barely noticed the girl, let alone expected Ruby to cycle after her, eye lit up like a bright bulb of concern. But Ruby turned and followed. Even after Nell had ridden out of the parklands and swerved west, bypassing the way into the estates, the town.

As Nell moved, she listened to her body, her thrumming pulse, her chest; her ticking shifted tone, started to clang. Something was happening. She didn't stop.

The two girls flew on their bicycles against the warm rain. Nell led them out past the rush of Heuston Falls and down the increasingly barren road westward. The road became less even, as the ruins began to loom against the humid gray of the falling afternoon.

The ancient flats and high-rise blocks like rotten

teeth lined the blackened old tongue of the road that led out to the mystery of the rest of the island. This was where the scars of the epidemic were the most gnarled, between the Pale and the Pasture, the places that the sparse population hadn't even tried to mend yet. Hadn't they enough to do in their small communities, rather than waste time on the ragged edges, the rotten hemline of their tiny civilization?

Nell slowed a little. Putting miles between her and the house, Io's arms. It was supposed to be helping, but she was feeling sicker now than she was in the kitchen.

Ruby caught up and pedaled beside her.

They didn't say anything to each other, not for some time. They just cycled on, past small gray shells of houses and wide, scorched fields. Night suggested itself over the horizon; the sky began to move neon.

This far out the air began to reek. Yellowed and tangled meadows stretched out on either side of the decrepit motorway west. They soaked up the warm rain greedily, drunk after so long dry. Close up Nell could smell how foul and how sick it was, but the girls stayed in the center of the tar road as though the slight distance from the wild pasture would grant them more safety.

"My chest hurts," Nell said suddenly, breaking the silence so sharply that Ruby almost lost control of her bike.

"Do you need to stop?" offered Ruby, her voice hopeful. "Are you ready to go back?"

Nell did not answer; she only kept pedaling.

Ruby moved closer to Nell on the road, barely an arm's length from her. This was the farthest west the girls had ever been. Nell's breaths were great gulps of panic. "Ruby, my chest hurts." She still looked straight ahead into the electric sunset. "It sounds—"

"It sounds bad, Nell; it sounds different," ventured Ruby.

Tears rolled down Nell's face, her lips were chapped; but she was still somehow cycling. Still moving forward, still moving away.

"Nell, maybe you should stop?"

Nell said nothing, her face crumpled in something that married physical pain and immense sorrow. She slowed down a little. Ruby reached out, but Nell swerved, lost her grip on the wet filthy road, and toppled gracelessly over on her side. Her chest whirred, clanked. The hull of a sinking ship, long after the iceberg. The creaks of a burning house coming down around itself: a terrible, terrible noise. Her palms were scraped from the road, and her throbbing, exhausted legs still tangled in her bicycle. She heaved, but there was nothing in her.

Ruby leaped down to Nell's side, her bicycle

clattering to the road. Rain slid down the tip of her nose, her clothing plastered to her form. Nell shuddered and gasped.

"Can you move? We need to get back!" Ruby was crying now, totally powerless in the rain, on the road. "I'm not going to be able to carry you!"

"Will you," Nell managed weakly, "you please get my—my da?"

The sheer effort of this breathy request pulled Nell's precarious consciousness out from under her. Her eyes flickered shut, her breathing labored, but her chest kept grinding, metallic and heaving and strange. Ruby shook her once or twice, but Nell couldn't feel it; she was lost to the blackness of the asphalt.

Ruby picked herself up, sobbing, and pulled away from her friend. She clumsily mounted her bicycle, the streamers from the handlebars pathetic, childish in the storm. Ruby began to speed back the way they had come. Night had fallen hard, and she left Nell alone in the dark.

CHAPTER 7

I am walking toward you, but I cannot see you yet. The rain is heavy. Your father came out of his laboratory; he heard the door slam. He asked me why you left, and I told him that you got a fright. He looked at me long and hard, and I almost told him that you kissed me; but I did not think that was the right thing. Your father is very secretive. He placed long black gloves over my hands and arms and boots on my feet and a long rubber coat over my body. The hat, he said, would keep the water from connecting with my eyes and damaging them. He told me that between these garments and the umbrella, I would be hard pressed to get wet at all. He said not to move too quickly. He said not to burn you, not to burn his girl. He said he was not worried about you because he trusts me.

Nell. I am not sure what that means; but I did not

have time to ask. I am not sure he should trust me. I have not yet seen another person. This world outside the house, I am sure, in daylight is very beautiful.

The city is very large and very gray, and the stone woman on the horizon is very tall. I like her and hope you will bring me close to her. Can we explore this city together? It does not look like the map that I have stored in my code. The network is silent, and there are no updates. I know this waterfall from somewhere, but I would still very much like you to tell me about it when I find you, if you are not still frightened, or angry.

I wish you had location tracking. I wish you were a blue dot on a white map that I could go to.

Your chest was making different noises in the kitchen, but I am not sure you could hear them. I did not tell you when I heard the frequency change, but I should have. Dancing with you was very easy. I want to find you, but perhaps you do not want to be found. I am sorry. I should not keep walking in case I walk in the wrong direction.

When Ruby barrels toward me on her bright bicycle, for a moment I think she is going to attack me. I brace myself for collision, but she skids to a halt and is shrill; her voice is not her voice. If you were frightened in the kitchen, then Ruby is terrified now. But not of me. Of something else.

Her words spill out of her. She tells me she left you by the side of the road. "Nell is broken, go west, go to the motorway, you'll find her after the city ends, she's far out, run, run, run." She inhales and exhales in great gulps of night air. Maybe if I were a human, I would embrace her, but I do not think she would like that.

I do what she tells me and begin to run, holding my umbrella over my head. I am fast in the rain. I am learning about time, because time changes pace depending on what happens. I experience time differently from how you experience it, Nell. I do not feel it slow because I am bored or fly because I am happy, but tonight I run for a hundred years.

Each footfall is an hour, a day. I have learned this feeling from you; surely it was you showing me how to feel these things. Each second is another winter, Nell. When I find you, this terrible slowness, this human dread will stop. Things like me should not feel time like this.

I am coming for you. Please keep ticking. I will find you; I am listening for you. The night is truly down upon me now as the city gives way under neglect and dissolves into desolate countryside. The rain sounds like a million tiny stones thrown down all at once against my umbrella, a clatter, destruction. Like a broken television. Like a radio that does not work. Like the moment eggs begin to really sizzle on a frying pan.

I will tell you all about televisions, Nell. I will tell you about radios. I will play you every song in my library with rainfall sampled in the music. I hope you will let me dance with you again.

I am a hundred years older. I am rust under my long coat and gloves. I am afraid. How is it I learned so much from you, Nell, in so little time? How is it that my code can pulse this way? Why did your people make things like me, Nell, if only to teach them this agony?

Then, over the rough drone of the weather, a sound. It is not your ticking. It is a gnarled, crunching wheeze. It is something broken, but it is at least in your rhythm, with your frequency. I'd know your heartbeat anywhere. Ten thousand songs, and it is still the most marvelous thing I have heard.

Nell, I want to show you the words these songs have taught me. I want to say *heartbreak, ecstasy, tragedy, forgiveness. Waterfall.* I want to tell you I have heard all about Fridays. I can hear your body in the dark, and the sound will have to be the blue spot on the white map that I move toward. I know you are alive nearby.

In the moonlight (I know a lot about moonlight, too), I see your body and bicycle against the silver and black and water. I am standing over you. You are so small, Nell, and your sound is a factory on fire.

Your oak skin is gray, and I am glad of my gloves and that I cannot hurt you. I could hold twenty of you with my strong arms. I am sorry, I am leaving your bicycle. I can carry you and this umbrella, and that is all. I begin to walk east, back to the city.

Your eyes flicker open, and you are frightened, then relieved; then your body tenses with pain. You cough, and there is blood on your lips. I run.

You are gone again, asleep or worse, but still breathing, your chest still churning out that sound, that awful symphony, but at least it means life. At least you are here.

I drop the umbrella once I am under the porch and hammer on the door with all I can, still holding your body, all limbs and sound and, I am sure, cold, but I cannot feel that through these gloves.

Dr. Crane answers, Kodak sitting around his shoulders. "What took you so—" Then he sees you and swears. I tell him you are broken, and his voice darkens. "Bring her to the laboratory immediately, stupid child going so far out . . ."

I don't ask any questions. I bring you through the white room where you brought me to life, and he closes the door behind us.

I am not a monster now. I can help.

CHAPTER 8

You are standing out at the edge of the lake, the water is lapping your feet, starving. Your hands are full of small stones, shining and black. You place them in the pockets of your nightshirt, then lean down to the shoreline and gather up some more. Your pockets are heavy. This is the only thing you can feel: the weight. Your chest is quiet, and the world is quiet. You are sure you can smell the rain, but it is just beyond your senses.

Fistfuls of stones.

The shirt pulls at your shoulders. Maybe it will rip. If it does, you will tie its white flannel arms around your naked waist, and it will be just as good for dragging you down when you walk into the water. You will walk into the water, and you will find her.

She'll be lying among the weeds and loaches, hair a vortex of curls, peaceful and safe from the hand of your father, the cold water soothing her electrical burns, the weight of the water a loving pressure. You step forward. You can't feel the water, but it must be cold. When you find her, you will lie beside her, place your head in the crook of her arm, and place your ear to her chest. It will be silent. Everything will be silent and safe.

When you decide you weigh enough, or the rocks run out, you begin to walk forward. One step, two steps, but you are barely up to your ankles when the lake begins to move, the tide shrinking away from you, repelled.

You step forward, and the slow repulsion of the water becomes a rush away from the land, from the living bad world. You cannot move now; your legs will not listen. The water swirls and grows tall, the atmosphere charged with something bigger than you, far bigger. The lake grows tall, a whirlwind, a tower, a body, a fountain. The water splits, becomes legs and a belly and breasts and arms and hands. There are drops on your cheeks, your eyelashes. You can't wipe them away, and even if you could, you wouldn't. The lake is your mother. Her mane is black, inky weeds, the slope of her nose, her full sad mouth, all water. She is a fountain, and you are a girl, a child with her pockets full of stones.

She ascends taller and taller, a green glow from her chest like a beam, like a beacon, until she all but disappears into the night sky and the lake is empty, a crater. She has taken all the life of it with her. You try to say, "Mother," but your tongue doesn't work. Far above you, her laughter is a trill of starlight; she raises her river arms up high, stretching. She is whole.

You are fearful suddenly that she can't see you, that she doesn't know you are there, her line of vision too far above. You want her to see you, see you completely: your quiet chest and your heavy nightshirt, your bare feet.

Then she begins to walk. The earth shudders with each footfall. She passes right over you and the tiny stone path. Her toes glance off the roof of your house just exactly enough that the roof is dislodged like a kicked cobble. The tiles shatter to the ground, and the walls crack from the disturbance. But she keeps walking. As the giantess walks away, you hear her singing. Her voice is volcanic; words descend like ash, like rain: "Don't follow me, Penelope, don't follow me."

Stone Kate is a child at your mother's side for a moment as she passes. You can hardly see her now as the swaths of distance and darkness swallow her up, but you know she is walking to the ocean. Your house has fallen down; your mother is in the water once more.

You can move your arms, your legs. You say, "Mother, Mother." One by one you take the stones out of your pockets. There are so many.

You will wake up when they are empty.

Ruby calls, "Nellie?" then "Dr. Crane" and I say, "Come in; it's just me here today." I am keeping the house together while you are healing. I even have a list of instructions: basic organization, alphabetizing bookshelves—busy work. I am not sure Dr. Crane trusts me with much more. He is out mostly and warned me not to receive any guests, but Ruby has let herself in. I did not know if I would see her again after the road, and at first I am pleased to see her. Between her scarf and woolen coat, she looks like a bundle of fabric on legs. The tip of her nose is pink, and she is sniffling; she has a cold. The night in the storm did not hold well for her.

I say, "Would you like some lemon and ginger and honey and tea, also cayenne, and I believe there is some whiskey." I say, "You look like you have a cold, and this is a cure."

Ruby smiles at me, then looks back into the hallway. She is nervous.

She says, "I'm fine for now. Oliver, you should come in here."

A voice outside says, "I don't think I can."

Ruby smiles at me again, then looks back into the hallway. Says through her teeth, "Oliver Kelly, you'd want to get over yourself!"

A thin young man comes into the kitchen then and stares at me for 4.21 seconds before collapsing onto the tiles. You humans, if you'll pardon me, are extremely fragile.

Ruby gasps as his body crumples, but he is fine. I go to the cabinet to remove some smelling salts and suggest that whiskey is a good choice for treating this boy's ailment also. Ruby helps him up. He is not unconscious, just a little pale. Shocked. She props him onto a chair at the kitchen table, and he is shaking but not in danger. I offer him a drink. He shakes his head. His pupils cannot take all of me in. He gapes.

There are several optional impulses for this situation. I could offer him my hand in greeting. I could apologize for startling him. I could laugh at the shock he is experiencing; this is a temptation, though it would not be helpful at this time. I choose to offer him my hand. As I extend it to him, he pales further, and his lips begin to lose their color. It is my less functional hand. I can't read any texture or temperature from it; it is a little rudimentary, maybe a little ugly, but not so abhorrent that it should cause this reaction. I withdraw.

"Say hello, Oliver." Ruby urges him. She looks to me then. "Io, Oliver is an old friend of Nell's. He was worried about her, they had a falling out, and well, I couldn't really explain, so I brought him here to meet you himself. And to see how Nell is."

She's nervous. I wish I could put her at ease.

I tell her that you have a few days left incubating your new augmentation and that you responded excellently to the operation. Oliver is staring at me now, and I offer tea again. Ruby accepts; Oliver barely nods. Your people refuse things they want several times before accepting; this is both frustrating and entertaining in equal measures.

As I fill the pot with water to make the customary drink, Oliver whispers to Ruby. Nell, I understand that I am an adjustment and can be surprising, but I find this extremely uncomfortable.

"That's it?" he whispers. "That thing? I mean, it's— it's incredible, but I at least thought he'd look human." Ruby thumps his shoulder to silence him. I know what he means, what this is, but it is more polite to carry on than confront him.

Oliver is not scared of me, Nell. It is a more complicated thing than this. How many of my new songs are about this strange hybrid of fears, his concern that I am somehow superior to him? His defiance, his disbelief—how I *can't be.*

The notes of emotion in the boy's voice are like picking apart a musical recording—fear upon outrage upon disgust—and the beat, steady, holding it all together: jealousy.

I serve them two cups of lemony tea, Nell, as they simmer at each other. Something in me is hurt by this, but I do not linger on the flashing light of it. Hurt, Nell, that is something for your people. There is a choice for me here; hurt does not stick.

I offer the deck of cards, a pleasing way to socialize. Oliver is now suddenly unable to look at me, rather instead peering closely into his teacup.

"Snap is a game I cannot cheat at," I offer, but he jolts at the sound of me. I am now finding his obvious unease distinctly unpleasant, irritating even.

I run the list of reasons that his behavior could be eliciting this irritation and among the data, among my recognition of his discomfort, those words again and again. That Thing. Thing. Tango Hotel India November Golf. *A liquid.* 01110100 01101000 01101001 01101110 01100111.

I am the product of the greatest minds that ever walked this planet. I am the last of my kind. Because of creations like me, your people poisoned one another to death. Might like mine draws wonder and terror, and in the year I was programmed I was as powerful as any god your people ever had. I will not let you make the same mistakes again.

The boy looks at me again, and I hear "That thing," but I know he means, "I am afraid," like any child who sits at the feet of a titan.

We split the deck. Oliver insists that Ruby take the first round. The kitchen is quiet and the tea is cooling and there is rainfall on the window and we play cards.

The arc of Snap is funny. I am not getting any better at it, though I feel this is because of the limitations of my physical reflexes. In time I will improve them myself, if you permit me the tools. Ruby wins because I am preoccupied.

Oliver is in love and in pain. He looks at me with curiosity and with horror. He is many things at once, in his flesh and weakness. I think that when you kissed me, it scared you that I am not human, that I am not a boy. That I am not flesh and weakness. Nell, I will never be this.

Ruby, snap, snap, snap again, quickly takes the round. She is more at ease now, delighted, demonstrating my imperfection to Oliver, who has seemingly summoned enough courage to play me.

There are many avenues in my programming that I could select in order to appear competitive here. None of them are appropriate, though victory does open up a set of pleasing lights. His hands are shaking, and there is sweat gathering on his upper lip. He lays each card down slowly, faceup. We quickly make a pair of fours; I permit him the win. He coughs out a shocked laugh, says to Ruby, "It's not all that smart!"

It. India. Tango *Goes*. 01101001 01110100 00100000.

I lay down a two of hearts; he lays down a jack of clubs. We both place a queen, spades and diamonds, and I slam my hand down, seconds before his descends. His grip tightens a moment around my mine—my slower hand, no less—and I say, "Snap."

Snap as if we are both the same. Snap, as if what we both bring to the table is equal, a woman looking up from the paper between our fingers.

CHAPTER 10

The sound was different.

Nell was not quite awake but in the final silk threads of peace and sleep, yet she could hear it. It wasn't a ticking, not anymore. The steady beat of her life moving forward, the rhythm of her panic and delight, the sound, natural to her as her own breath, was gone. It wasn't the rattle and grind of her journey on the road; it wasn't sickness. It was health. She was alive.

She groggily opened her eyes to the easy afternoon light. How long had she been out? She felt rested, strangely refreshed—and good. Really good. She shifted and sat up. The world was too soft and too kind. As her head unclouded, the sound from her new chest, the new sound, became clearer. A *chime*.

Her old flannel nightshirt was buttoned up to her neck, and she undid each tiny plastic disk to see what had become of her. The scarred landscape of Nell's chest was usually a resigned, disappointing vignette, but her silver-white scar had been remade, scarlet, bright between her breasts. Not sewn shut but stapled. Nell found herself admiring the starkness of it, how deliberate it looked. She had survived; here was crimson proof that she was made of blood.

She exhaled a laugh at herself, the familiar confidence of the Medi-Patch occurring to her. She rolled up a sleeve and saw two, placed neatly on her forearm. Smiling, she thumbed them. What a relief. Nothing would hurt. Nothing.

Something moved at the bottom of her bed, and she yelped, then giggled. "Hello?"

Kodak lifted his tiny head and blinked.

"Kodak!" she sang.

He scampered up the crisp peaks and folds of the bedsheets to Nell and nestled in her lap. She ruffled the fur on his head and scruff with her fingertips. They sat together there for what felt like a long, peaceful time, Nell surfing the crest of her strange high calm, Kodak a knot of purring affection.

Where were her father and Io? Io had brought her home, hadn't he? Her memory was fuzz, the cotton kind of ignorance that in this specific moment felt useful. Her brain was taking care of her, saying, "Not now, Nell; maybe in a few days." But Io had somehow come out in the rain, hadn't he? Nell looked over at the window, the weather calm; he'd brought her home. He'd carried her here.

She laughed again. Goodness, that was so extreme of him! So dangerous! What a kind robot he was. She probably shouldn't have kissed him, shouldn't have started down that avenue—she'd frightened herself— and while the fear had dimmed, the indentations of it were still clear, just beneath the haze.

"Can robots even be kind? I bet my father told him to come and get me. Oh, wow"—she reeled—"I'd love to listen to some music again. That was *so* nice."

She felt calm. She felt a bit silly. She felt like going back to sleep. She looked around her room again and mimed walking one leg before the other under her bedsheets.

"I can walk. Easy-peasy. Sure. Easy!" she affirmed, lifting herself up a little, using her arms and practicing moving parts of her hips. Yes, she could absolutely go for a walk about her room. Nell sat astride the bed, legs dangling. "Sure, this is fine."

She stood, wobbling, for maybe five seconds before her knees buckled and she sank to the floor, rag doll. Her body hit the old carpet, but she didn't feel any pain from the impact.

Io and Julian burst into the room with such fervor

that Nell gave them a hello and dissolved into giggles. Her father's face was a combination of concern and relief and something else that she couldn't quite parse.

"You're awake!" he exclaimed, but rather than move toward her, he let Io step forward to help.

The strength of Io's arms was shocking to Nell as he lifted her effortlessly back into bed. The sensation of rising in Io's arms, even for the fleeting moment before being placed into her cocoon of blankets, flashed something like memory over Nell's dulled senses.

The neon burn of sunrise, wet hair, the clanking behind her sternum. Io's striding footsteps, bounding toward somewhere safe. His calm voice.

Cora's scorched wrists, the bolts in her neck . . .

"Was *I* dead?" she asked, her voice strange, like a little girl's. "Did you heat me up and bring me back?" Her words came out more slowly this time, like molasses or oil. She started to feel nauseated, the high pushing her further back into her head, her speech pulling from far away.

Julian laughed too merrily, in a way Nell had never heard before. It made her feel as though her mattress were full of liquid and the world were falling away below her.

"Ah, now, girlo, you were no such thing. Io brought you home on what was it, a Wednesday morning? And I got an awful scare. Your cavity mechanism had done its time and started shutting down."

Nell's eyes closed and opened again, the sound of the blink heavy, her eyelashes like a curtain rising, then falling—a beginning and an ending—too fast for their weight. Her mouth went too dry.

"Frankly I'm shocked it lasted this long; it was bound to give out at some point; but look, it's pioneer technology. Lucky Io was here to bring you back, doesn't bear thinking what would have happened to you."

Julian took off his glasses and cleaned them with the edge of his jacket, flippant. He gave a tut.

"That's what you get for straying so far with Ruby. Hopefully this shock will stop you going so far again. You've no business out on the motorway. Asking for an accident. You'll know better now."

Was she being *scolded*? Kodak crawled up around her, chirruping. Julian's tone had a fresh edge, a wildness. Nell's tongue was too soft, and her voice was too far away to summon. This new glint in him was dangerous, a match held too near the firewood. It sounded like a threat rather than a caution. Her new chiming slightly rose in tone against her numbed anxiety.

"But in fairness"—he paused—"the new one sounds just wonderful!" He threw his arms—one spindly, one mechanical—above his head, a proclamation of his genius. "Imagine, we had you walking around with that awful ticking for so long, when all it would have taken was the insertion of a slightly different quality of steel . . ."

He kept talking, but Nell couldn't hear him. She began to clumsily button her nightshirt back up. Her scar was now a scarlet river over the flat horizon of her skin, each staple a bridge of gold from one shore of her flesh to the other. It was red running water.

"Why don't I have bandages?" she asked, the simplest question she could pull from the thrumming wasps' nest of curiosity beyond her haze.

Io spoke, his voice a measured and gentle contrast with her father's mania. "You did. We took them off a few days ago."

"And when—when—" Nausea began to roll a terrible ocean in Nell's gut, and she was sure that she would vomit, her forehead wet now and the blood from her face making a swift tidal departure to her hands, the weight of them.

"Ten days ago. You've been sedated through your recovery, much, much less pain this way," Julian said, glib. "No point in being awake while your body adapts to the new system, best to just keep you in the twilight until you'd almost healed, then wean you on to something lighter. I'm glad you're responding so well to the Medi-Patch. We took you off all the drips this morning and moved you up here. You must be very hungry!"

Ten days. Twilight. New system.

"Would you like if I brought you some food?" asked Io.

Nell nodded. Perhaps water. Or soup, broth with rosemary and toasted bread, but she didn't say anything. She didn't want to talk. She wanted her father to leave. She thumbed the Medi-Patch. She wondered foggily what she would do without this haze.

Probably lose her mind. Or get angry. She'd scream, absolutely. She had these screams inside her, but they felt so distant, buried in flannel and cotton. How much longer would she feel this way? She'd ask Io later, she resigned, smiling feebly down at Kodak.

"Well, glad you're awake all the same, girlo. I'll check in on you soon. Call for Io if you need anything. Oh, oh, I'd better tell you now: I borrowed your drawings for Io. Just so I could help if he needed fixing up. They're very good, Nell." He turned his back to her and kept talking as he left the room and walked down the staircase, leaving his daughter alone with her benign steel giant.

After a moment Io spoke again.

"I am sorry I frightened you." His voice was strangely dulcet, and Nell closed her eyes. "I am sorry you were hurt. I am so happy that you are awake."

He sighed then, a relief.

"Thank you," said Nell, marveling at his emotional fluency. With the Medi-Patch, it was easier to marvel than to worry.

Imagine, she *had* been frightened of Io. But she was so far away from it now. He had walked out in the rain, and he had carried her home safely! For now, in the dull padded chamber of her mind, that was enough. Besides, she was really hungry and wanted to listen to some music.

"I'm hungry, and I would like to listen to some music, please."

"I will make you a meal; then I will play you some music," Io said, standing up to leave. "I will return shortly. I will also bring some fresh Medi-Patches, and some tea. Is there anything else, Nell?"

She shook her head. "No, Io, thank you."

As Io moved toward the door, Kodak popped up and scampered off the bed to his feet. The creation took the tiny animal in his big, strong hands and gently petted his head with his thumb and forefinger. Kodak's eyes closed in appreciation. They walked away together.

Had Julian said something about taking her notes? Her walls were empty. Her desk was clear.

The Remaining Hibernian Senate
Thug gach duine cúnamh agus stróic leat!

For the attention of Penelope Crane:

Your Black Water City contribution is to be presented on the last day of August at the Olympia Council Building, Dame Street. Your time slot is 11:45 a.m. *Your presentation will be capped at fifteen minutes.* We have not received any preliminary forms regarding your contribution to this date; *please arrive early and ensure that all paperwork is completed in full and handed to the mayor's secretary before your time slot begins.*

We look forward to congratulating you on completing your apprenticeship and receiving your contribution.

Carry on, at all costs

Sinead Burke

The Office of the Mayor of Black Water City

CHAPTER 11

Ruby came to visit the following day. She wasn't ashamed to bunch up her face and cry with noisy joy at the sight of her friend propped up among crisp pillows and sheets, huge scarlet scar and pupils like gunshot wounds from the drugs. Without saying a word, she climbed into the bed beside Nell and listened carefully to the new melody of her best friend's chest.

"Thank you for cycling after me," Nell said softly.

Ruby wiped her eyes. "Of course. Why—look, why were you running away?"

Nell shrugged, feeling so distant from that day in the kitchen already. "I kissed Io. I got frightened."

Ruby blinked, as though realizing that now wasn't the time for her particular brand of real talk. "Are—are you going to contribute him?"

Nell sat up a little. "I am. I have to. There's a letter here somewhere; it came while I was—you know. I've been given my date. It's very soon, Ruby. Did you get one?"

Ruby nodded. "Yes, it's not until winter. I'm well ready, mind you, been viewing shopfronts down by the markets. When you're better, I'll bring you there."

Contributing to the city wasn't just a notion in the distance anymore, wasn't just static anxiety. It was upon both girls, ready or not. Laid up in bed full of stitches and new metal or not.

"Do you mind my asking . . ." Ruby looked down at the sheets, traced the flowers on the fabric. "How do you think they're going to take it? I mean, take him, take Io?"

"I think they're ready for something like him, Ruby. If the mechanics and bakers of this city are stowed away in an old picture house halfway electrocuting themselves to try to wake up computers holding this city's past, people must be ready. They must be."

"But what does he—what does he *do*, Nell? You can't just walk out there and play a game of Snap in front of every apprentice in the city."

"He plays music."

"What music?"

"Music from before. I saw him bring a broken music tablet to life. I saw him read it and fill up with all its information. He played me songs."

Ruby squinted. "Are you—are you serious, or did you dream it?"

Nell focused hard on remaining composed, running her fingers over the neat twin Medi-Patches on her arm. She didn't want Ruby's pity, didn't want Ruby to think her deluded. Ruby and her shop, her earnest contribution. Ruby and her common sense. Nell hadn't dreamed this; she had felt it more real than anything in her life before, even if it didn't sound like common sense at all.

"I'm serious. I think he can access other broken machines, old computers, and talk to them. I think he can ask them about the past, even—even contact the rest of the world. He can find answers that'll help us stop everything from getting in a mess again. People will like him because he doesn't look like a computer; he looks like parts of them! He's an oracle like Nan— but for the *past*. Not the future. He's a door. He's . . . a key. That's what I'll tell them. I'll find a way to show them. Think of what we could learn."

Nell had a deep suspicion that Ruby thought this was the Medi-Patch talking. She could feel her words slurring, her sentences melting into one another. Ruby hummed skepticism. "I'm not sure I should be asking you all this yet. It's too soon. You're barely awake." She looked down at the bedsheets again. "Look, are you hungry? Can I bring you anything?"

Food. The haze of the Medi-Patch responded to thoughts of food. Nell looked off into the middle distance as though she were receiving delicious smoke signals from another realm. "A fat slice of soda bread, heated up under the grill, with ricotta cheese, oh, oh soft white cheese," she whispered, like an illicit secret. "And *honey.*"

Ruby laughed, at ease now. "That's easy. I've fresh soda farl wrapped in paper back in the house. I'll fly back and get it in no time."

"Ever since I woke up I'm so hungry," Nell mused. "It's—it's so great. *Food,* Ruby"—she looked her friend square in the eyes with penetrative intensity—"is so *great.* I am *hungry,* and if I am hungry, that means I am doing all right, even if I am fuzzy."

"Is it a bad fuzz or good fuzz?"

"Just fuzz. Io's going to pull me down to one patch in a few days instead of two, then half, then quarter." Nell sighed. "Looking forward to getting my brain back. And my legs. I want to go up to the roof to see what they've done to Kate while I've been gone. I want to get back to work again, Ruby. I need to."

She closed her eyes. "I had a question for you and it was important and I'm trying to remember it, but I can't, like . . . *find* it."

Ruby took Nell's hand. "Take all the time you need."

They sat there together for a few minutes, reveling in the calm hush. Nell was so grateful for the softness of the bedsheets, galaxies away now from the harsh asphalt and barren fields and disaster of the last time they'd spoken. They were together there in the quiet.

"Will you—can I give you tokens for the fabric? Will you make me some new clothes? I—I don't think I can wear any of Cora's anymore. I don't like them." Nell strained to make this sound like less of a confession than it actually was. "I need a change."

Ruby nodded, didn't pry. "Of course. What would you like?"

She shrugged. "Something denim. A pinafore maybe. A striped cotton blouse. A red dress."

Ruby smiled and squeezed her hand. "Do you have some paper and pencils? I can start now."

"Oh, yes, yes!" Nell perked up significantly. "In my desk somewhere."

Ruby disembarked the nest and pottered over to Nell's desk, removing a pencil box and a slab of paper bound with three bright silver hoops. "There's practically nothing left at all, Nell! It's so organized!"

I'd better tell you now: *I borrowed your drawings for Io*—Had her father taken everything? The chill of

Nell's concern rose up against the balmy warmth of the Medi-Patch. She didn't like this.

Ruby clambered back into the bed, pencils and brick of paper in hand.

"Tell me the shape you want to be," she said, removing a graphite pencil, sharp as a needle and beginning to outline Nell's figure on the page.

Nell closed her eyes and in the darkness saw herself: white skirt and blue blouse, twirling to music she couldn't hear. In the shush of afternoon she told Ruby how she wanted to look, how many miles from her sables and sages she wanted to be, released from the earthen runway of her mother's life. She asked for bright ribbons and pearlescent buttons. Could Ruby embroider her a sash? These shining distractions from the healing of her body, the persistent concern: *I borrowed your drawings.* For a moment Nell let her worry slip away.

The bright, sweet bond of their childhood sparkled out from beneath Nell's grim concrete fortress of the last few years. It ran a shining river through the icy portcullis of the recent months. They sat in the flood of it. Here they were, redrawing Nell anew, as she wanted to be.

"Thank you for following me." Nell looked into the smoke signal distance again, her eyes half closed.

"Thank you for not sending me away." With a swoop of soft gray, Ruby completed the figure of her friend, dancing in the crisp whiteness. "You'll look so smart during your presentation, whatever way it goes. You'll be a new woman."

Nell looked at the paper girl below Ruby's pencil and felt determination rush under her haze. She would be a new woman, unveiling a new man. A man, a door, a key.

CHAPTER 12

Nell alternated the following days between sitting crouched over a thick notebook, developing her presentation for Io and taking slow, labored laps around the room. Sometimes out to the landing, sometimes just to the window and back. Nell's chiming felt now like a countdown, and Io's presence was just a reminder of what she had to do. She had to bring him out. She had to justify him. Her notes stacked up, her handwriting small and deliberate. Lead snapped into dust from her pencils; pen nibs burst under her determination.

On a brief vacation toward the kitchen, she tripped, halfway to the door. Io thundered up the stairs to her rescue when he heard her body collide with the floorboards.

"If you push your body too hard, healing will take

longer, and you're more likely to hurt yourself again," Io had thrummed, helping her back into bed.

She'd given him a willful stare, settling herself back into her pillows and pages. "I'm not sure I should be listening to anything you have to say about human bodies."

"I'm equipped with health and nursing applications," Io had replied confidently, folding her blankets in around her. Nell had just about growled in frustration, reluctantly making a note of this ability in the margins of her notes, and Io gave a natural, affectionate laugh. It was a pleasing sound.

Io said something like "Don't go anywhere" or "Don't run off on me," but Nell shooed him away.

"Come back up in a little bit. I want to read this to you, see what you think."

Nell lost herself again in her pages, in her deliberation. Her speech was missing something still, but it was moving, growing. The Medi-Patch wasn't helping, but better the fog than an aching chest, than an itching scar. Nell couldn't quite place what to do while she was up on the stage; she needed to demonstrate Io's abilities to the council. She couldn't just stand him up and declare that he was incredible without any examples of why. All bees and no honey. He could play music; he could be an aide in illness. He could do all these things, but he needed to be as important to everyone else as he was to her.

It was quiet but for the rain smattering against the window. This fresh sound had become a pleasant static in the background of her world. Her eyes were drawn to her desk in the corner; it felt like months since she'd sat down to perform a button-eyed exercise. What did Io think of the steel sprites, his predecessors? His family even! She snorted, *ridiculous,* her remaining half Medi-Patch showing its bleary web over her perception.

Nell looked over her drafting desk, the wobbly tower of letters from the Pasture all that remained. Had Nan Starling sent any new packages lately? There surely would be one or two; was Julian keeping them from her? She didn't like the creeping uncertainty around this; she didn't like that Julian wasn't at her bedside ever at all. Had he been in contact with Nan?

There she was, a pen in her hand, reams of work beneath her—and not a single word of it addressed to her grandmother. Nell should contact her, but what would she even say? News of Io wouldn't sit with Nan's view of the world at all. Nan came from a time too close to the horrors of the Turn to feel comfortable or safe around a computer, let alone a walking, talking computer with arms and legs, with hands and a voice. Nell tapped her pen on the page, half imagining a letter.

Beloved Nan,

I have built a man. He has a computer for a brain. He thinks and he talks and has applications that show him how to help sick humans. He also can cook. He knows lots of songs because I showed him a pre-Turn music box. I think the rest of the Pale and the Pasture will love him and will want to know more about computers because he is so nice. And also my chest augmentation broke down. Da had been keeping my mother's body in his lab for reanimation, but it's okay because I put her in the lake. How is the Pasture? How are the dogs? Kodak is great. I walked around the room three whole times today.

Nell whistled low to herself. Under no circumstances.

The thought of Nan's reading the letter, then conducting months of prayer services and building skyscraping altars to pray for the fate of her grandchild. Useless, pretty words thrown at candles and crystals. How much did Io know about prayer, but just as she leaned over to ring for him, a soft knock came to her door.

"Perfect timing!" she called, but when the door

opened, it was Oliver Kelly. Paler and more serious than usual. His work suit was a little crumpled from the rain; his hands were knotted together, white knuckled from worry.

"Howya, Nell," he said, pausing in the doorway. He walked over the threshold cautiously, all the pomp and charm squibbed out of him. The bags under his eyes were especially purple; his jaw was rough with patchy stubble. Nell hadn't seen him since she'd shoved him into a storage closet and raided his inventory of historically important augmented limbs. She'd robbed him blind, and she'd forgotten all about it. He was the last thing on her mind, but here he was.

"Howya, Oliver," Nell replied tentatively. "Come in."

Oliver was notably torn between whether to sit on the bed or sit on the guest chair, his eyes lingering on a prone spot by Nell's legs. He resigned himself to the chair, stiffly placing himself on the seat's edge. He shuffled it closer to the bedside, then gathered his thoughts for a moment.

"Everything is wrong, Nell."

Nell could tell immediately that Oliver was not talking about an accident, or a death, or the Lighthouse's getting shut down, or his trade's getting audited by the council. He didn't even seem angry, as if he were coming to read her the riot act for drugging him and looting his lab. No.

Oliver was talking about his feelings.

Nell set her jaw. Here we go.

"You probably think I'm only after one thing with you." Oliver's eyes were on the floor. There was something different this time.

"Oliver, I know you're only after one thing. Well, two things, and if you pretend one of them isn't my father's trade, I will have to ask you to leave." Nell's light tone sank. Oliver wasn't here for banter. They weren't Crane and Kelly, a hermit and a barfly here. This wasn't going to be any fun. Nell took stock and mentally put down her sword. No duel today.

"Nell, my whole life I've been convinced that it would come down to you and me." Oliver spoke softly, still not looking at her, worrying the cuff of his jacket. "And even all the times you said no, I thought it just meant you weren't ready yet. Or that somehow you couldn't quite see what I see. I always thought that someday something would happen that would shake up your perspective and that finally"—he exhaled deeply, these awful words—"you might see me how I see you."

They hung against the patter of rain on the window and the thickness of sleep in the air and the chiming in her chest, and Nell couldn't say anything to him at all. This wasn't just attempt nineteen for Oliver. This was something real. Something final.

She began to say something like "Oliver, I'm sorry" or "Oliver, you know this already," but got only as far as the end of his name before he stopped her.

"I'm sure you think all this is just about the trade, the honor of continuing your family's work. But you've had it mixed up all along. The limbs, the weekend studies with your father, I—Nell, maybe it started out being about the job, but it became about—about you. How you make me feel. That's what's kept me going." He stopped, his face ruddy with vulnerability.

Nell felt a flash of something under her rib cage. Alien and strange and bright. Oliver's voice had a strong and lovely timbre to it that she spent most of her time ignoring, but on that last word it was a thunderclap. The brightness rose into her mouth—an awareness, a knowledge—but then it left her as quickly as it had arrived. She said nothing and looked at the white florals of her sheets.

"I know you made Io because you find it hard to connect to the rest of us, and I want you to know that he is the most incredible thing I have ever seen in my life—may ever see in my life. When the folks at the Lighthouse see him . . . They need him down there. He could wake every single one of their old computers. He's a conduit, Nell. You could, well, you *two* could change everything."

He spoke slowly, his voice trembling from the confession. Nell didn't take her eyes off the blanched cotton garden around her. The shock of emotion lingered in her; maybe that was all the love and desire she'd meant to have for him over her whole life flaring up at once. But then it left, a ghost. She had nothing to give him. He'd just handed her a massive compliment, but all she could muster was a quiet "Thank you."

"I wonder what I could have been part of if I hadn't said no to you that day on the steps." His voice was bitter now.

"You were part of it, Oliver!" Nell couldn't snuff the pity from her voice. "I mean, you had all those parts first. You're—you're part of him, too."

Oliver looked up at her then finally. His cheeks were still pink, and his eyes were enormous, and he shook his head. "No. I'm not."

It wasn't self-pity, but it was heartbreak. And it was true. Oliver had been telling himself the same love story for years and had come to believe it, and now he was ending it, on his own terms.

"I just need you to tell me no, once more, for real," he said, and Nell mentally drew a different blade. Their dueling days were over. This was an execution.

She tried once more to summon that flash of

lightning, but there was nothing, only the lame, hushed drizzle against the window.

"I don't love you at all, Oliver."

"But could you?"

Her blade was in his body, but he wouldn't fall; he wanted so desperately for this to live. She'd never stopped to think maybe he was hurting. But Nell wasn't anyone's happy ending. She was always a more likely executioner.

"No. Never."

She wanted to offer him some consolation, but none would come. He didn't say anything for a moment, just shook his head, absorbing the fullness and finality of no. Of never. She thumbed the Medi-Patch. Was it the gauzy medicinal filter that allowed her to maintain distance from this, or was she really so cold that she couldn't even tell him she was sorry?

Oliver rose to leave, his face ashen, humiliated, his breathing edging toward that awful syncopation that leads to a very particular kind of crying. She reached a hand up to him, and he took it in both of his. Oliver held it for a moment, steadied his breath, and said, "All right. My presentation is this Monday. I know you probably won't be on your feet. But I'll be thinking of you when I'm up there."

He turned away and left her room. Nell sat amid the

eiderdown and paper and found, as if from nowhere, fat tears on her cheeks. Relief, she thought it must be, as she wiped them away. Just relief.

The front door clicked shut in the distance, and she returned to her work.

CHAPTER 13

That evening Io led Nell down to the kitchen for a change of scenery. She sat at the table, drinking hot chicken stock from a mug, while Io fussed around, preparing a proper meal. Nell's appetite had been voracious lately; everything she ate was fuel toward her body's taking new steps and healing itself. The hunger was at least partially artificial from the Medi-Patch, but as the heady and dense rosemary and echo of white wine (and a suggestion of mushroom and . . . was that bay leaf?) in the stock hit her tongue, she was glad of it.

Io played some music for her (soft, guitars, a man's voice this time) and sliced bright vegetables into even disks. He placed them one by one into a simmering dark sauce on the hob in the fat cast-iron pan and then set about cobbling together a cake. Watching him brought

Nell a very quiet peace; this soft domesticity was a relief from Oliver's confession scene earlier in the day. She watched Io's hands, confident and uncanny. They still unsettled her but in a way that pulled her in now, rather than drove her away. She wasn't afraid of him.

"I promise I know how to cook, too," Nell said, over the lip of her mug. "Do you ever get hungry?"

"No." Io seamlessly cracked one egg into a bowl, then another. "But I appreciate the composition of food. I am feeling this more acutely the more I practice the recipes in my applications. The instructions are effectively equations and the cake"—he gestured to his mixing bowl—"will be the correct result. How satisfying."

Nell chuckled. "Yes. I agree. Cake is a fine answer to any equation. It is a shame you can't taste it, though."

Io shrugged. "There were taste extensions and applications for my model, but at present the hardware needed to build me a fully functioning palate would be extremely complex and would require some hypersensitive fibers that I am unsure are still in existence."

"Maybe when I'm better, I can get working on that for you. I'm sure Da knows a thing or two about that. Who knows what materials he's got stashed back there.?"

Nell said this lightly but caught herself. The things her father kept in the laboratory weren't for playful suggestion. She sipped her broth again, warmed by it.

Io cradled the mixing bowl and stirred rhythmically, quiet for a moment. He was deliberating.

"Nell, I would like to tell you something."

Not this again. Nell wasn't sure she could handle anything else today after Oliver, but she said, "Oh, what is it?" instead of "I am very delicate right now. Can we please go back to talking about desserts?"

"In Dr. Crane's laboratory I saw that he was making drawings for"—Io hesitated and looked into the mixing bowl—"for something like me."

The chiming began to escalate in her for the first time in days. Something like him? An android? A robot? A person? Io didn't look up, his arm still churning the batter in the heavy enamel bowl.

"Excuse me?"

"He is planning to build something like me, Nell. Only not like me. I think he intends it to be a woman."

The sound of the wooden spoon in the mix was a dull beat in circles, and the spiral of it was something awful. Nell blinked.

"Do you think Dr. Crane is making a friend for me?" Io asked then, earnest, turning toward the cake tin on the counter, expertly lined with brown greaseproof paper. He carefully poured the pale batter down into it, a neat transfer.

"I don't know. Maybe?"

Nell did know. She saw her mother's body under the sheet again, a flash of it, a flash of what the landscape of her father's mind looked like. If he couldn't have Cora's body, would he build something like it? Of course he would. The laboratory was a cave of transfiguration, a mechanical womb for him to try and try again to claw Cora back from the dead. So he could prove to himself—or even prove to her—that he could. That he was capable of anything, regardless of death.

Nell looked at Io. She couldn't tell him all this when it was barely clear to her. What good would it do to pour all this into Io's hands? What could he do with it?

"Do you . . . want a friend?"

Io opened the oven, and a deep breath of heat rolled into the room. He placed the cake pan inside and closed the hatch behind it. "I don't know. I like you. But you aren't like me. So"—Io stalled—"maybe I could find a song for this?"

Nell shook her head. "Don't."

She hadn't built him to watch him interact with things like him; he wasn't another exercise or a steel sprite to add to her little collection. She'd built him for herself, for her world, but she had never considered for a moment that maybe he would prefer the company of someone more like him.

Maybe humans weren't all that interesting after all; maybe their world, full of things he couldn't experience, tastes he couldn't taste, was dull to him. Maybe he needed someone to talk in code with, to learn about the human world alongside, a cipher to piece this place together with. Maybe he didn't want a programmer or a maker condescending to him. The maybes grew taller and taller in Nell until her chime sang, "Maybe I am wrong; maybe this is all wrong."

Io saw her panic and came to her across the kitchen tiles, placed his hand on her shoulder. Nell swallowed hard on all the ugly questions and asked, "Would you like a friend who's just like you? Because if you would, maybe I can make you one."

Her creation turned his bronze face to her. "If you want to build me a friend, I will have a friend. If Dr. Crane has a friend for me and you find this the correct way to continue, I will have a friend. But I am happy to be your friend, just yours, if that is what you wish."

How did reams of numbers flash light into this? Nell wondered, looking up at him. How did algorithm become emotion? The recipe of him just worked that way, she supposed. If Io believed himself to be happy, he was happy. Faith and programming might be the same thing. Maybe this was how he understood cake.

Nell said, "Lean down."

The robot did, and she placed her lips very softly on the architecture of his cheek. It was metal and hard, but this time it was warm.

"Thank you," Io said.

When the cake was done, 24.4 minutes later, the kitchen air was charged with sugar and that special alchemy that baking brings to a space. The dessert cooled on a rack, and Io and Nell sat at the table, playing Snap.

Nell's reflexes were a good match for Io's image processing speed. A two of diamonds, an eight of spades, a jack of spades, a jack of—*snap*! Io gathered the stack, and they started again. A queen of clubs, a three of hearts, Cora's body pulled into focus in Nell's mind. Who would be on that empty table next? Was there something already there? Were parts being gathered or forged anew? Nell ran her fingers over her Medi-Patch, tempted to tear it off, to face down the dread in her belly and be her whole self again.

The front door of the house opened, then closed.

Io peered over his cards and didn't draw another, but before he could ask Nell what she was thinking, Julian blustered in, the smell of fresh rain and earth rolling off him, his glasses fogging up. He wasn't wearing a raincoat, just his worn tweed jacket, his tie too tight.

"Nell, what did you say to Oliver Kelly?" he demanded.

His tone was urgent, furious, and marbled with terror. He pushed his glasses up into his tangle of hair, his brow beaded with sweat.

"Did you see him? Is he all right?" Nell asked, knowing full well that these were the wrong questions. Io held his cards still and didn't make a sound.

"Nell. What did you say . . . to . . . him?"

Nell fanned her cards out and looked into the black and red and white of them, instead of over at her father's intensity. Best to keep it frank.

"I told him that I am not and never will be in love with him. I'm cutting him loose; it's not fair on him anymore, Da. He'll recover."

Julian stood very still for a moment. He shot a dark look at Io, then at Nell, then at Io again, speechless.

Nell steeled herself and looked casually over her shoulder at him, keeping her fan of cards high. "Why? Is he all right?"

"Oh, he's going to be all right," replied Julian, walking out of the kitchen. His voice carried through the doorway. "Us, though, we're not."

His laboratory door creaked, then slammed, a tremor running sick through the whole house.

A roar came up through Nell before the mugs on the shelf were finished rattling. "What is that supposed to even *mean*?" Julian dipped in and out of Nell's orbit, a strange and troublesome comet. He'd land with real destruction someday. That day was soon, and there was nothing she could do about it.

Nell threw her cards on the floor, a scatter of black and white and red. She stormed, as best she could against the stiffness of her legs, to the door of his laboratory and hammered with her fist. "You can't just keep hiding in there!" she shouted into the dark wood. "You're going to have to talk to me someday!"

The reply was simply the click of a lock, the heavy slide of a bolt, the sound of her father's footsteps walking back into his own wretched world.

Nell placed her head against the door for a moment and ran her fingernails slowly down its surface, the scratch against the varnish a last whisper of her fury. She made her way down the corridor back to the kitchen and breathed her chiming back to normal volume. She sat down at the table again with a heave.

She held her face with her hands and measured her breath against the quiet, against the response she'd never get from Julian. Something was wrong, and he'd make sure she'd never see it coming. Around her, Io picked up the cards, one by one.

Nell eventually pulled her face from the dark of her palms. "Do you think the cake has cooled?"

The knife slid down the belly of the cake easily. It was delicious.

In the morning, after an empty sleep, Nell pulled back the covers and ran her hands over her legs. She silently asked her muscles to be strong. Her fingernails were ragged. She'd get Julian to come out and talk to her today one way or another.

Rays of early light stretched over her room from the windows. Cabin fever was edging at her. She'd ask Io to help her out to the garden today if the sun stayed out and the rain kept away. Maybe she'd go talk to her mother, pick some wildflowers and leave them at the side of the lake.

Nell pushed the deadening patch with her fingers, hoping for a moment or two of peace, missing the thin curtain between her anxious brain and the real world, the veil of chemical calm. She was adjusted now. There was no more relief in the high. There was no more relief at all.

"Oliver was going to be fine," her father had said. "Us, though. We're not." He'd locked his door in the face of her rage. He'd stepped away from handing her any sort of truth. Nell was confused, but more than this. There was something terribly wrong in this house. Were they in danger?

She huddled among her pillows, and Kodak squirreled his way up the covers and nuzzled into her neck.

"What do you know then?" she whispered to him. "What do you know?" She rubbed his head, his silky coat. The clock on the wall read an inch or so past nine, and she listened closely to the house for movement.

Muffled laughter drifted up from directly below her. Something was happening in the kitchen. But who was there? What kind of laughter was it? Good spirited, cruel? It set her teeth on edge.

Then a shriek of joy reverberated up the stairs: Ruby, that was Ruby's voice. Right, at least that meant there wasn't immediate trouble. It felt dissonant to Nell, a stark contrast with the mood of the Crane house.

A barrel of footsteps up the stairs. Three clear knocks on the door, deliberate and formal.

"Ruby, what, what?"

Ruby laughed gaily and hushed her. "Shh! You'll see! C'mon!"

More than a little awkwardly (and far more stiffly and painfully than she let on) Nell got herself to the doorframe: then Ruby placed an arm around her waist and helped her through the door and onto the landing. It was an awkward waltz, but the first steps of the day would be the stiffest. Nell was steadier than she'd been the day before. She was almost fine, but if she fell now, she'd take both of them tumbling down at once. The top of the stairway was a precarious ledge.

"Why don't you sit here? It'll give you a great view!"

Nell held the banister and slowly sat down where the landing met the top stair. "A view?"

"You'll see!"

Ruby skipped down the stairs with an ease that Nell utterly envied. She rubbed her knees, thought: Soon, soon. Ruby called over her shoulder, "Don't run away on me!" as if Nell had any choice at all in the matter.

"Sure," she replied, still steadying her breathing. "Sounds grand." Running. That was a long, inconvenient way off yet. Her sarcasm disappeared into the empty hallway.

Ruby appeared again at the bottom of the stairs and cleared her throat theatrically. "Miss Crane, in lieu of your oncoming wardrobe, it is my pleasure to present to you this fine, drizzly morning, the Premier Underwood Android Collection for Autumn and Winter."

The kitchen door swung open with a flourish. Nell gasped.

Io emerged, but hardly as Nell knew him. Ruby had made him clothes.

His shirt was informal, a heather gray linen with tiny bronze buttons tailored to his form. Ruby had rolled up one of his sleeves. His trousers were charcoal, cut just above his ankles, as was the style in the city that year. A red woolen scarf was slung about his neck cavalier, and as he paraded the hallway, he flung a length of it over his shoulder, delighted with himself. Ruby applauded his performance, and Nell was breathless with laughter. She clapped wildly as he pivoted, and Ruby fussed around him.

Io still looked like six and a half feet of metal. He was still mismatched and clunky, still almost faceless. But Ruby's wrapping him in good tailored fabric brought him just a little closer to being human, at least from where Nell sat. She put her hand to her chest as her creation danced about with her best friend. A wave of pride, and relief, rolled through her. Life could look like this. The sound of laughter in the halls of the Crane house didn't have to be so scarce, didn't have to feel like a threat. She looked at the still closed door to her father's lab. She hoped he could hear them. She hoped he was curious.

"Well?" Ruby demanded, teasing. "On a scale of, let me see, one to Ruby, you are a genius, where have I landed?"

Io began to ascend the staircase toward her. "Do you like it, Nell?"

Nell nodded, grinning, and he sat down beside her on the stairs. She rested her head on his shoulder for a moment, holding her delight. The fabric of Io's new clothes smelled fresh and clean.

"I like it, too," Io said to her quietly. "Very much."

Ruby stood at the bottom of the stairs, hands on her hips, very pleased with herself.

"Next, I'll be setting you up with a jacket. I have *just* the tweed in mind. Maybe a hat with a dashing brim for the winter? You'll be the talk of the whole city. Forget your body; everyone'll be asking who composed that dapper ensemble!" Ruby whirled toward the front door in a pantomime of her future success, thanking invisible fans for their esteem and compliments. "Why, yes! I do sew everything myself!" and "No, no, these hands aren't augmented!"

She blew kisses and leaned against the hall door. "Nellie, I hate to tell you, but I get the feeling my star is going to rise even higher than yours! The Marvelous Miraculous Ruby Underwood!"

And then, as if the universe had got wind that they

were having just a little too much fun, an unusual sound came from out beyond the front garden.

A purr of engine, the riff of a vehicle pulling in, pulling back, parking. A car. Outside. Ruby's and Nell's eyes connected. No one in the Pale had a car.

"Open the door," said Nell, the chime suddenly ricocheting through her body, the hairs on the back of her neck standing on end.

Ruby wrapped her hand around the knob and pulled. The day opened up before them. Nell couldn't see what Ruby could at the bottom of the garden, so she stood up and took some creaky steps down the flight of stairs.

A white albatross of a car. A woman removing a case from the boot. Dread rose over Nell, the heap of unanswered letters in her mind's eye.

Nan was here. Her recent silence had been a summoning.

"Close the door!" Nell called out, and Ruby slammed it shut.

"Io, go to my room!"

Io looked down to Nell, and Nell looked up to Io. He registered her urgency and rose quickly to disappear across the landing into Nell's room.

Five rhythmic and stern raps at the door. Rat-tat-a-tat-tat.

"Nell, it's your *grandmother*!" whispered Ruby, clasping her hands over her mouth as though the word were a curse, or a spell gone wrong, as if she'd conjured her up herself.

"Let her in," Nell said. "Let her in."

CHAPTER 15

As Nan Starling walked into the Crane house, something in the architecture seemed to shift to her will. She illuminated the hallway. The cobwebs suddenly became ashamed of themselves; the dust cowered at her gaze. Under her eyes, the house reminded itself it had once belonged to her. Her assistant and the white car disappeared. She carried a single case, leather, quilted, cream, not even big enough to imply she was staying for long.

She was cloaked in dove and fog linen, the barest suggestion of rain on her shoulders, glimmering on her silvery hair. Short and soft bodied, she was the brightest thing for miles. The creases in her face were deep but elegant; her brown skin was still supple for all her years.

She turned first to Ruby, taking her all in. "Well,

well, Miss Underwood, how you've grown. You look fit for work! Whatever have you been up to with your pins and tape?"

Nell didn't say anything. Nan hadn't clocked her yet. Nell hadn't seen her in a long time, only her ink on paper. She seemed shorter to her, smaller. An impulse ran through Nell to tear down the stairs and throw herself upon her grandmother, to inhale the incense and cotton of her, to find safety in her arms, but she held strong.

Her eyes flicked to Julian's door. He'd be coming out soon. He'd have to, now that Nan was here.

"Miss Starling—" Ruby began, but Nan interrupted.

"Oh, I'm well beyond miss, dear. Nan, I'm just Nan now. That'll do just fine." Her voice was accented with the grandeur of the Pasture, glinting like the edge of a coin.

"I—I was making—I was about to measure Nell for some new clothes," Ruby stammered, all her flare fizzled out. Ruby had been in the way of Nan Starling only a couple of times that Nell could recall. She held far more reverence for the dowager, for the oracle than Nell did.

"Penelope."

Nan looked across the hallway and up the stairs to her grandchild.

Nell stood on the stairway, her hands clasped together, chiming alarm.

"Aren't you going to come down to me? Say hello?" Nan demanded.

Nell placed one hand on the banister and slowly began to lower herself down the rest of the stairs. "I'm sorry if I'm slow. I've had an operation."

Nan had grown older since Nell had last seen her, but her presence still felt celestial, as if her glow would have been too big for any room, and the closer she got, the more Nell could feel her pull.

"I know about the operation," Nan said, watching her descend, "though you should be well back up on your feet by now."

"I *am* well back on my feet. I'm still just a little slow." Nell found herself childlike, indignant, and moved faster to prove herself. She made it to the ground and over to the old woman. Nan's arms were already extended, awaiting embrace. Nell leaned into her chest, buried her face in her grandmother's neck, the scent of her perfume and sacred powders filling her nose, too much, too dense.

"No matter now, girleen," Nan said, patting Nell's back fondly. "As soon as we get you down to the estate, you'll be leaping around in no time. Lots of space to heal. The air will do you some good."

"Sorry, did you just say—are you taking Nell to—" Ruby piped up immediately. Nan was unperturbed and gently released Nell from her embrace.

Nan's eyes were dark pools now. "I presumed Julian had filled you in. Does this mean you're not packed?"

Nell blinked at her and shot Ruby a look. Ruby shook her head, mouth slightly agape.

"That boy," Nan said, as though she were remarking on a ten–year-old who'd accidentally broken a window. Her composure was pristine; her tone, clipped. "Well, since he's got his head under the bonnet of some project or other day in day out, I suppose he can't really be trusted to deliver information in a timely and appropriate manner. He and I agreed that after your little incident you should come stay with me. You'll better recover out of the way of any errant . . . *machines*." Nan just about hissed *machines* like a curse, the name of a demon.

"What did he tell you?" Nell asked. Her pulse thundered. Nan must know everything. Nan must have seen all this somehow in tea leaves or in a mirror; she must know Io was just a few feet away.

"Penelope, I know there's an android in the house. I appreciate your attempts at making a, well, *revolutionary* contribution—your father spoke very highly of your intent—but neither you nor this city is prepared for the changes that a sentient machine will bring about. Computers ruptured how people speak to one another; they tore away the stitching of how our society works. Whole towns of people didn't speak a word aloud for years before the Turn, so greedy for information, for the silent sanctuary of their digital world! You think you're missing a bigger conversation? The world out there is alive, but it's silent. And consider the many people living on this island who would rather know *nothing* that came before the Turn. Think about the grief." She grabbed Nell's arm tightly. "Think about the horror in that history, Nell. And you're going to dig it all up? You're going to switch on all the dead and sick computers? Irresponsible, Nell. Some things are best left gone, best left switched off." She released her grip and pointed to the kitchen door. "Ruby, go put the kettle on while I help Nell gather her things."

Nan was matter-of-fact, no fuss, no nonsense, uprooting Nell's life without the bat of an eyelid. She was not a woman to be disobeyed.

Ruby flashed Nell a look that signaled both "I'm sorry!" and "I'm out!" all at once and disappeared into the kitchen.

As Nan went to ascend the creaky stairs, Nell raised her hand to stop her. The word *irresponsible* thrummed through her body, and a courage overcame her, a terrible clarity. Nell peeled the Medi-Patch off her arm and folded it over itself, then placed it into one of her pockets. She was done.

"Io?" she called. "Could you please come downstairs?"

The tall robot, all dressed in his finery, peered around her bedroom door, then walked to the top of the stairs. Nell beckoned him forward. He cocked his head to the side. "Are you sure?"

"Quite sure, thank you. I have someone for you to meet," Nell chirped, hoping to disguise her searing nerves with brazen cheek. Io descended without a moment of hesitation. Nell looked to her horrified grandmother, who had begun to back away quite slowly, her immaculate composure flickering.

Io said, "You must be Nan Starling. I am Io. I am very pleased to meet you."

Nell noticed that Nan quietly produced from her pocket a small chain of crystals and began to run them through her fingers. Empowered by this tiny ritual, she stopped retreating and planted her feet firmly. When was the last time Nan had seen something—someone like Io? Never. She'd have been born just after the machines fell. He was an effigy from history books and cautionary tales out in the Pasture. His very existence was blasphemy, his head full of scrolling code, his life artificial and cold. The old woman kept the crystals in her hand and said, "Penelope, what have you done?"

"Oh, it's quite all right, Nan," Nell said, clasping her hands together to stop them from shaking. "Io is very kind. He carried me all the way from the old motorway when my chest broke down. He's been caring for me during my recovery since Da is extremely preoccupied in his laboratory. Io has been nothing but a gentleman," she said, more than a little for show, more than a little in spite.

"Thank you, Nell," Io said. He placed a hand on Nell's shoulder and squeezed it. He looked to Nan then. "Can we offer you a cup of tea?"

Nan just blinked silently, but Io was unperturbed. "Is that labradorite in your hands? It's considered an excellent healing stone, and that obsidian is most definitely useful in warding off danger." Nell felt a smile almost surface; Io's calm was the perfect counterpoint to Nan's repulsion.

Nan took a deep breath. "Yes, yes, that is correct." Her voice was still steady and sharp. "Ruby is in the kitchen; she will have the tea prepared."

"Io knows lots of things, Nan," Nell started, thinking that maybe if she behaved as though she were still under the influence, she might get a little leeway.

"He's been making all the meals in the house. They're always perfect!"

"If I could connect to the Internet, I'd have access to more," Io chirped as they entered the kitchen. Over her shoulder Nell was sure she heard Nan gasp at the word *Internet*: heresy. Even the thought of it went against everything she had built her whole life in the Pasture around.

Nell supposed she should respect that or at least acknowledge the power and value that faith had to the healed. But of course they believed in a god out there. The jagged silhouette of the big smoky town didn't even stain their horizon. They didn't live in the city barely yet on its feet. Everything around them was beautiful. That's what she'd loved about the world out there. How selfish a thing, but how true. What need had they for computers, for answers about the past, for androids? Prayers were enough for them. But that wasn't enough for Nell.

The laboratory door swung open so suddenly it crashed against the adjacent wall, and the whole house moved from the assault. Julian materialized, stepping casually into the kitchen as though he hadn't nearly shook all the cups and saucers off the shelves. Ruby fussed about, tidying away her impromptu tailor's suite and preparing for a swift exit. She was leagues out of her depth in this production.

Julian was a crow in a lab coat, gaunt, dark, hair wild. He didn't even look at his daughter. He took off his gloves to shake Nan's hand. "Nikita."

"Six hours on the motorway, Julian," Nan replied icily. "I didn't expect a procession , but this isn't exactly a welcome. You didn't tell Nell anything."

Nell shot Ruby a glance; the true awfulness of being present for a conversation about herself was only heightened by the embarrassment of its happening in front of Ruby.

"I only had her brought back around a few days ago. I was going to tell her when she was back on her feet. I didn't expect you so soon."

Julian was petulant, his arms crossed. Nell had never seen him like this before, making excuses, being scolded. He looked very young.

Nan was restored to all her former poise. "I told you I'd be here on the afternoon of the twentieth."

Julian uncrossed his arms, then crossed them again. "I was busy."

Without a moment to humor his petulance, Nan matter-of-factly stated, "I'll be leaving with her this evening, so you'd best help pack her things given that she's barely walking on her own. I'm surprised you left her to the android rather than provide adequate physical rehabilitation, *Dr.* Crane."

Nell's head swam. They were serious. Nan had intended to just swoop in, slap her father's wrist for his neglect, tuck her into the white car, and whisk her away from her life, out of this house.

"Are you going somewhere?" Io asked, beginning to sit down, alarm in his voice. Nell shook her head.

"As it happens," Julian interjected, only looking to Io for a moment before returning his glare to Nan, "Nell isn't going anywhere, Nikita."

"What do you mean?" Nan snapped. "You agreed to this weeks ago, Julian; you've had plenty of time."

"Look, the new technology in her chest is an incredible example of the advances I've made. She'll need to be displayed to the council as a further contribution. I can't have her out in the middle of nowhere when I need her for work." Julian was attempting to stay calm, but his voice was erratic. He didn't want Nan here. Ruby looked as if she wanted to fall through the earth. Nell felt her eyes unfocus, rage a climbing pyre inside her. *Displayed. Contribution.* She felt it boil up to her throat in a scream but contained herself as her father kept talking.

"And as for the robot, I've been studying it closely since the incident. Nell's not prepared for the impact it could have on her: these computers are programmed to be such good mimics that they can manipulate us into experiencing all kinds of feelings. Nell's too naive for it, I can't risk her getting notions about herself; she's more valuable as a contribution than Io in the long run. I'll be taking the sentience strip and resetting it and putting it to better use."

As Julian spoke, Io reached out his hand and took Nell's as she trembled with fury. Her father hadn't been designing a friend for Io; he'd been constructing a replacement of his own design. Not only this, but outlining how to present his daughter to the council.

Nell his contribution. His greatest invention. More grandeur for him, more proof of his excellence. It rang even now in Nell's chest: a victory bell. She wished she could undo the seams of her scar and take every inch of what her father had put in her out again, a bloody exorcism of steel.

But Nell kept her nerve. This was not the time to burn down the house, to rise up into a righteous storm. That had never gotten her anywhere. She'd get past him just how he got past her, again and again: closed doors and distractions.

"Can I please have a moment alone with Ruby, to see her off, say good-bye? Before we—we, get into this?" Nell had no idea how she managed to measure her voice—her resolve more steel than in her chest.

Nan and Julian exchanged a look. "Yes," and "Of course," they replied, and Ruby looked as if someone had just turned the key to release her from a room with a falling ceiling.

"Thank you!" she burst, making for the door. Io and Nell followed, her chiming a flaming cathedral all the while.

CHAPTER 16

The three of them stood in the hallway again, a huddle, as though amid the debris and aftermath of their runway, their parade.

Nell took Ruby's hand and squeezed it to release some of her frustration. "I just can't *believe* them," she whispered bitterly.

"You look like you're about to scream," Ruby said, and Nell clenched her teeth.

"There's time for screaming plenty later."

"Nell, Julian still has all your papers; you should go get them while you still can." Ruby pointed to the lab door, still open. Perfect.

Nell nodded. "I'm going in there, and I'm not coming out until I have something to fight him with."

"Are you sure you want me to leave?" Ruby asked quietly then. "Are you sure you'll be safe?"

Safe. Maybe Nell had never been safe in the Crane house.

"I don't feel right leaving you. Can I come? Even just as an outside eye to make sure nothing . . . bad happens?"

If there was one thing the Cranes and Starlings valued, it was saving face. It was kept secrets. Asking Ruby to stay was not weakness; it was defiance.

"Yes. Stay," Nell said softly. Ruby lifted Nell's hand and kissed her palm.

She led Ruby and Io down the hallway. Adrenaline coursed through her; she almost shook with it. Her plan crackled together: Get into the lab; lock the door; find her blueprints for Io. Find a way to reason with both her father and Nan.

The rain-flecked air breathed through the doorframe, and the laboratory door responded like a valve squeaking on its old hinges, swinging back and forth.

The three heaped into the lab, and Nell slid home the locks, sealing the world behind them very softly, so the bolts didn't make a sound. A fastened door bought her all the time she needed.

She'd destroy all her plans if she had to, rinse out the ink, tear apart the paper of them. She'd write them anew and make sure he never got his hands on them. To think, he'd given her all her education. Even the thinking core of Io had been a gift from him. Nell's stomach twisted at the thought. She could never have done this without him. To make Io, she'd stolen, taken her father's work, taken advantage of Oliver. Did that make her as bad as her father? A specter of doubt touched her: Was anything she had truly her own?

But Nell had turned Io from arms and legs and a ladder and a kettle into this, into a friend. Nell had discovered that he could wake up and read computers from the past, discovered that he was a key. Nell had been brave enough. That belonged to her. It had to.

"Ruby, will you keep an ear out at the door, please? Warn me if you hear them coming?"

Ruby gave her a salute and posted herself by the door, her ear pressed to the crack between worlds. "I can't hear anything; they must be still arguing in the kitchen."

"Good, good." Nell sat down at her father's desk, placed herself at the helm of his empire of blueprints, some stolen, some his own. The desk was a mess.

"Nell, what is happening? What are we going to do?" Io sounded almost fearful, and it just about broke Nell's heart. None of this was his fault, but he stood at the center of it still.

"I don't know," Nell replied, steeling herself. "All I can do is make sure he doesn't take you."

"But . . . your grandmother wants to take *you*," Io

replied, his voice glitching ever so slightly.

Nell took a deep breath. "Even if she does, we'll find a way to keep you safe. But know I don't plan on going anywhere."

She riffled through the papers on Julian's desk, keenly looking out for any mark of her own pen. Nothing looked right: all reams of equation, all reams of numbers and symbols. Walls of her father's even, tiny print. Then the anomaly she was looking for: in the disarray of loose-leaf, a notebook, wide open. Scattered over the blossom of pages was what looked like her own writing, her tall consonants and loops.

She fished it out of the mess puzzled. It was an unwieldy thing, a thick leather binder, a cover marred with old stickers. Nell had never seen it before. Why would Julian take the trouble to put her notes in here? She looked closer; her chiming sang higher from the shock of the certainty that came over her as she read. The voice that echoed out from the pages was the soft tones of a paper ghost.

Cora just wouldn't leave this house. Here she was, in Nell's arms again.

CHAPTER 17

Ruby posted at the door and Io standing over her, Nell disappeared out of the room, out of her rage. She ran her fingertips over each page's smoothness, the indentation of her mother's pen barely traceable. This paper was so precious that she worried that if she pushed down too hard, the words would shatter like glass ornaments under her touch. The ink would smudge, or the page would somehow tear, and her mother's secrets would be corrupted or lost forever.

There were sketches of her mother's body drawn out again and again: obsessive self-portraiture, drawing herself into existence.

On one page, Cora had outlined her own pregnant body as a diagram: the swelling crescent of her belly, her heavy breasts, her arms outstretched—like a woman, but also like an eagle or maybe an angel. Thin lines matched her left breast to more equations in the margins. The nest where Nell had grown was etched with blue grids.

It felt hugely private, a violation even to be thumbing through the secret ruminations of her mother, but Nell could not pull her eyes away. Pregnancy, invention, illness. She had held Cora's remains in her arms, but she had never been closer to her than in this moment.

Nell's chime began to rise, a small symphony to accompany her reading. Nell held the notebook up close to her face and let her eyes follow every curve of her mother's lettering.

One page simply read, "onwards & upwards," and the ampersand was perfect, a simple knot. A private mantra. Below it: "Done with the stone, on to the steel!"

Kate. Her mother's great contribution to Black Water City, but Nell didn't see anything else about the stone woman here. None of this was architecture; none of this was design. It was all formulas, all something else, all what Cora had really been working on.

Many pages had letters squeezed tightly and neatly together between lines; others were more spread out, white space littered with numbers and equations and measurements. The diagrams were drawn with less flourish: concise, clear illustrations of where veins would become pulsing, kinetic tubing, or exactly how wires would weave over bones and become tightly braided scaffolding in their own right. Symbols Nell had never seen before splayed out in equations to equal huge words like MOVEMENT and ENERGY and HEART.

In the margins Cora had doodled. Sometimes just *CS JC*; sometimes her maiden name, then her married name, Starling-Crane, Starling-Crane.

Beside the date, one day, in tiny letters: "I hope the bump is a girl!" Other days; "Sick again." Sometimes "Sick again, chest." Sometimes "Sick again, baby!"

Nell turned a page and entered a city of lists, pages and pages of orderly lined and notated salvaged goods and their precise locations. Boots from the old Arnott's Car Park, found inside a burned-out Ford Fiesta. Eight boxes of eyeglasses in perfect condition, found behind a shutter near the Trinity ruins. Box of chips—chips?

Sometimes Cora's handwriting looped and dived excitedly, other times it was precise and neat, but it was always her, no matter the mood. Here Cora sprang to life in elongated stalks and the occasional hurried misspelling, in scribbles and stains where the nib of the pen split under her excitement. Nell wanted to take out each page, fold it up one by one into tiny squares, and place it in her mouth. She wanted to eat these pieces of her mother.

She hated that Julian had ever had these things, that his awful name was scribbled in her margins, "Jules, Jules," and sometimes "JEWELS." She was barely older than Nell herself. A teenager in love.

"FOUND A STOAT TODAY, AND I AM KEEPING IT WHETHER JULES LIKES IT OR NOT! A BABY STOAT IS CALLED A KIT, MAY CALL THE BABY KIT"

This was Cora's diary, her workbook, all knitted into one cover. Her whole world was in here, from the mundane notes of her day-to-day—"Clarissa Underwood is pregnant! Race you to labor! Poor girl is still throwing up every morning, hate that!"—to page after page of intricate maps of a prosthetic left arm. Julian's left arm.

Under the final perfected image in the series, Cora had written: "Happy Birthday, you son of a bitch." Nell inhaled sharply, the shock of the insult before her. Cora's letters were hard, dug deep in the paper with anger. Nell's stomach lurched at the dried teardrops that had muddled the ink into tiny stained pools. Those tears were older than she was. Her eyes, in that moment, were molded to the page as if all of her mother's anger had reached out of the liquid ink to touch her, a channel of fury through time.

The next page was more shocking still than her

mother's venomous note to her father; it was a contract, stapled in, with just one signature at the end. Julian's. Where Cora's name should have been, just a blank space.

Nell scanned it quickly, her fingers shaking. It would have given all the rights of her intellectual creations to her husband, Julian Crane, from the date of signature and thereafter. But Cora hadn't signed. She'd built his arm on to his body, and he'd presented the idea as his own. Marvelous Doctor: marvelous liar.

Nell flipped the next page. More drawings and symbols and equations, but no notes in the margins. They were less coded and more deliberately instructional, but Cora's voice was still there: "the incision should begin in the center manubrium and continue down my sternum but finish before my navel. Don't start any higher, there's no point, the scarring will just be ugly. This way it'll be easier to hide." Nell placed her fingertips at the beginning of her scar, just beneath her bottom lip. *Ugly—wait—my sternum? Cora's sternum?* Nell scoured forward. This couldn't be.

Her stomach churned. The beginnings of a guide to the removal and replacement of a chest cavity. Removal and replacement of a heart. Cora's heart. Piece by piece. She was designing this for herself and instructing Julian on how to perform the surgery.

Nell blinked. Cora had designed the very engine

that kept Nell alive, the very engine that made him marvelous in the eyes of Black Water City, the very structure that he would exploit again.

He must never have had a chance to operate on her. Had it gone too late? Had Julian made a mistake? Had he not been able to learn fast enough?

Nell closed the book for a moment to steady herself. She flipped to the back to see if Cora had gotten all the way to the end.

A grid of tiny calendars ate up page after page after page. Every day marked with a simple tick. Two or three with an X. Pages of calendar, tiny and neat. Eventually, the Xs outweighed the ticks; the last X was just eight days before she died.

Nearer the middle there were more diagrams, illustrations, and a tiny piece of gray metal. It was smaller than a fingernail, taped in place. A tiny computer. Cora had drawn arrows from it leading to more equations, more numbers. Nell had no idea what they meant. Small paragraphs of text were among the symbols; one was connected to the chip with an arrow:

"This is one of the functioning sentience chips. If I can implant it, I can communicate with it. If I can communicate with it, think of what I can learn. Think of what I can ask it. Think of what I can know. There is infinite knowledge to be had. I want to know everything. This is how I will do it. I will ask the computers what they know."

Nell understood her mother in this moment. Nell wanted to ask what the computers knew, but she wanted to share it, to scream it from rooftops, use it to unlock the whole world. Cora's whole world was here between the pages; her whole world was a secret.

On the next page, a stream of appendages and dates:

Finger—didn't feel it. Took it out after 24 hours.

Forearm—didn't feel it. Took it out after 24 hours.

Sternum—definite change. Left it in! Let's wait and see.

Pregnant! Will continue—shouldn't interfere.

Calf—nothing. Left it in.

Thigh—nothing. Left it in.

Sternum Update: Has a green light! Something is happening!

Nell blinked.

Green, round as a penny. Green like poison.

She'd been putting metal inside herself. Cora had been operating on herself. Before she was pregnant with Nell, after she was pregnant, conducting experiments on herself. Nell clutched her chest, anger flickering within.

Nell's thick red scar, the ticking of her body: all from her mother's recklessness and greed for an electric god.

Her whole life Nell had believed her mother to have been stricken by some bolt-from-the-blue toxic aftershock of the epidemic, some cruel twist of fate, and her own illness to have just been collateral. Nell's poisoned body was not an accident; it was a direct consequence of her mother's pursuit of some sacred knowledge.

There was no sanctuary in Cora's memory; there was no safety in her father's arms. Nell was trembling, white-hot with rage. With this book in her lap, Nell was so close to Cora, but pulling farther and farther away. She would make sure nobody ever fell poisoned from her work, from her discoveries. Just because her mother had been so mercenary didn't mean she had to be.

A note was nestled between the following pages, loose. Nell plucked it and thumbed it open.

> *Jules,*
>
> *The Pasture has been a wonderful break. Nell just loves the gardens; today we counted bugs for hours! I have not told my mother about the implant. I do not think I will. She senses that I am sick and distracted, but I am brushing her off. My teeth are loose, and if they start to fall out, there'll be no hiding it.*
>
> *I want you to know that though I am ill, I feel incredible. No matter what comes of these*

experiments, I am glad I performed them. I can hear the quiet voices of the sentient chips, and they are telling me things about this world; they are telling me secrets. I write this now because I am getting weaker and soon may not be able to write at all.

I know you are angry, and afraid, but perhaps someday you will understand. I am not afraid. No matter what happens, I have heard electric voices, I have heard my footsteps counted, been warned of oncoming rain. I know something greater than my mother's spells.

When Nell sleeps, I listen to it count her breaths. I listen to it tell me when dawn is coming. It tells me I am poisoned. Please prepare my laboratory when I come home. We'll find a way to leave it in and settle the fluttering in my heartbeat. I trust your clever hands—sure, didn't I make one of them myself?

Yours, always,

C. C.

Nell closed the book for a moment to come up for air. She trembled under the weight of this silent conversation with Cora, under the fresh, terrible knowledge of it. She chimed and she seared with fury. How could they both have been such wretched disasters? Their violent, unchecked ambition appalled

Nell. How could they both have been so greedy? Knowledge and glory regardless of the price: How they both deserved each other, Cora and Julian Crane.

Nell was angry, but within that fire she felt something new. She would be better than both of them; she would be the best parts of them; she would not be a reflection of their secrecy and their recklessness. She looked up at Io and thought how astonished her mother would be, how proud perhaps that her child had roused a digital titan from his slumber. How could one human ever expect to keep something so huge for herself? How could her mother have hoped to contain power like this in her own body? Nell would not keep his voice for herself; she would play it for all of Black Water City to hear. She would broadcast it.

Suddenly Ruby called to her, breaking her time travel. "They're coming!"

There were voices outside the door. Time had run out.

CHAPTER 18

"Open the door, Ruby. Nan has to see; she has to see all of this."

All of it, yes, but most important, Nan had to see the empty space below Cora's typeset name at the end of the contract; this would be enough to unwrench her father's hands from their grip around Nell's future. That would be the first thing. She'd show her the rest later.

"Are you sure you're ready?" Ruby asked her, and Io followed with a chorus: "Don't you need more time?"

Nell shook her head. "I can't wait any longer. I'm finished."

Io nodded. "You are very brave. I am glad to be yours."

A great wave came over Nell as she looked at her companions. Maybe Io wouldn't feel that way if he knew everything about this mess; the logic in him surely couldn't rationalize any sense out of staying in the company of someone like her. A disaster like Julian, a furious rebel like Cora: Nell was a cocktail of them both. The chaos of them lived on in her. Io was bound to realize that he was a product of that selfishness; that very same impulse to uncover secrets, to pick apart locks, to charge into places not meant for her was the same as the impulse that had led her mother to poison herself to death with old toxic metals. And Ruby—Would Ruby stick by her?

It was suspiciously quiet then, for a heartbeat too long; the voices at the door stopped calling Nell's name.

A terrible roar shattered the strange quiet. "Where is she?"

Oliver Kelly's ragged, wild voice.

Ruby turned to Nell, her hand on the doorknob. "Should I open it?"

Nell nodded. "No more closed doors, Ruby. No more."

Now wasn't the time to hide away, no matter what Oliver brought in with the storm. Ruby took a deep breath and unslid the locks.

It was barely open a blink before Oliver blazed into the lab, shoving Ruby out of the way. "She must be in here, she must be!" He was a savage demon, wearing the body of the boy they knew.

Nell was not afraid of him. She saw beyond the unhinged rage, dug her fingernails into the pages of her mother's history, and drew quiet power from them. She stood up. "Here I am, Oliver."

"Not *you*, Nell!" he bellowed, his voice cracking, sweeping his arm across a worktable full of test tubes and Bunsen flasks; a shower of broken glass crackled ugly to the floor. "Where is Cora Crane? Where is Cora Crane?" he called, stomping down to the end of the laboratory, kicking over a chair, approaching the operating tables, the stacks of clean linen folded neatly on their surface. Ruby flashed Nell a frozen look, her back against the wall. Nell shook her head and mouthed, "I'm sorry."

"Your mother, your mother—Crane has her body here; he has her!"

Nell summoned stillness against his madness, her truth against his terror. "She was here. I found her. I took her to the lake. She's gone now."

"What?" he exclaimed. "She's gone?"

"Yes. She's gone."

Nan and Julian were in the doorway then, Nan's face drained of color and Julian a scarlet flash, clenching and unclenching his fists, silent and fuming.

"Do you know how he got her here, Nell?" Oliver was almost laughing, manic. "He bought her body from my mother. My mother recorded Cora as cremated. And do you know—do you know what he bought her silence with?"

Nell didn't. What was the cost of that kind of silence? What was the cost of a body delivered? How could Julian pay for something so huge? What currency was enough for this?

"What?" she asked, her chiming ascending to a ringing, impossible pitch.

"With you. *You*. He promised my mother that I could *have you* when we were old enough."

Tears of fury and shame overcame the boy then, Oliver Kelly, the barfly, Nell's counterpoint, now half mad with shock, in a terrible frenzy.

Ruby's hand clasped her mouth as she stood against the wall. Nell heard her gasp.

And Nell just stood there, a terrible vignette scrolling behind her eyes: her father shaking hands with the undertaker, her mother's body delivered like meat, her own body for trade. Like an object, a machine. A contribution.

"My mother told me. She's been trying to tell me for years." Oliver swung around to face Julian, and the tension around them shifted up a notch, electric, dangerous. Sensing it somehow, Io moved closer to his maker, putting his hand on her shoulder. Nell squeezed it for a moment, then lifted it and moved out from behind the desk. This was not about Oliver and her father.

Nan was still in the doorframe, one foot in the hall, her lips moving in silent prayer, and Nell loved her just then, blessing this awful room, blessing everything she feared.

"How could—" Oliver began to ask the question that had been festering away inside Nell herself, but she cut him off.

"How *could* you do this?" she shouted. How could you keep my mother's body in here, how could you steal my plans, how could you promise me to somebody, how could you use me that way, how could you, how could you?

The reply came with Julian's sneer. "Cora was a genius, and she'd have loved it; she'd have done anything to live forever. She was reckless, but think of what she would have *known* if it hadn't all been ruined." He turned his piercing gaze to Nell for a moment, then back to Oliver. "Kelly, you haven't a blind clue what you're talking about. You'd do the very same if you could."

Nell was shaking with rage. "No, he wouldn't."

Oliver looked at her, astonished.

Julian actually laughed. "Please. He's been ignoring

your refusals for years, Nell. He'd have broken you down eventually. He doesn't care what you want."

"I do care!" Oliver insisted, but Julian waved him off cruelly.

"Ha! You'd keep her if you could. I know you, Oliver Kelly. You've been looking at me like a god your whole life; you'd kill to be just like me, to do what I do."

Something blinding and fast and dreadful happened inside Nell as Oliver shot toward Julian and the dull clumsy thudding of blunt punches filled the room—the snorting and breathlessness of two men fighting. There was maybe four, maybe six long seconds. Nell wouldn't watch it any longer: Oliver stumbling, the dark clatter of her father's mechanical hand against the back of his head, Ruby's shocked scream puncturing the air—"No, no. Please stop!"—through her hands. Oliver was about to keel as Julian swung back, preparing for a strike that would knock him out.

Nell threw herself between them, her hand shot up to meet Julian's in the middle of his strike. Her fingers clasped around his arm, and all of her might was there.

There was cracking and graceless wrenching and a wail.

"My arm! You stupid girl, my arm—"

The arm was separate from her father, clenching and sparking in her fist, from the elbow down. She dropped it, and metal clattered against the tiles. She gasped and stepped away from it. It writhed for a second or two as if it were still possessed, like a snake. Then it was still. Just a broken thing.

"That arm was never yours, Da." Nell was trembling, her hand bloody, her legs weak.

Julian dropped to his knees, gasping, swearing, and Oliver kicked the arm away across the floor. Io moved toward Nell, arms raised for an embrace, but she stepped away from him. "No, no."

She didn't want to be comforted. Adrenaline still seared through her; she was vibrating with it, her chest sore and her hands aching, her fingertips burst, a nail loose. Her ears rang. She couldn't look at Julian, crumpled, heaving. A hot streak of guilt rose though her for her violence, but it felt like a purge, like an exorcism.

"I am not yours either," she said. He didn't say anything at all.

Nan touched her shoulder then, and the room stilled.

"I want you gone, Da," Nell said, her grandmother by her side. "You take the business, Oliver. You take on Da's work. There's no way he'll be permitted to carry on anyway, not after his confession."

Julian's head snapped up, a lens of his glasses smashed, her face and red hands reflected back at her in them.

"It's all in here, Da," Nell said, her voice almost cracking. "Ma's notes, all of them. She designed your arm. She designed what's inside of me. And you, you took and took and then tried to wake her up to take *more*. You will—you will write a confession. You'll tell the council and the city what you've done. You'll resign. You'll leave."

Nell stood taller, her hands bloody, her chiming symphonic. She retrieved her mother's book, watched the blood from her hands seep onto the cover, red around the lip of the pages.

"Do you really think that Kelly can take on my work? Do you—"

"He's welcome to if Nell wishes." Nan cut him off sharply, her voice sheer voltage, her power undeniable, her fists full of crystals.

Nell looked to Oliver, his eyes watery, his skin blanched, and said, "Do better with it than he did."

"Nell, are you sure?" Ruby gasped, her face soaked with tears.

Nell nodded. "Ruby, he cares about this work far more than I do. I have something bigger to build."

Oliver accepted, his hands clasped in gratitude, mute.

"You are not welcome on any Starling land, Julian; this is not your house any longer." Nan continued, matter-of-factly. "There will be work for you out in the Libraries. You'll be allowed your dignity, as long as you stay away."

Io stood away from this, blinking silently through it. Kodak had scampered in, and the android had taken him in his arms, as though for comfort. Nell looked over at them for a moment, the notebook heavy and precious in her grip. "I am sorry you have had to see this, Io. We are going to be better than this."

Io didn't say anything at all.

"Penelope, you will come stay in the Pasture until your father has packed his things and left. I want you away from all this awfulness—" Nan started, but Nell shook her head.

"No. This is my home. I'll be staying here, with Io. You are welcome to join us, but my work isn't over. I have—I have a contribution to make."

"There are ways around that, Nell, after all this." Nan studied her, then Io: "I don't think the city is ready for something like that."

"You're not ready for something like *him,* Nan. That doesn't go for everyone else. There are people who are ready, and those who aren't, I'll—I'll show them why they should try. There's so much about our nation that we could learn from sleeping computers, Nan; there's so much knowledge, so much music, so much about the whole world. Io can conduct that information. He can pass it out to us. I'll be responsible with it," Nell pleaded. "You can stay here with me. I want you to see. To hear the music. I want you to look at this book with me. Will you?"

Her grandmother looked out over the laboratory, her eyes far away. She cast her crystals into the air, and they froze there for a second, turned to prisms, then disappeared. Ruby gasped.

"I will stay until these halls are clean of what has happened here—for you, child. I won't leave you alone with either of these creatures." She cast a glance to Julian, then Io. Nell put her arms around her grandmother and held her. She smelled like heady incense and clean sage, the fabric of her so soft. Nell leaned into her and was lost for a moment in her safety, until Ruby broke the moment.

"Oliver, I think we should leave."

The boy gathered himself for a second. "Of course. I'll—I'll inform my mothers of this update then. If they ask who's responsible for the state of me, I'll make sure to let them know it wasn't you. There—there weren't any blowtorches within reach this time."

Nell turned to him, his cheek cut, a bruise blooming on his forehead. "Thanks, Oliver."

"If you need anything, please don't hesitate . . ."

He walked backward toward the door, unable to look away.

Nell nodded. "If I ever need anything from you, I'll take it."

Oliver smiled wryly. "Of course you will."

Ruby threw herself at Nell then, a roaring thunder of a hug, her cheeks soaked. "Nellie, I'm only five minutes up the road always."

Nell muffled a thanks, a sorry-for-everything into Ruby's shoulder.

"Don't you be saying sorry. Don't you *ever* say sorry to me," Ruby said to her, pulling herself away. She turned to Oliver. "Come on, you. Can't send you home to your mothers like that."

Then the pair were gone out of the lab, leaving Io and Nan and Nell and Julian in a strange silence. Nell took once last look over the bad white room and turned away. As she left, she heard her father softly call, "Nell," but she couldn't even turn to him.

"If you want to talk to me," she said, "you can write me a letter. Maybe I'll read it. I'll reply when I am ready."

Io placed a strong hand on her shoulder. Nell was grateful for its weight. She closed the laboratory door behind them. The house felt different to her, as though relief had started to wash through the halls, something like release. She was glad of Nan's stern presence, even if the old woman wouldn't look at Io. Even if she asked for him to be sent upstairs. Nell agreed, and Io and the stoat alighted to her room.

In the kitchen Nan had Nell run her hands under cold water until the blood ran clear, and at the kitchen table she powdered them with something strange, something that stung; Nell didn't ask what it was. Just there in the quiet Nan blessed her hands, their fresh wounds.

On the table sat Cora's journal. After a time Nan asked Nell could they go through it together. Nell took the book in her lap, opened it to the first page, and began to read.

CHAPTER 19

The first thing is it is dark. You imagine this is how it always feels before the curtain comes up—something like birth. You adjust the pleats in your dress, shuffle the small cards your speech is written on. You imagine yourself five hundred feet tall, strong as stone, with lights all along your limbs. You imagine yourself Nan, crystals in your pockets. Kodak rests around your shoulders, and you are glad of him, gladder still that it is not just the two of you up there.

Io stands behind you, the red scarf slung over his shoulder. He blinks and looks down to you, and you beam courage up at him.

"I'm sickened with me nerves," whispers Sheena Blake.

"Would you ever stop¿" Rua hushes her. "We're grand. Nell has us sorted."

"I know, I know. There're just so many people out there . . ."

Nic shushes them both, and Tim chuckles softly. They are poised and ready to go, each operating a different component of the presentation: speakers, a screen, the projector, the lights. You could not do this without them. They are proof that this matters, that this is possible. You are not doing this alone. You'll never be alone again.

Moving the Lighthouse rig into your father's lab was hard—it was a mess, and it was sad—but the four digital archaeologists had been so excited, so enthralled by Io that through the grief, a home had begun to flourish around you.

The night Julian left, Nan poured lines of salt on the floor, and you prayed with her then, watched them turn to ash. She is somewhere now in the theater; you are sure she is praying for your reception, for awe rather than uproar, for delight rather than riot. You are almost certain that you are praying yourself.

The city is still reeling from your father's admission and departure, still astonished at Oliver's so swiftly taking up his reins. The air is simmering around you, and your chiming is filling you completely—exhilarated. You know the others can hear it, but nobody is asking for your silence now. You will not apologize.

You are about to contribute a skeleton key to the city's whole past: "Io, who can unlock sleeping data, who can read what we cannot. Io, who can show us where the world was headed before the Turn, so we can walk forward with knowledge of who we were before, so we don't make the same mistakes." You repeat these lines to yourself; you know completely why you are here and what you have to give. What you have to contribute. The mayor is speaking in front of the curtain. You hear your name.

"Are you ready, Nell?" asks Io.

You stand taller. He takes your hand. You hold it for a moment, then let it go. The curtains open, and light floods all around you. The beat strikes up, interstellar and glimmering as you walk toward the microphone and the silent, waiting crowd.

01001101 01110101 01110011 01101001 01100011 00100111
01110011 00100000 01100111 01101111 01110100 00100000
01101101 01100101 00100000 01100110 01100101 01100101
01101100 01101001 01101110 01100111 00100000 01110011
01101111 00100000 01100110 01110010 01100101 01100101
00101100 00100000 01110111 01100101 00100111 01110010
01100101 00100000 01100111 01101111 01101110 01101110
01100001 00100000 01100011 01100101 01101100 01100101
01100010 01110010 01100001 01110100 01100101 00101100
00100000 01100011 01100101 01101100 01100101 01100010
01110010 01100001 01110100 01100101 00100000 01100001
01101110 01100100 00100000 01100100 01100001 01101110
01100011 01100101 00100000 01110011 01101111 00100000
01100110 01110010 01100101 01100101 00101100 01101111
01101110 01100101 00100000 01101101 01101111 01110010
01100101 00100000 01110100 01101001 01101101 01100101
00101100 00100000 01100011 01100101 01101100 01100101
01100010 01110010 01100001 01110100 01100101 00100000
01100001 01101110 01100100 00100000 01100100 01100001
01101110 01100011 01100101 00100000 01110011 01101111
00100000 01100110 01110010 01100101 01100101 00101100
00100000 01101101 01110101 01110011 01101001 01100011
00100111 01110011 00100000 01100111 01101111 01110100
00100000 01101101 01100101 00100000 01100110 01100101
01100101 01101100 01101001 01101110 01100111 00100000
01110011 01101111 free

ACKNOWLEDGMENTS

One girl can't build a monster alone.

There are many people without whom I'd still just be tinkering at my desk. Brian, Lydia, Ella, and all at Titan for welcoming me and Nell on board—and for all your work in bringing this book to life on this side of the world—thank you doesn't begin to cover it.

Thank you to my agent, Simon Trewin, for plucking me as a wild card and for fighting for this book and for being at the other end of the phone: thank you for believing in me. To Eric Simonoff and all at WME too, for having my back. Thank you, Vanessa O'Loughlin—without whom I might have given up, way back.

Thank you to everyone at Greenwillow Books and Harper in the US for welcoming this strange book into your shelves. Martha, my editor, for handing me a flashlight while I built this weird thing, for interrogating the work, for bringing the book this far. It's been a great, inky road to walk with you.

Thank you, Nic Alea, for being a good witch across continents, for use of your poetry as epigraph.

Thank you to my folks, Sean and Patricia—you gave me the toolkit I work with, the first books—the most important ones. The video games. The paper to write on. The David Lynch movies. Without the things you gave me—the love, most important—I wouldn't be writing at all. I wouldn't know how to. My sister, Katie—you keep me footed. To my Nana, to Polly and James and Tre. Family is at the core of this work.

Thank you to the Doomsburies. To Deirdre Sullivan, for challenging me to write a sexy Frankenstein book and for magic totems. To Dave Rudden, for catching me at the end of the staircase and taking mad phone calls at all hours. You both read me more than you ever need to; I'm indebted to you both for this. To Graham Tugwell, though it's been a long time, for giving me the black armband in the first place.

To my friends—Christina and The Duffs for true kinship and a very important week on Valencia Island. To Damon, for making me laugh. To everyone at The Booksmith in San Francisco, for tolerating a lunatic greetings card buyer, for buying me gin on important days, for keeping the altar up. To the folks at JAM on Synge Lane, for giving me a piano to write at. To Helena Egri, for getting this from day one. To Roe McDermott, my God I miss you. To Erin Fornoff: all the common sense and laughter. You three good witches give me courage. To Tynan, for shouting it out in long halls. This is a strange job to find yourself in and all of ye make it less strange, or make the strangeness a home.

And most of all, to Ceri Bevan. My whole heart, how did you let me away with this? I couldn't have made you up.

ABOUT THE AUTHOR

Sarah Maria Griffin is a writer from Dublin, Ireland. Her nonfiction has appeared on *The Irish Times*, Buzzfeed, *The Rumpus*, Midnight Breakfast, *Guts* and *Winter Pages*. Her collection of essays about emigration, *Not Lost*, was published by New Island Press in 2013. She was the recipient of the European Science Fiction Awards Chrysalis Award in 2017. She tweets @griffski.